Beau & Becca,

Thanks for all the
Support!

Never lose your
Rebel Souls!

Jenny C. AM

A percentage of the profits from *The Brother's Creed* series will be donated to Colors of Heroes®.

Freedom is never free!

Colors of Heroes is a 501c3 nonprofit foundation dedicated to rebuilding confidence for combat wounded veterans and gold star families through new relationships and outdoor adventures.

Learn more at: *www.colorsofheroes.org*

BAD COMPANY

THE BROTHER'S CREED
BOOK 4

JOSHUA C. CHADD

Published in the United States by
Blade of Truth Publishing Company

Cover art by Johnathan Chong

Contact the author via email at:
joshuacchadd@outlook.com

ISBN-13: 978-1-64248-005-4

You're the one who taught me to be a man, to stand for what I believe in, and to do what is needed to protect those I love. I may have killed off your character in the first book, but don't think you haven't been present in all of them. Your influence is a part of all the characters—especially Emmett. You've taught me more than you'll ever know and helped shape me into who I am today.

I would not be the man or author I am without your constant guidance and teaching!

This one's for you, Dad!

PROLOGUE

Zeke looked through the heavy-duty fence at the town beyond. It was impressive to see how well the government actually worked when the country was at risk. Considering how much the two political parties argued, they normally couldn't get anything done. When he'd come over to America all those years ago, it'd been a different country. There had still been the pointless arguments, but the country and its government had stood for something. All that was gone now, and it was instead a melting pot of hate and chaos, which reminded him of home.

Inside the ten-foot-high fence, a guard walked by, glancing out into the night. His gaze passed by where Zeke lay and then moved on. Even with the night-vision goggles the guard wore, there was little chance he'd see Zeke. Zeke had been trained at a young age to move without being detected and had mastered that skill a long time ago.

The town in front of him had been turned into part-compound and part-military base. The fence, which was almost like a wall, was secured by stationary guards every hundred yards, as well as roving patrols. They weren't taking any chances. The fence itself was impressive and looked like it could withstand a lot of punishment before going down.

Between the patrols and the fence, he didn't think his current group would be able to sneak in and out without getting caught. That left them in need of a new plan if this was the town where those cowards were hiding.

He stood up and continued to sneak around the fence, careful not to get too close. Coming to the southwest corner, he followed along the west side, heading north. The thumping of a helicopter sounded in the distance and Zeke merged with a small divot in the field, expertly disappearing from view. The chopper flew in from the east and settled into a clearing just inside the fence. Without shutting the engine down, soldiers brought six civilians to the chopper and loaded them up. As it took off and headed back in the same direction it had come, his mind began to ask questions about what they were doing and where the chopper was going.

Zeke shut his mind down.

He had one task that night—locate the people who'd decimated their group and report back to Jezz. They'd been searching for over a week and had come up with nothing. They knew the group was heading north, but had they continued on or stopped somewhere along the way? The latter would be the only scenario that allowed Zeke to find them; otherwise, they were all on a wild-goose chase.

More than likely they would've come through this town, but whether or not they were still there was the question he'd find the answer to tonight. He waited for a few minutes after the chopper left before rising to a crouch and continuing his circuit.

Drawing even with a street that ran through town

to the east, he pulled to a stop and brought up his binoculars. Sitting outside a white-roofed house was a black Ford F-450 with a topper and shooting platform welded to the top. It was one of the survivors' trucks they'd stolen back from the Reclaimers. They were there.

Zeke smiled. Finally, after all this time, he'd found them. The search was over.

Moving closer to the fence but still staying hidden in the shadows, he stopped and watched the house. Before too long, an older man carrying an M4 rifle approached the truck from a side street. He went up to it, put his rifle in the front seat, and then went into the white-roofed house. Zeke didn't recognize him since he hadn't seen any of the people when they'd been captured. Still, he knew these were the ones they were after.

The group had stopped on their journey north, taking refuge in the border town of Coutts. It would be the biggest mistake they ever made. It wouldn't be easy for Zeke with a town this well-fortified and guarded, but he'd find a way in, and then he'd teach those punks a lesson that they'd remember for the rest of their lives, however short those lives were.

Movement caught Zeke's eye and he looked along the inside of the fence. There was a squad of six soldiers heading his way at a jog. There was no way they'd spotted him, but still, he faded farther back from the fence, lying down in the field once again. The soldiers reached the spot flush with where he'd been and looked out into the darkness.

"The sensors picked up movement here," said one of the soldiers, his voice carrying a hundred yards to

Zeke.

"Probably just a raccoon or a deer like most nights," said another soldier.

"Still need to check it out and make sure it's not an infected or hostile," said the first soldier.

They waited for a few minutes before splitting up and going down both sides of the fence. One stayed behind, scanning the darkness through his night-vision goggles. Zeke didn't even twitch until after the lone soldier had moved off while speaking into his headset. They must have motion sensors along the fence. That made things even more difficult but still didn't affect his plans. No matter where these people went or how secure they thought they were, he'd find them and have his revenge. He didn't care that Jezz wanted them reclaimed. He had a debt to settle.

And a debt couldn't go unpaid. It just wasn't how things worked.

Zeke moved off into the night, heading back to where he'd meet with Jezz and the rest of her Reclaimers. The new group wasn't nearly as strong as before, but the added bodies would help in the end. He didn't like them as much as the last ones. Jezz tended to reclaim most of the people they stumbled across now and only recruited the vilest she could find—the kind of people Zeke used to be hired to kill. He itched to do the same now but held himself back. He wasn't that man anymore. He was a survivor, and if that meant playing second fiddle to a psychopath, then so be it. As long as it helped further his goals, he'd play that fiddle the best he could, and when he no longer needed Jezz, he'd do the world a service and reclaim the Reclaimer.

1
THE RISING SUN

Post-outbreak day 17

James burst through the front door, Beretta M9 .22 handgun leading the way. Immediately, he noticed two zombies crouched over, eating something a few aisles down. With two rounds from the suppressed handgun, they were on the floor, sporting small holes in their heads. Tank followed James into the room, sweeping left while Connor swept right. James could barely hear the almost silent gunshots from their M9 handguns as they moved off to either side. His attention was focused ahead as three more zombies rounded the end of the aisle, heading towards him. With the handgun shooting subsonic .22 LR rounds, the sound of the three bodies hitting the floor was louder than the gunshots. James ventured further into the grocery store, stepping over the five bodies, and saw that the first two he'd shot had been feeding on the body of an emaciated golden retriever.

His brother and best friend joined him by the door leading into the back room.

"Clear in here," Tank said.

Connor nodded at the door and James moved up,

readying himself. He looked to Tank and then his brother, nodding. Connor opened the door and James entered, flashlight shining into the partially dark supply room. He moved into the room, Tank on his heels and Connor covering their six. His head on a swivel, he scanned the shadows, looking for any signs of hostiles. Large shelving divided the room into three sections. James took the middle while Tank took the left and Connor the right. James had made it halfway to the back wall when he heard cursing, followed by suppressed gunshots to his right.

"I got a bunch of 'em over here!" Tank yelled from the other side of the eight-foot stack of crates and boxes.

James turned and ran back to the front of the room, ducking around the corner to join Tank. His friend was a few steps ahead of him with dozens of zombies shambling towards him. Tank had holstered his handgun and was now letting them have it with his fully automatic SAW machine gun. The suppressor kept the shots from being extremely loud in the confines of the room, but it was far from silent. James moved up to Tank, quickly holstering his handgun and grabbing the ACR combat rifle hanging at his side. Looking through the four-power ACOG optic, he acquired his first target—a large zombie weighing over three hundred pounds. It made a loud smack as it fell face-first to the hard floor. The sound of Connor's suppressed ACR rifle soon joined James and Tank's, and the zombies began to drop like flies.

Tank fired a small burst, dropping the last one. The spent 5.56 casings tumbled to the floor, clinking in the now silent room. James watched the downed hostiles to make sure none of them moved while Connor turned around to check their six. The three of them stood there for a few seconds as adrenaline coursed through their veins.

"Nothin's movin'," Tank said, eyeing the pile of corpses.

"Clear back here," Connor said, lowering his ACR.

"So this is what I've been missin' out on?" Tank asked, turning to the brothers with a wide smile on his face.

"Feels good, doesn't it?" Connor said, a smile tugging at the corner of his lips.

"Hell yeah, it does!" Tank said.

"It just feels good to be out here again," James said. "I was feeling cooped up back there."

"I agree," Connor said. "I didn't want to lose my edge with all that sitting around."

"Well, thanks for the assist, boys," Tank said. "Shall we finish clearin' the room?"

"Roger," Connor said.

The rest of the back room was clear. They'd only found a fresh corpse in the corner where the zombies had come from and all the supplies seemed to be intact. Either no one had thought to look in any of the boxes and crates piled in the room, or they didn't have the equipment to haul them off.

Meeting at the door leading back into the grocery store proper, James pulled a small hand-drawn map of the town from a pouch on his plate carrier and circled the grocery store they were in. "Let's gather all the small stuff scattered around," James said. "We'll leave the crates for them to get later." He moved off to the front to grab a shopping cart.

The large grocery store had been ransacked and most of the shelves were bare. Wrappers and empty boxes were strewn about, but a few intact items were also in the mix—a bag of chips here, a can of corn there, a package of hot dog buns buried under the refuse.

James pushed the cart to the far right aisle where Tank was digging through a pile of cereal boxes. James's ACR rested on the small basket at the back of the cart, allowing the flashlight beam to brighten the aisle ahead. The windows in the ceiling cast scattered light down onto the floor, poorly illuminating the large room.

"You ask her out yet?" Tank asked, dumping a few cereal boxes into the cart.

"Not yet," James said.

"C'mon, bro," Tank said. "What's holdin' ya back?"

"It's just… complicated," James said.

"Ya scared?"

"No," James said but hesitated. He wasn't scared; he was terrified. "Maybe a little."

"Why be scared? She's just a girl, and girls aren't nearly as scary as fightin' off hordes of undead!"

"Are you sure about that?" James asked.

"Oh yeah, they're not that bad," Tank said. "Or is it Emmett you're afraid of?"

"I'd be scared of him," Connor said from the next aisle over. "He'll probably kill you if you hurt his daughter."

"Thanks for that, bro," James said.

"No problem," Connor said. "If you do have to

break her heart, just make sure you're *very* far away."

"Although he could probably shoot that far," Tank said.

"Yeah, over a mile with the right setup," Connor said, coming around the end of the aisle to deposit a box of assorted dry goods into the cart.

"Maybe just break up over text," Tank said.

"Phones don't work," Connor said as he moved off to another aisle.

"Right," Tank said. "Okay, maybe you *are* screwed."

"Enough!" James said. "I haven't even asked her out yet, and I'm not afraid of that."

"Then what is it?" Tank asked. "What's holdin' ya back?"

"What's the point of dating? It's not like we can get married and have a family and a normal life. There's no such thing as a normal life anymore. Either one of us could die tomorrow."

"Precisely! You might not get another chance," Tank said.

"So then, what's the point?"

"It's called livin' life," Tank said, looking directly at him. "As you said, you might die tomorrow, so there's no point in wastin' time bein' afraid. If you want to experience life, you have to live it."

"That's oddly profound."

"You know me. I'm not just full of wisecracks but deep insight as well."

James barked out a laugh. "That's true," he said.

"Plus, if you do die tomorrow, at least you'll have one date under your belt, and maybe somethin' more," Tank said with a wink.

James laughed. "It'll just be a date, nothing more."

"Not even a kiss?"

"Well, maybe that, but not the other stuff."

"Oh, trust me, I know that. You've been adamant about that since middle school. God forbid you let yourself slip up now at the end of the world."

"I've been holding to my convictions this long. I might as well stick to them till the end now."

"And I respect you for that," Tank said, defensively. "But it don't mean I have to do the same."

"I know that," James said. "I never meant you had to. *I'm* just choosing to stick with it, is all."

"Good," Tank said, moving around the end of the aisle and into the next one. James followed, pushing the cart.

They finished cleaning out the store, ending with two carts full of supplies. Connor exited the store first, with James and Tank each pushing a cart behind him. Outside, there were a few zombies gathered in the parking lot. As soon as they saw movement, they started their slow shuffle towards the storefront. Connor made quick work of them with his rifle, and within a minute, the way to their vehicle—Scourge— was clear. James and Tank pushed the carts over to the large armored LAPV while Connor continued to cover them. They loaded all the supplies into the back of the rig, filling up a quarter of the available space.

Tank drove out of the parking lot onto Railway Street, heading north. With the rising sun backlighting them, various zombies could be seen shambling around the streets farther into Milk River,

Alberta. Groups of zombies were also beginning to form and head towards the sound of their vehicle. They hadn't been able to check the rest of the town yet and wouldn't be able to now. James marked the other stores they hadn't made it to on his map so they could come back later. Their main mission was to do reconnaissance and search for large amounts of food and other necessary supplies while also getting an idea of the number of infected.

They pulled up to a pump at a gas station on the northern outskirts of town. James exited the rig and drew his handgun, walking closer to the three zombies stumbling towards them. At ten yards, he opened fire, and in four shots he had them on the ground as a suppressed gunshot went off behind him. With the hostiles taken care of, Tank began to fuel Scourge.

"You two can head inside and check," Tank said with an edge to his voice. "I'm gonna stay and fuel up."

"Sure thing," Connor said, moving to the station building. "C'mon James."

James looked at Tank and then followed his brother. They'd done something to piss him off. At the front of the station, Connor banged on the door, then waited a few seconds and opened it as James trained his handgun on the doorway. Groaning sounded from inside, but nothing came out to greet them.

"There's at least one," James said, moving into the building. "Must be trapped or something."

"Careful," Connor said, following.

James holstered his handgun and drew his

tomahawk, looking around the interior. The groaning came from the back of the room so he moved farther in. One of the beverage coolers had fallen over and a zombie was trapped underneath. It looked like it'd been trying to claw out for a while because its fingers were broken off and streaks of blood covered the floor in front of it. Bringing the tomahawk down on its head, he ended its torment. Unexpected emotion rose in his chest as he looked down at the creature. It had once been a woman, and probably a beautiful one at that. Now she was dead—fully dead—not stuck in some half-existence. This woman had once been a daughter to someone, maybe even a wife and mom. She'd once had dreams of her own. She'd loved, feared, hoped, and *been* someone once. She used to be *alive*.

That could be Alexis, James thought. *Or me. Or any one of the people I love.*

Tank's words from before came back to him, and he was struck with sudden clarity. He had to live each day like it was his last or he wasn't truly living—he was just surviving. He said a quick prayer for the woman as he moved to check the rest of the building. There was a sadness buried deep inside him that he hadn't realized was there until then. He'd thought he was healing and growing used to all of this, but in reality he was trying to stay busy to keep the feelings at bay. This past week had been a struggle for him in that regard, but now that these emotions were starting to surface, he was afraid of what they would bring. He'd done things to survive that he didn't know if he could reconcile.

"Clear," Connor said, checking the bathroom.

James scanned the room with his eyes. The station had been effectively raided and nothing useful was left.

"What'd you say to Tank?" Connor asked.

"I don't know," James said, thinking back. "I made a comment about how I wanted to wait until marriage to have sex."

"Let me guess—you said it the same way you always do?"

"Well, yeah."

"James, you say things with such intensity sometimes that it comes off as judging."

"I don't ever mean it that way."

"I know, but you do realize Tank and Chloe have been hooking up."

James stood there, stunned. He knew they'd been spending a surprising amount of time together lately, but he hadn't realized that.

"Damn," James said. "He thinks I was judging him."

"Yep," Connor said.

"That makes sense."

He thought back to the past decade he'd been friends with Tank. They were too similar sometimes but also completely different, which caused them to butt heads when they spent too much time together. Their friendship had even been compromised by arguments a few times. It was funny, Connor and Tank never got that way, only him and Tank. He knew what he needed to do, even though he didn't want to. It wasn't his fault people always took things the way they did when he spoke. He was just an intense kind of guy, and it tended to lead to the misunderstanding that he was arguing when he was really just stating an opinion. Okay, so maybe he *was* argumentative at times.

"Let's go. I'll fix it," James said, walking towards the exit.

"Good, because I always seem to get stuck in the middle," Connor said, following.

Outside, Tank had finished fueling and taken down five more zombies that had strayed too close. There was a small horde of them coming from town a few hundred yards away.

"You ladies finally ready?" Tank asked, starting the diesel engine.

"Born ready," Connor said.

James just nodded. He hated it when Tank called him things like that. It was like his friend didn't respect him at all. Biting back a response, he realized it was just the friction between the two of them. Normally, he would laugh at a comment like that, but not when things were like this. He needed to clear the air before it got worse, like it usually tended to.

"Hey, bro," James said, "I'm sorry about earlier. I didn't mean to imply anything with you and Chloe. I was just stating what *I* wanted to do. I never judge you for the way you live; in fact, sometimes I wish I could be more like you. You're so good at interacting with women and living the way you want."

"I know," Tank said, glancing back. "I wasn't upset. I just wanted to stick with the rig, but thanks."

Even though Tank had spoken like it wasn't a big deal, James knew he'd accepted the apology and things would go back to normal soon. He'd just have to watch what he said for a little while.

Tank pulled out of the gas station back onto Railway Street, heading north again. There was another small town on their map they were supposed to scout out. They turned onto Highway 4 and continued on their route to Warner.

James was still surprised that the leaders in Coutts had let them come out on this recon mission unsupervised.

It's because Emmett has pull and he talked with the right people, James thought.

That was why they had their gear and Scourge back. The first couple of days after arriving in Coutts, they hadn't been sure what would happen, but after being interviewed a few more times, they'd been told they could have their necessary gear, but all the surplus went back to the black-uniformed people it belonged to. Luckily, they let them keep their two ACRs, the SAW, uniforms, and Scourge. After a week in town, they'd finally been assigned their first mission as a test—the one they were on now.

"Is that smoke?" Connor asked.

James looked to the west where Connor was pointing and saw a thin line of gray rising into the sky. The smoke didn't look like much from this distance, but he knew it was a large fire.

"Looks like it," Tank said.

"We should go check it out. Someone might need help," James said.

"Really, bro?" Connor asked. "Haven't you learned anything in the past two weeks?"

James bit back his immediate response. Was the potential life of a stranger really worth risking his life or the lives of his brother and best friend? It could be a trap. There could be people waiting there to ambush whoever came to check on the fire. James could even put Coutts and the rest of the survivors in jeopardy, but something deep inside told him it was worth the risk because life was precious. At the same time, he couldn't ignore the potential danger to those he loved.

"You're right," James said, sitting back in his seat. "We have a job to do."

2
LIFE GOES ON

Alexis looked around at the other women in the kitchen and couldn't deny that she felt out of place. Most of these people hadn't been fully exposed to the harsh realities outside the safety of the fence. It wasn't their fault; they'd been fortunate that the government had stepped in and made this a safe haven early on. Still, she felt like an outcast, especially in this kitchen. She'd never been much of a cook, opting to either eat out or just get some cheap TV dinners, but there was a limited selection of jobs in Coutts. Her dad was talking with the higher-ups about letting her go out on runs, but so far he'd made little headway.

He'd been able to convince them to send the boys out though, Alexis thought.

She had half a mind to think her dad wasn't trying very hard, or at all, because he didn't want her out there. For the first couple of days in town, he'd barely left her side, but once he'd established that it was truly safe, he left her alone. After all they'd been through, she thought it was almost comical that he was being so overprotective when they were safer than ever. It was beginning to drive her crazy though, and she had to remember that he was doing it out of love, however misguided.

Even though it *was* truly safe in town, she constantly had to remind herself of that. Her mind flashed back to the last time she'd thought she was safe—they'd been taken captive to be executed by a zealous priest and his pet zombies. Now it was hard for her to let her guard down.

It could happen again, a part of her whispered. Shushing the voice, she went back to the task at hand. She had pasta to make, and it was proving to be disastrous.

Two hours later, she exited the kitchen, smelling like burnt noodles. Cook—the lady in charge of the kitchen—had been impressed. She'd never known anyone who could burn noodles before. Walking out of the diner they'd turned into the Mess Hall, she stopped on the street, feeling peaceful. A light breeze rustled her brunette hair, which gave off the fresh scent of burning food. There was definitely a shower in her plan for the evening.

The summer sun was low in the sky. It'd be setting in a few hours and still they weren't back. She headed towards the house she shared with her dad and Abby. As she walked, she had to keep her mind from worrying about them—well, worrying about James mainly. The feelings that rose within her every time she thought about him were getting out of hand. She'd rarely felt this way before. There'd been a few boys back in high school, but none of them had lasted very long. They were too young, and she didn't have any patience for idiots or egotistical guys—except her ex, Patrick. He'd fooled her and broken her heart, taking some of her innocence with him when he left her high and dry.

"Alexis," someone called from behind her.

She turned, reaching for the handgun holstered at her hip. It was her father, walking down the street towards her from the large Border Services building the military had claimed as their headquarters. Relaxing, she slowed so he could catch up.

"You finally get me out of that cursed food factory?" Alexis asked as he joined her.

"Roger, I—" Emmett cut off, flaring his nostrils. "Is that you that smells like a charred corpse?"

"Yeah, I burned some noodles today," Alexis said. "Oh, and the sauce. The bread came out edible at least, mostly."

Emmett laughed. "You got my cooking skills and not your mother's."

"Maybe I should use your technique and fool them all with MREs," Alexis said, chuckling.

"Worked for me."

"So, any good news?"

"You start working in the infirmary tomorrow."

Her father beamed at her like it was the perfect outcome. She was a little pissed that she wouldn't be going out on runs—she didn't like to be coddled— but as she thought about it, she realized she'd rather be helping people than going back out there anyway. However much she didn't want to be caged, she was also weary of always being on the run and constantly alert. It'd be nice to do something she loved and put her years of training to use.

"I know you want to go out, but I thought you'd like this even better," Emmett said.

"It's a huge upgrade from the kitchen," Alexis said, "so I'll take it."

"Good. You know the building just south of our house?"

"Yeah."

She'd seen it often but had never known why people were coming and going from there. It was always under guard and had the same type of fence around it that surrounded the town. It made sense; they had to treat every wound as if the person could be infected, especially those coming back from runs.

"That's where you'll be working," Emmett said. "Head over to HQ tomorrow morning at eight and they'll get you your credentials."

Alexis nodded as they arrived at the door to their house. She stopped and turned to her dad, smiling up at him. "Thanks, Daddy. That sounds perfect," she said, hugging him.

"You're welcome, sweetie," Emmett said.

"I need to wash this nasty smell off," Alexis said, ending the embrace. "See you tonight at dinner?"

"Not tonight," Emmett said, his face clouding. "I have a meeting, and it'll probably go late."

"That's okay. I'll see you in the morning. Love you."

"I love you, too," he said as he turned and left, making his way back to headquarters.

Alexis entered their house, thankful no one else was inside. Sharing a bathroom with her father and Abby was difficult when everyone wanted to use it at the same time. The house was small—three bedrooms, a kitchen, tiny living room, and the one shared bathroom. Her room was the first to the left and her father's was next to hers. In front of her room was an open living room with a kitchen directly to her right and the third bedroom just beyond the kitchen. Abby, one of the survivors from Burns, stayed in the third room. She was fun to stay with because she'd lived a long life and loved to share stories with Alexis, but she also tended to take forever in the bathroom and repeat those same stories over and over.

She made her way to her room to gather her things before showering. When she left the bathroom some time later, steam came pouring out from inside the confined room. Entering her bedroom, she shut the door and flopped down on the bed, wet hair and all. Showering had felt good, almost too good. For a few moments, she'd been able to forget about everything and believe that things were back to normal, or at least what she remembered of "normal." It was getting more and more difficult for her to remember those days. It was almost like her mind didn't want to think about what it'd been like before all this. Now all she could remember was the last two weeks, which seemed like a lifetime. Closing her eyes, she made herself relax. They were safe; *she* was safe. She just had to remember that.

Recalling what her dad had told her, she grabbed the alarm clock from the small nightstand next to her twin bed. She had to make sure she was up early in the morning. Her dad had practically beaten into her the fact that to be on time was the same as being late, and she wanted to make a good impression on her first day.

She wondered what it would be like to work in the

infirmary. From outside, the place looked more like a prison than a hospital. It made sense that she had to get credentials first; they wouldn't let just anyone in there. With that thought, it fully dawned on her that her dad had gone to a lot of trouble to get her this position, maybe even more trouble than letting her go out on runs. He'd known that even though she wanted to go out, she'd like this more, even if she didn't realize it at first. Her heart swelled with the love she felt. He'd always taken care of her and kept her safe. Maybe his protectiveness wasn't such a bad thing after all.

She put her alarm back down on the nightstand and rested her head back on her pillow, letting her mind wander. It was crazy to think they'd been in Coutts for nine days already. The past week had gone by in a blur of nothing but sleeping, eating, and interrogations. Then they'd been allowed out of their partial confinement and welcomed into the community. Most of the people were friendly and had been there since the beginning. Everyone contributed to the community in some way by volunteering at the different places around town. It was almost like people had jobs, and that created a sense of normalcy, which she was thankful for.

The higher-ups mostly left everyone to their daily lives, but there were a few rules, and the influence of the military was unmistakable. There were scheduled meals, food was rationed, and people weren't able to leave the town without permission, which most didn't seem to mind. The only part she didn't like was that everyone was kept in the dark about how the outside world was faring. She was also suspicious of the buildings that were off limits and the constant string of helicopters coming and going each day.

Her train of thought moved on to another topic that she'd been spending a lot of time on lately—James. She wondered when he'd begun to occupy so many of her thoughts. It was like he was always there now, in the back of her mind. She couldn't get him out, and she wasn't sure she wanted to. Did he feel the same? It seemed like he did, yet he hadn't made a move. He paid her a lot of attention when they were together and she often found him sneaking glances at her, but he never did anything about it. Her experience with guys was the opposite. They would come sauntering up to her, lay on some stupid one-liner, and expect her jump into their arms. They never succeeded in their quest, but they tried anyway. James was different, and maybe that was why she felt the way she did.

As all these thoughts chased each other in her mind, she eventually dozed off, the softness of her bed lulling her to sleep.

3
DEER IN HEADLIGHTS

James watched as they passed through the northern gate into Coutts, headlights illuminating the soldiers stationed there. Most of the border patrol and some of the civilians who'd lived in town before the outbreak had been evacuated to Calgary, one of Alberta's more fortified cities.

Tank drove them south on the interstate towards the Border Services building the military had made their HQ. James looked down at his map again, preparing his report. It felt weird to be reporting to an officer when he wasn't in the military. His brother, on the other hand, had easily fallen back into his training. Captain Miller, their commanding officer, liked that about Connor, but at the same time he didn't fault James or Tank for not having the same training. It was probably one of the reasons they were content to let them go out alone. Even though Connor wasn't enlisted anymore, he was still one of them; once a Marine, always a Marine.

It made James happy to see his brother fulfilling the role he'd always wanted but couldn't retain after his injury, although it didn't seem to be making him any happier. Over the past week James had begun to see his brother close off more, even to him, which was never a good thing. It was like how he used to be right after being medically discharged from the Marines, and it wasn't a good place for him to be. Connor seemed fine to most people, but James knew better. They'd never been very good at hiding things from each other, and he'd have to talk to his brother about it soon.

Tank pulled Scourge to a stop in the parking lot. Two Marines stood guard outside the door to the large, glass-walled building that was lit up from the inside.

"Let's report in," Connor said, stepping out and leaving his ACR in the seat.

James and Tank followed suit. The three of them headed towards the front door of the building.

"Back from a run?" asked one of the Marines.

"Yes, Corporal Lewis," Connor responded.

"Any bites, scratches, scrapes, cuts, or other injuries to report?" Cpl. Lewis asked.

"No, sir," Connor responded.

"Follow me, Captain Miller is expecting you."

The three of them followed the Marine inside. James looked around. Military men and women sat at their desks, talking on radios and satellite phones. Cpl. Lewis led them to the staircase and they went up to the second floor. There was a hallway with offices lining both sides. The first office to the left had a name taped on the outside of the door—Captain Miller. Cpl. Lewis stopped outside the door and knocked.

"Come in," a voice said from inside.

"The three civilians have come back from their

run, sir," Cpl. Lewis said after opening the door.

"Thank you, Corporal," Cpt. Miller said from behind his desk.

Cpl. Lewis nodded and headed back to his post outside the front door.

"Come in and sit down, gentlemen," Cpt. Miller said.

"Yes, sir," Connor said as the three of them sat down in the chairs across from the desk.

"What do you have for us?" the captain asked.

"We went north as requested," Connor said, glancing over at James, who pulled the map from a pocket on his plate carrier. "Our first stop was Milk River."

"How was the town?" Cpt. Miller asked.

"Overrun," Tank said.

The captain cursed. "It was clear a few days ago."

"We found the grocery store on the south end of town," James said, passing his map across the desk. "We gathered all the miscellaneous items lying around, but there were whole pallets and boxes of food in the storeroom. By the time we cleaned the place out, a horde had started to form around us, so we didn't have a chance to check the rest of the town."

"Good," Cpt. Miller said. "At least we have that. The whole town will have to be cleared soon or it will just cause us issues in the future."

"I agree," Connor said.

"Anything else?"

"We checked Warner as well," Connor said.

"Also overrun," Tank said, "but there weren't as many undead there. I think most had already evacuated."

"We took everything from the grocery store, but there wasn't much," James said.

"Oh, and the fuel station on the north side of Milk River had workin' pumps," Tank said. "Not sure if they're on a different power grid or a backup generator, but they worked. The one in Warner didn't."

"Good, we'll take the tanker to Milk River and the fuel truck to Warner," Cpt. Miller said. "Anything else?"

"We saw smoke west of the highway between the two towns," James said. "Quite a bit of it."

"Did you investigate?" Cpt. Miller asked.

"We didn't want to risk it, sir," Connor said.

"Probably wise," Cpt. Miller said. "We'll have a Black Hawk check it in the morning. I shouldn't be surprised because of what Sergeant Wolfe said about you, but I still am. You did well."

"Thank you, sir," Connor said.

"No, thank *you*. If we can send out trained civilians to do the recon runs, that leaves more of our men to see to the protection of this town."

"We're glad to get out 'n get some exercise," Tank said.

"Indeed," Cpt. Miller said.

"Thank you again, sir," James said. "And for returning our gear to us, as well."

"It seems like it was a wise choice and will continue to be so long as you use it to help us."

"We will, sir," Connor said.

James wanted to add that they would until they decided to continue on, but he held that comment back. Cpt. Miller might not like it if he knew they wouldn't be staying long, not after giving them all their gear and a huge asset like the LAPV.

Should we stay longer? James asked himself.

It was the question that had been nagging at him for the past week. This place was as safe as any they had seen so far, and it might be one of the safest places left.

"That's all, men," Cpt. Miller said. "Take tomorrow for yourselves and report back here Wednesday at 0800."

"Yes, sir," Connor said.

"Will do," Tank said as the three of them stood up.

James led the way out of the office and into the hallway, the other two exiting right behind him. They walked out of the building in silence and loaded into Scourge.

"That went well," James said.

"Yeah, it did," Tank said.

"We're showing them we can be helpful," Connor said. "They aren't gonna like it when we're ready to leave."

"My thoughts exactly," James said.

"We still plannin' on that?" Tank asked.

"I think so," James said. "I know this seems safe, but I don't think it'll last."

"And something doesn't feel right," Connor said.

"I'm glad I'm not the only one who feels that way," James said.

"I just think you two are crazy and can't handle the peace," Tank said with a smile, starting the rig and driving into town. "I'll make sure to let a few undead in tonight to keep you on your toes."

James chuckled. "Or not."

Scourge rolled past the store with a large sign that read "Duty Free," and turned onto First Street. Coutts normally held around two hundred and fifty people, but with their group, other survivors who'd ended up there, and all the military personnel, there had to be over four hundred. Living space was limited, so much so that groups of people had to live crammed together in one house. That's why the three of them were staying in a small, abandoned store. The authorities had cleared out the space and put in a bunch of cots. The good news was that it was warm, dry, and they each had their own cot to sleep on, complete with a foam pad. Plus, they were the only three living there so far. Once more people arrived, they'd get shoved in with the three of them, but until then they had the run of the place. Tank turned onto North Avenue and began the short drive through town to their place on the outskirts, not far from the west side of the fence surrounding town.

"Oh, hey," James said, an idea popping into his head. "Can you drop me off at Alexis's house?"

"On one condition," Tank said, that mischievous glint in his eye as he looked in the rearview mirror. That wasn't good. "Only if you ask her out. Tonight."

"I… this is hardly the—"

"Cut the crap, man," Tank said. "Nut up or shut up."

"But—"

"If you can't stand the heat, get out of the kitchen," Connor said, cutting James off.

"Ya know Troy has his eye on Alexis, and I bet he'll be askin' her out soon. So you better get to it!"

Tank said.

James clamped his mouth shut. He couldn't get a word in. Tank turned north on Third Street, driving away from Alexis's house and theirs. He was giving James time.

"Guys, I just can't..." James began but faltered.

"Bro," Connor said, looking back at him, "we've faced down armed men, taken on dozens of zombies, and driven hundreds of miles through shit-storm after shit-storm. I'm pretty sure that if you can do all that, you can ask a girl out."

Those were all very good points, but why was Connor always telling him how it was? That was supposed to be his job as the older brother, but it never seemed to be like that. It was more of a give and take in their relationship, and even though Connor was younger, he still helped James just as much as James helped him.

"You're right," James said, taking a deep breath. "I'll do it."

"There ya go, Jamesy Boy!" Tank exclaimed, flipping a U-turn in the middle of the street.

"It's about damn time," Connor said.

"I mean, what's the worst that could happen?" James said.

"She could crush your heart with her bare hands," Tank said.

"Or Emmett could kill you," Connor added.

"Holy crap, guys," James said. "That's not helping."

"Oh yeah, right. Happy thoughts," Tank said, chuckling. "Nothing bad has ever happened when a man offers a woman his heart."

"It's just a date," James said.

"Is it?" Tank asked. "I thought you were all about only dating someone when you knew you wanted to marry them."

"That was before the end of the world," James said.

Was that still true? He didn't exactly know what his feelings were. Tank pulled up outside the house, parking next to Emmett's truck.

"You guys comin'?" James asked.

"Nope, gonna head on down to the saloon," Tank said.

"You got this, bro," Connor said.

"Thanks," James said hesitantly as he stepped out of the vehicle.

As soon as he shut the door, Tank took off down the street. James slowly walked towards the house, his steps laden. Why was this so damn daunting? It wasn't as if he was in danger here... or maybe this was the most dangerous thing he'd ever done. His heart pushed him forward while his mind told him to run into the night.

The front door opened, spilling light out onto the small porch, and James stopped dead in his tracks like a deer in headlights. Alexis was standing in the doorway, dressed in a pair of jeans and an olive-colored t-shirt, her undone hair glowing in the light from behind her. He couldn't see her eyes in the dark, but he knew they were locked on him. A smile grew on her face as she recognized who was standing at the bottom step.

"Who's out there, sweetie?" Abby asked, trying to look out into the night from the dining room table. "Is it that boy you—"

Alexis quickly stepped out, shutting the door behind her and cutting off the older woman.

"Hey, James," Alexis said, standing on the porch.

"Uh, hi," James said, still glued to the ground where he stood.

He knew the awkwardness he felt was exuding from inside of him. Opening his mouth, he tried to speak but then shut it again, like a fish out of water. He had no idea what to say. As soon as she'd opened the door, all of his thoughts had flown from his head. What the hell was he going to do now?

4
BOOTLEGGER SALOON

Connor walked into the Bootlegger Saloon with Tank. They were quickly becoming regulars at the place. Tank led them over to a table in the far right corner, the same one they always sat at. It took only a minute until Chloe was heading their way, a smile on her face and a shot of Captain Morgan and Jack Daniels on her tray. They definitely came in here too often if she already knew what they'd order.

Setting the rum in front of Connor, she went over to give Tank the whiskey and acted like she was about to give him a kiss on the cheek but stopped herself.

"No James tonight?" she asked, starting back towards the bar.

"Nah," Tank said. "He might finally be askin' Alexis out."

"Took him long enough," Chloe said. "She's been wondering if he even still liked her."

"He just had to work up the courage," Connor said.

"Chloe!" yelled the owner of the saloon, an angry man named Durt.

"Better go," Chloe said as Tank handed her some

cash. "I'll be right back with your next round of shots."

"Thanks," Tank said with a smile, watching her as she retreated to the bar.

It was still hard to believe that those two had turned from enemies to lovers so quickly. Or maybe they'd never really been enemies, just so similar that they often bickered. Either way, they were ideal for each other and Connor was happy for his best friend, although he was still curious as to why they were keeping it under wraps.

"So," Connor said. "You and Chloe."

"We have shots to take first," Tank said, raising his glass and downing the liquid.

Connor picked his up, eyeing it. Alcoholism was in his family's blood, and he knew he was going down a slippery slope.

I only drink for the fun of it, he told himself. *It's just something to do.*

He shouldn't have anything to worry about. It wasn't as if he was getting drunk every night and stumbling home. He was just having a few drinks. Raising the small glass to his lips, he tipped it. A familiar burn accompanied the liquid down his throat, and he sighed. No, this wasn't bad—just a way for him to relax at the end of the day. As soon as he set the small glass down on the table, Chloe was there with another shot for each of them.

"Another round after this?" she asked. "Or are you ready for your drinks?"

Tank looked at Connor, who didn't even hesitate. The thoughts still scratched at the back of his mind.

Connor nodded. "Two more shots."

"That's my man!" Tank exclaimed, handing Chloe more cash as she deposited the new shots and went back to the bar.

It was funny—just over a week ago he'd thought they'd never use money as currency again, yet here they were using it to buy drinks, one of the only things they had to pay for in this town. Their housing and food were paid for by working for the military leaders. The only way to spend the money they found on runs was at the saloon or the duty-free store, which didn't have much of anything they needed.

Connor took his shot first this time and Chloe brought them another round as soon as they were done. It wasn't like the place was busy. There were usually a few soldiers and Marines in there when they had the evening off, but tonight it was just him and Tank, along with the regulars. Chloe was the only server working there. No one else would work for Durt because he was such a prick, but Chloe didn't care. She just gave it right back to him. It kept her busy and she'd learned how to make drinks quickly. It was just another thing she and Tank had in common.

They continued to drink as the night wore on. They had the next day off so Connor didn't care how late it was. He still didn't want to drink too much, but after a few hours he was feeling good, and those annoying thoughts in his head were gone. For now.

"You still wanna leave town?" Tank asked.

"Yeah," Connor said. "It can't last long. Soon, this whole place will fall apart."

"How? They have tons of firepower, that fancy fence, and good leadership."

"It'll just happen. Every time things start to look up, we get hit. This'll be no different. It's the cycle we live in now."

"So it's less that you think this place'll fall and more that you're just waitin' for somethin' bad to happen?"

"Maybe," Connor said, taking a sip of his Dark and Stormy. "But it'll happen."

"I hope you're wrong."

"Me too."

This place was too good to be true, and while he would love for it all to work out, he doubted it would. Even with the military in charge and help from the government, this place would fall, given time, and he didn't want to be around when it did. If they could just get to Alaska and out to the bush where they'd be alone, then *maybe* they'd be safe. Unless that fell to pieces, too. Then they'd have nothing left. But he'd make sure that didn't happen. With just a few of them, they could survive and make a life for themselves, but they couldn't trust others. They'd have to keep their haven a secret, hidden away from the rest of the world. It was the only way it would work.

Glancing up from his drink, he noticed Chloe wink at Tank.

Those two, Connor thought, shaking his head.

"Why hide it?" he asked as Chloe walked back to the bar.

"What?" Tank asked, moving his gaze from Chloe to Connor.

"You and Chloe."

"Hide what?"

"Allen," Connor said. Tank looked around quickly to make sure no one had heard. "I know you and Chloe have a thing going on, and so does everyone else."

Tank looked pissed that Connor had used his real name, but the look faded. "Because we're just hookin' up."

"And you don't want people to know because then you'll have to take it more seriously?"

"No, it's just no one's damn business."

"Brother, I know you, probably better than you'd like me to. You were calling James on his crap earlier, so now it's my turn."

"This isn't—"

"Nut up or shut up," Connor said, looking his friend directly in the eyes. "You're afraid of letting anyone close because then they have the power to hurt you. So instead of having an actual relationship with Chloe, you're just keeping it physical. But that won't last and you know it. You'll either have to move to the next stage or end it. Not only do I not want to see either of you getting hurt, but I actually think you two belong together, even if that sounds cheesy as hell. It's been a long time since you let anyone really get to know you, and that was my brother and me. It's time to do it again. The world is ending, and we could go out on a run in two days and not come back. You owe it to yourself and Chloe to let her in."

After his uncharacteristically long speech, Connor took a swig of his drink.

"You always were an insightful bastard when you drink," Tank said, subdued.

"It's almost like a superpower that's powered with alcohol."

"What *is* it with today? First James gets all his issues shoved in his face and now me? I think it's your turn next."

"No need. I know my issues."

"Really?"

"I drink to silence the voices in my head, to cover up the fear and worry growing inside, and to run from what I know is true. I drink because it's necessary to survive in my current state. I've got a lot of shit I don't feel like dealing with right now."

"Okay," Tank said, chuckling. "I guess you're right."

"I usually am," Connor said, smiling at Tank, and they both started cracking up.

It'd always been easier for him to open up and say what was in his heart when he drank, but he guessed that was how it was for most people. They finished their drinks and sat at the table, talking about things that didn't matter anymore—video games, movies, TV shows—anything that kept the conversation from getting too serious again. They were there to forget, not dredge up more of the past.

When the last call came, Connor left and walked back to their place two blocks south. Tank lingered and helped Chloe close down the saloon. He'd be staying with her that night, and maybe he would open up and let her in. Connor truly hoped he would.

If James and Tank could be happy—the two people he cared about the most—then maybe he could look past the hole growing inside him and be content with that. He knew it wouldn't last long, but maybe he could hold it together until they made it to Alaska. After that, he'd finally deal with everything he was trying to cover up.

5
THE LEAP

Alexis smiled and walked down the steps past James. Could she sense his fear like a predator? If that were true, he was in a world of hurt.

"Wanna go for a walk?" she asked and turned back to face him.

"Yeah," James said as she started down the street.

It only took a few steps and he caught up with her as they walked down the narrow sidewalk together. The only light was cast by various porch lights in small pockets, as well as the sliver of a moon above. James felt himself relaxing as he breathed in the cool night air. He always felt more comfortable outside, even if it was in the middle of town.

"How'd the run go?" Alexis asked, breaking the silence after they'd walked for a minute or so.

"Good," James responded, glad to get out of his mind. "We found quite a few supplies in one of the towns and even a working gas station."

"I hear those are becoming increasingly rare," she stated.

"They are. Most have lost power, and it's going to make heading north even more difficult."

"Dad thinks we can stay here. It's safe, and it's

sounding like the government might be able to get this whole thing under control."

"Yeah, so they say."

"You don't believe them?"

She glanced over at him as they continued to walk, side by side. James almost stumbled when his eyes met hers, and his heart gave a small leap in his chest.

Get it together! he chided himself.

"I don't know," he said. "It's just hard to wrap my mind around. Nine days ago we thought the whole world was falling apart. Now we hear it's not that bad. It just doesn't register with all I saw out there."

"They said the western states got hit a lot worse. The east coast wasn't nearly as affected."

"That's what they've said, but then why are they still here? Why not just get everyone east where it's safe?'"

"That's a good point," Alexis said as they arrived at the last block before hitting the western fence.

They turned north, passing by a large open lot to their right with a couple of houses to their left. After walking awhile in silence, James realized it wasn't nerve-wracking like before; it was almost comfortable. They didn't need to talk to enjoy each other's company. Something clicked in his mind. He didn't know what it was or even how to explain it, but something just felt *right*. It gave him the courage to continue.

"How was cooking today?" James asked as they turned to the right, following a different street back to the east.

"It was fine," Alexis said.

"It smells like you burnt something again."

"Really? I still smell like crispy noodles? I spent fifteen minutes in the shower washing my hair!"

James leaned over and sniffed her hair.

"Yep, still smells like you set somethin' on fire." He smiled, and then realized how weird it was that he'd just sniffed her hair. His smiled faded, and when she glanced over, the look on his face caused her to burst out laughing.

"That look," Alexis said, giggling.

"What? Was it that obvious?"

"You looked like a kid with his hand caught in the cookie jar."

"Oh."

"Lighten up, James. No need to be so stiff."

"I just haven't spent much time around..."

He didn't finish the statement. Why was he acting so weird now? Hadn't he just been thinking how right it felt?

"Women?" Alexis supplied.

"Yeah."

"That's okay." She smiled over at him. "It makes you sincere."

"I feel like it makes me weird."

"A little, but being weird hasn't ever hurt anyone."

Her smile was infectious, and soon he was smiling along with her.

"I guess that's true," James said.

They turned south on Third Street, heading back towards her house. If he didn't make his move soon, he'd miss the perfect opportunity. His mind battled with his heart and his hands began to sweat. Why was asking one simple question so hard? Probably because he was offering her a small piece of his heart and she had the ability to crush it. He was under no illusion that he already loved her, but he did have strong feelings, and if she said no, it'd be devastating. In his life up to this point, he'd just avoided situations that gave others that kind of power over him. It was safest. But now nothing was safe, and since this could quite possibly be the last time he saw her alive, he'd be damned if he chickened out now.

"Alexis?" James asked.

"Yes," she said, stopping and turning to face him.

Oh, hell, James thought. *Why'd she have to do that?*

He felt like he was standing in the path of a charging grizzly bear, unarmed and naked. It would've been a lot easier if they'd kept walking and he didn't have to look into those gorgeous hazel eyes. She'd stopped in one of the few pools of light on this block and he could see her face—the way her brunette hair caressed her cheeks, the small dimples that formed when she was about to smile, and those lips. His gaze snapped back up to her eyes. He would not succumb to her charm, not right now. He had a mission to complete. Staring her in the eyes, he leapt from the cliff, praying he could fly.

"Will you go out on a date with me?" James said, the nervousness gone from his voice, replaced by determination.

The growing smile on her face told him the answer before she even spoke, and his heart began to soar. Maybe he did have wings.

"I'd love to," Alexis said. "What'd you have in mind?"

"I honestly haven't given much thought to it. I've

been trying to work up the courage just to ask," James said, smiling from ear to ear.

"Were you scared of me?"

"More so than anything in my life."

The sincerity with which he said it made her laugh, and he joined in. All he'd faced, yet asking her out had been the most frightening thing he'd ever done. He had some serious issues. They arrived at South Avenue and turned back towards her house, the porch light shining in the distance.

"When will this date be?" Alexis asked.

He hadn't given much thought to that either. He was still shocked that she'd said yes.

"How about tomorrow night? Seven o'clock?"

"That sounds perfect."

They arrived at her house and she went up to the porch while James stayed at the bottom of the steps. She turned around and smiled down at him. By all things holy, she was beautiful.

"I'll see you tomorrow night," James said.

"Goodnight, James."

"Night, Alexis."

She gave him one last smile before opening the door and entering her house. James stood outside for a few minutes, his mind unable to process what had just happened. He turned and jumped as he saw a shadow walking towards him from across the street. His hand slipped to his hip where his 1911 handgun was holstered, but he calmed quickly as he recognized the man walking towards him.

"Evening, sir," James said.

"Evening," Emmett said, walking up to James. "I heard the run went well today."

"Yes, sir," James said. "We were able to find a stash of food and scout out those towns."

"Good job. I'm glad to see you and your brother are doing better. This break from being out there seems to be fixing you right up."

"Yes, sir."

James didn't want to tell him the truth. The downtime was tearing him apart inside, not making him better. But maybe that was what he needed in order to get closure and prepare for the rest of the trip. They still had a long way to go.

"Well, you have a good night, son," Emmett said, "and enjoy your free day tomorrow. We have a lot of work ahead of us."

"Yes, sir, I will," James said as Emmett continued on his way. "And sir?"

Emmett turned around. "Yes?"

"I hope it's okay with you, but I asked your daughter out on a date."

Emotions flashed across Emmett's face too fast for James to follow. Finally, Emmett gave a small smile and walked back to stand face to face with James. It registered in James's mind that he was a dead man. What had he done? But just as quickly, the irrational fear faded, and he stood up straight and looked Emmett in the eyes.

"I see," Emmett began. "I think you've been around me enough so I don't have to give you the tough-dad speech. You already know that if anything happens to my daughter, I'll leave you bleeding in a ditch. You also already know that her safety is my biggest priority in all I do. You know all that, and I know you know that. So I'll just say this—treat my daughter with the respect she deserves and protect her with your own life."

"I will, sir," James said.

"I know you will. That's the only reason I'm allowing this. I trust you."

"Thank you, sir. I won't let you down," James said, reaching out his hand.

"Make sure you don't," Emmett said, taking James's hand in a firm grip and giving it a shake. "Now, get some shuteye."

"I will. Night, sir."

Emmett gave him a pat on the shoulder and walked to the house. He opened the door and walked inside, not looking back. James went down the street towards his place, an assortment of emotions swirling within him. The meeting with Emmett had somewhat dulled the elation he'd felt before. There was responsibility in taking this on. Maybe it would be just one date and after tomorrow night they'd go back to being friends, but he doubted that. If things did continue, he'd have another person close to him that he'd have to protect with his life. But he'd always felt that way about her, so things weren't changing that much. After another block, the pure joy of it caught up with him and he practically skipped back to their place to tell the guys.

6
TRAINING

Post-outbreak day 18

Alexis awoke to her first alarm and sat up in bed, wide awake. Today was a big day, for more reasons than one. It was her first day at her new job, and tonight was her date with James. She thought about their walk the night before, and it still surprised her that he'd finally asked. She'd wanted him to, of course, but with the way he'd been acting lately, she hadn't been sure he ever would. Then, when he'd asked with such confidence, he'd suddenly been the same man who'd taken charge of the survivors in Burns. Given his actions in that situation, she sometimes forgot that he was only twenty-one, just a year older than she was.

Climbing out of bed, she dressed and got ready for work. She wasn't sure what to wear so she opted for a tan pair of cargo-style pants and a tank top. If yesterday was any indication, it would be hot and sunny again today. She decided to grab a plaid button-up shirt in case the infirmary had AC. She was out the door and heading to HQ by seven-thirty. It was always better to show up early rather than late, although she more often tended to do the latter like her mother. Thinking about her mom brought up emotions buried deep within her, and she had to spend the five-minute walk getting them back under control.

She stopped outside the catwalk that led to the second floor of the Border Services building. Two soldiers stood out front. It was nice to see that both the Marines and the Army had a presence there and were working together, but it also didn't bode well for how things were going beyond the fence.

"Morning, ma'am," one of the soldiers said. Hines was the name on his tag.

"Morning, Hines," she said, smiling. "I'm here to get my ID for working in the infirmary. Not sure who I'm supposed to meet though."

"You must be Alexis Wolfe," the other one, Donn, said.

"Yes, sir," she said.

"Right this way," Hines said, opening the door for her.

"Thank you," Alexis said as she stepped inside.

He took the lead and led her to the offices on the north side of the building. She walked down the hall behind the soldier, watching as a few men and women walked in and out of the doors lining each side. It was surprising that she saw very little military presence in the town proper, with the exception of the three barracks they had set up, along the fence, and here. None of them seemed to go into town besides the odd patrol here or there. They didn't mix with civilians such as herself unless someone had a job that required them to work together. They didn't intentionally keep everyone separated, did they?

"Right here, ma'am," Hines said, stopping outside a door and knocking.

She read the name on the door—Captain Miller, her dad's old squad mate. The captain responded from inside and Hines opened the door, ushering her in. She entered the threshold and stood just inside as Hines closed the door behind her. The man sitting behind the desk had gray hair at his temples and an exhausted air about him. From what her dad had said, this man was in charge of the day-to-day running of the town while another man, Captain Sanders, was in charge of the military operations. Colonel Briggs was in charge of all of them, but she'd never seen the man.

"Morning, Ms. Wolfe," Cpt. Miller said, looking up from his paperwork. Even in his exhausted state his eyes were sharp and alert.

"Morning, Cpt. Miller," Alexis said, walking farther in and sitting down in a chair.

"You need an ID card for the infirmary, correct?" Cpt. Miller asked.

"Yes, sir."

"Good, take this," he said, handing her the paperwork. "This is a contract. Read through it and then sign."

"You don't mind?" she asked, looking at the twenty or so pages.

"Not at all. I'm used to signing everything that's dropped in front of me, but we expect you to know what's in that and agree to it."

"Perfect," Alexis said, beginning to stand.

"You can stay in here, Ms. Wolfe. I'll just be

reading over and signing my own paperwork," Cpt. Miller said kindly.

Alexis settled in. Halfway through, a nagging feeling began to grow in her stomach. Most of the first half was a basic kind of doctor-patient confidentiality stuff, but now it was beginning to talk about what happened inside the infirmary. She couldn't share what she did, saw, or heard, and she had to follow orders as if she was actually in the military. It wasn't like a normal hospital, and there was even a part of the contract that said if she was infected she forfeited her right to live. They took this very seriously, and it left her a little uneasy.

"Is all this really necessary?" Alexis asked when she'd finished reading. "I mean, why can't I talk to others about what happens inside the infirmary?"

"For the most part, it doesn't matter," Cpt. Miller said. "But then there are those few cases when people are infected and have to be… put down. It wouldn't be good if people went around telling everyone else that we were killing people. Then no one would go to the infirmary and the first person to be infected in town would cause havoc."

That made sense, but she didn't like it. Not at all. "You just 'put them down?'"

"It's only happened once, to one of my men. He wanted it that way. All this is more theoretical. *You* won't have to do it if it ever comes to that. Someone else will handle it. Plus, I don't think it's much of a possibility. We have some highly-skilled doctors on staff and few people come back infected." The way he said the last part had her questioning if they *let* anyone come back who'd been infected. "If you'd like to change your mind, there'll be no hard feelings. You can always go back to the kitchen. I know Cook always needs help."

"No," Alexis said before she could dissuade herself. She wanted to help people. "I'll sign."

"It's your choice, Ms. Wolfe," Cpt. Miller said.

Once she signed, he took it, looked it over, and signed next to her signature. Then he handed her a single piece of paper.

"Take this down to the desk labeled *Exports* and give it to them. They'll get your picture taken and identification badge printed."

"Yes, sir," Alexis said, standing and offering her hand. "Thank you. And I really do want to work here. I'm grateful for the opportunity."

"You're welcome, Miss," Cpt. Miller said, standing and shaking her hand with a smile. "Your father is very persuasive."

She exited the room and headed to the stairs located at the other end of the hall from where she'd entered. She owed her dad big time for this. It'd taken a lot to get her this position, and yet she'd almost thrown it away because of some stupid contract. It's not like they were hiding anything. Leaving the stairwell, she walked into a large room with desks lining one side. She found the desk labeled *Exports* and the woman sitting behind it.

Thirty minutes later, Alexis left the building and made her way to the infirmary. It was a good thing she hadn't been required to be there at a certain time because it'd taken almost an hour to get her ID badge. The building that housed the infirmary was only a couple hundred yards away from HQ. It was surrounded by a fence, and she had to walk all the way back up the street and enter from the driveway across from her house. It was daunting, taking in the large brick building. It had an old, sinister feel to it. As she reached the driveway, she noticed an old sign that read "Coutts Community School."

She started down the driveway and soon reached the gate. Two black-uniformed men stopped her and checked her ID, then let her in. These were not normal soldiers. Their nametags looked like nicknames and they had no distinguishable ranks showing. Plus, one of the men had a face tattoo and that wasn't allowed in active duty military. These must be the same people James was saying they recovered all the gear from on the hilltop when they'd been captured by Bryce.

She walked past the lawn and noticed there were shelves full of books and items that had been thrown out of the building. The waste saddened her, but she couldn't blame them if they needed the room. Entering the infirmary, she noticed a young man standing in the middle of the room, glancing at his watch. When the front door shut behind her, he looked up and smiled. It was a genuine smile that spread to his eyes. He reminded her a lot of Levi, and she shuddered at the memories that rose within her.

"You must be Ms. Wolfe," he said, walking over to her and shaking her hand. "I'm Dr. Nelson."

"Nice to meet you, Doctor," Alexis said. "You can call me Alexis."

"And you can call me Henry," he said with that smile again. "You ready for your first day?"

"Of course," Alexis said as he led her to a small

room to the right of the entrance that still held shelves full of books.

"Today will be training. You'll be watching a lot of videos, and I'll be here if you have any questions," Henry said, going over to an old box TV on a stand. "It'll all be basic stuff, so bear with me because you'll probably know most of it."

He was right, and after the first hour of dated videos she knew it was going to be a long first day.

7
JUST ANOTHER DAY

James finished his breakfast in the Mess Hall and walked out into the sunlight with Connor following behind him. It was only nine in the morning and it was already hot. It'd be miserably hot later in the day. He always hated July in Montana. Growing up in Alaska, a hot summer day was in the seventies, maybe the eighties if it was really bad. But here it could easily get to a hundred degrees, and today wouldn't be far from that. He'd have to find something to do inside to get out of the oppressive, dry heat.

"What's your plan for today?" James asked his brother.

Connor looked over at him. James knew Connor had had a lot to drink the night before, and yet there he was, up early and looking normal. If James had drunk as much as his brother did last night, he'd be just about dead in his bed, not wanting to move. How did Connor always do that? Granted, James was kind of a lightweight, so that was partly it. But still.

"I was going to head back to our place and clean all the guns," Connor said. "Get our gear together for tomorrow. I think we'll need it."

"Sweet. You mind cleaning mine?" James asked, already knowing the answer. His brother loved to clean guns. Maybe it had to do with his days in the Marines.

"Why? You too busy preparing for your little date?"

"I still have no idea what I'm going to do."

"I got you covered. I'll get them all cleaned and then clean out Scourge. I'm still finding casings from your little stunt with the Reclaimers."

James laughed. Had that really been ten days ago? It felt like their time in Coutts was flying by, and yet, when they were out on the road, time seemed to drag on forever.

"We did fling a few rounds at them," James said.

"Yeah. I'll see you back at our place later," Connor said, walking off.

"See ya, bro," James said.

After a few minutes of standing in the sunlight, James began to walk around town with no destination in mind. He was doing his best to think of something special for his date that night, but he was drawing a blank. His biggest problem was that the options were limited. There was only so much that could be done in a post-apocalyptic town on lockdown. His mind began to try and formulate a plan of attack while he wandered the streets, nodding at those he passed. Eventually, he ran into someone he knew.

"Morning, Greg," James said as he noticed the big man walking toward him down the street.

"Mornin'," Greg said, pulling to a stop in front of him. "Look, James, I have a few things I need to say."

Great. And just like that, his morning had taken a turn for the worse.

"I wanted to apologize," Greg said. "I've been resistant to you ever since Burns, and while I still don't agree with everything you did, I do see that it has allowed us to get here safely. I already talked with Alexis and Emmett, but I haven't had a chance to catch up with you yet."

"Thanks, Greg," James said. "You've played a big part in getting everyone here, too."

"Yeah, I have," Greg said. "But I see now you also were a big part, so thank you."

"You're welcome," James said, shaking Greg's offered hand. "So what do they have you doin'?"

"When they found out I could weld, they sent me over to help out the town's metalworker and mechanic. It's nice to be doing something normal that I'm actually good at."

"I bet. Well, I won't keep you. Thanks again."

"Yeah, you have a good day, James."

He continued on his way. That was wholly unexpected but very welcome.

His thoughts returned to the date. Why was everything involving women so damn difficult?

~~~

Tank carefully climbed out of bed, leaving a sleeping Chloe curled up under the sheets. He dressed quietly, trying not to wake her. With Chloe working late shifts, she needed her beauty sleep. He'd accidentally awakened her once, and that hadn't been a good life choice. At the door, he pulled up short, Connor's words from the night before coming back to him. His friend was right—more right than Tank ever wanted to admit. Walking to the nightstand, he pulled out a piece of paper and a pen, scribbling down a little note. He left it sitting next to her alarm clock.

He took a quick shower because his place didn't have one and also because her two roommates were out of the house. The sun outside was already high in the sky, and it was late morning. He'd missed his scheduled breakfast in the Mess Hall. They had such a stupid system for that. Different people were allowed to eat at different times in order to accommodate the inflated population and because they only had the Mess Hall. That meant he'd have to wait for his scheduled lunch at twelve-thirty. He glanced down at his watch. It was only a couple hours anyway, so it wouldn't be that bad. Rarely had he eaten breakfast before all this, although now that he had a more active schedule, he was eating more regularly.

Walking down the street back towards his place, he ran into James.

"How'd it go last night?" Tank asked and James smiled. It must've gone well.

"Well, I'm walking around trying to figure out what to do for a date, if that gives you a clue."

"Right on, bro. Way to go!"

"Thanks, and thanks for the push. It was needed."

"It was nothin'," Tank said throwing an arm around James's shoulders. "I was just tired of seein' you spinnin' your wheels and gettin' nowhere."

"Yeah, I was, too. Oh hey, I just saw Greg and he's working for a guy who does metalwork. Not sure if he'd know how, but maybe he can make you a sword or something like Frostmourne."

"That's a hell of a good idea! Where's he at?"

"Forgot to ask. He was walking south on Third though."

"I'll head that way and see what I can find."

"See ya later, man," James said, walking off.

Tank turned back and headed in search of the blacksmith—well really a metalworker, but whatever. It wasn't hard to find the place. Third Street ended just past the mechanic shop and there were piles of the same kind of fencing that surrounded the whole town. There were semi-trailers sitting next to the piles, and soldiers were loading the fencing onto them. The trailer had a green logo of a box with an opening at the top and *HESCO* written next to it. It was presumably the company that made the fencing. As he watched them load, he realized just how nifty the stuff really was. The solid block that made up the bottom four-foot by four-foot area was empty until they poured dirt, gravel, or cement into it. It helped hold up the rest of the six feet of heavy-duty metal fencing with razor wire on top, making it almost impenetrable.

He entered the building and noticed Greg. The big man was welding what looked like reinforcement onto the front bumper of a Humvee. Glancing around, he saw an older man with short brown hair and a dirty plaid shirt who was bossing the other workers around. That'd be the man in charge.

Was he really about to ask this man to make him a sword? Tank shrugged. Might as well try.

He walked up to the boss when he'd finished

giving orders to a blonde-haired young man he recognized as one of the survivors from Burns.

"Excuse me," Tank said.

"Yes?" the man asked in a gruff voice, turning to face him.

"I have an odd request," Tank said. "I need a sword."

"You're kiddin' me, right?" the man asked, chuckling.

"No," Tank said. "I'm not sure if you've been out much, but I've been survivin' on the road for weeks now. I know ammo is limited, and sooner or later we'll all be relyin' on old-school weapons."

The man actually looked like he was contemplating it. "There are a lot of other weapons more practical than a sword."

"Yes, but it's not just about practicality. I used to have a sword and it meant a lot to me."

"How so?"

"Really? You want my life story right now?"

"You want a sword, and I want to know why you want it."

Tank sighed. Did he really want another Frostmourne that bad? This man was asking him questions he didn't like answering. In fact, only the brothers and his mom knew why.

"My parents divorced when I was young and my dad left. I haven't seen him in years, but for my seventh birthday—the last birthday he was around for—he got me a replica sword from my favorite video game. While I hate the bastard for leavin', it was all I had left of him."

"What video game?" the man asked.

"World of Warcraft. The sword was called—"

"Frostmourne," the man said. "My son had that sword. He died when this all began."

He pointed a finger at a replica of Frostmourne hanging on the wall of the workshop, the certificate of ownership hanging below it with a picture of the man and a young boy. Tank's heart ached. This man truly loved his son, but thinking about his own dad like this wasn't good for him. The wound was still raw after all these years. It reminded him of how much people could hurt him and reinforced the idea that he shouldn't get close to anyone.

"The name's Tom," the man said, sticking out his hand, which Tank took in a firm grip. "I'll make you your sword."

~~~

Connor tore down his ACR DMR, saving his baby for last. The SAW had been the worst to clean, and it had taken him a bit to get it done, but now he could move on to his own gear. He took good care of the other firearms he cleaned, but he cared for his like they were his own children. There was something about the smell of gunpowder and cleaning oil that calmed his mind. It was almost as good as the rum and without the side effects.

He let himself relax as he continued to clean while *Chaos* by I Prevail played through the little speaker hooked up to his iPod. The lyrics resonated with him, speaking straight to his heart. He'd find his way through all of the chaos and they *would* make it home. With the upper receiver of his ARC in his hands, he lost himself in the process of cleaning. If the cotton swab he was using came back with even a small amount of residue on it, he continued to clean.

Memories from boot camp swirled in his mind. Spending all day cleaning his M16 A4 service rifle came back to him and he smiled. Even though that had been one of the hardest few weeks of his life, he'd loved every minute of it. Those were his people and that was his calling. It was tempting to let himself go down that path again and ask to re-enlist in a time of crisis, or at least to be more involved, but something held him back. Maybe it was the inescapable knowledge that this town would fall and that nothing good could last in this new world.

Some small part of him registered that he was being dramatic, but that didn't change the deep unease he felt in his heart like a dark storm looming overhead, ready to descend on him at any moment. There were too many variables for this place to endure. Where were the remaining Reclaimers? There were at least two of them out there. One was the man who had shot at him and the other, he'd learned, was the leader, a woman named Jezz—a psychopath, according to Alexis and the others. She'd been the one who'd forced Ana to kill two of their own. He didn't agree with how things had gone down, but Ana should've come back. It wasn't like they would shun her. Connor would've done the exact same thing in her place, but by the way some of the survivors from Burns were talking, they didn't seem to mind that she was gone. In fact, they were happy.

They were idiots and liabilities he didn't need.

When they left this place, it would be with only his Wolf Pack, Chloe, Emmett, and Alexis. They'd probably have to bring Olive along, too, considering how attached his brother was. The rest would stay. They didn't need them, and he sure as hell didn't want them tagging along. They'd get them killed. Only a few had what it took to survive out there, and the rest just followed along under their protection. The question was, how would they leave? Should they talk to Cpt. Miller or just sneak out one night? He didn't want to leave like that, but he wasn't sure how the captain would take them wanting to head out after they'd proven themselves valuable. The longer they stayed, the harder it would be for them to get away.

Actually, they should've left as soon as they could after they'd arrived. The problem was they hadn't gotten their gear back until two days ago, so they were stuck here for that first week—sitting around, being interviewed and psychologically evaluated. He'd put on his happy face for the shrink. That man didn't need to know anything about what was going on in his head. Connor wasn't insane or unstable, just determined to do whatever it took to survive. It would've thrown a red flag if he started talking about repressing the thoughts and voices in his head. They weren't even so much voices, just his mind trying to reconcile all that had happened. He didn't want to reconcile it, and he didn't need to be fixed; he just needed to survive.

Glancing at his watch, he noticed he'd missed his designated lunchtime. It was easy to get caught up in the cleaning process, but it didn't matter. He could go

---

an afternoon without food. After the guns were cleaned, he started gathering supplies and putting together their daypacks and kits, including the plate-carrier vests that held their extra magazines and other gear. James and Tank would still check their gear to make sure they had everything, and James would reorganize his, but this would save them time. This way, when they headed out tomorrow, they'd be ready, and if things went south they'd have enough supplies in their daypacks to survive for a few days out there. He was tired of getting caught with limited gear and ammunition. They'd gotten lucky before when they stumbled into the pavilions with all the guns and gear. But luck couldn't be counted on moving forward so he made damn sure they were prepared.

~~~

James stopped outside the door to the community center they'd turned into an orphanage and school. Most of the kids and a few adults from Burns were staying there, and they'd turned a couple of the rooms into classrooms. It'd helped all of them to start back up in a normal routine. The kids were acting more like kids again, and the adults were doing better as well. Beverly, Neil, Mark, and Helen were in charge of looking after Olive, Felix, and the other sixteen kids staying there. He checked his watch. He still had another five minutes until their lunch break, and he knew better than to interrupt Helen's class. He'd caught some serious hell the last time he'd done that.

Going around to the side of the building, he sat down on a small retaining wall that was in the shade. That morning had been only slightly scalding, but now it was deadly hot. He preferred the mild summers and cold winters in Alaska. That'd come in time, though. Hopefully, they could finish resting up where they were for a few more days and help out the town, then head on their way.

His mind began to wander and memories from his past life rose to the surface—his family on vacation down in Mexico, their house on the lake in Colorado, going to the sports shows every year, and guiding with his father in Alaska. The memories with his parents hurt the most. It was at times like this that he truly missed them and wished things had turned out differently. That line of thought took him back to the courthouse where he and his brother had tried to rescue their mother.

Images from that night were burned into his mind. One by one, they came back to him as he remembered killing the sleeping men and women, and then seeing his mother beaten and bruised. He recalled the red that obscured his vision over the next few days, the barely contained rage, and his pure hatred towards the people who'd murdered his parents. It'd been easy to kill after finding their father and then their mother. But now those ghosts were haunting him, and he didn't know what to do about them.

The front doors opened and Neil and Beverly walked out.

"They done in there?" James asked.

"Yeah, Helen just finished up," Neil said. "We're

heading out to lunch."

"You should be safe to go in and see Olive," Beverly said, smiling.

"Perfect," James said, standing up. "I learned my lesson the last time."

"You have to watch Helen," Neil said. "Her bite is just as bad as her bark."

"I'll keep that in mind," James said, going to the door Neil held open. "Thanks."

"No problem," Neil said.

James entered the building and glanced back, watching Neil and Beverly walk across the street. They seemed to be growing closer despite the almost twenty-year difference in their ages. It was good; Beverly was a nice person and deserved someone like Neil, a true gentleman from the previous generation. He wouldn't be surprised if Neil had been in the military. Even though he was almost sixty years old, he was in great shape. There was also the way he acted with all this, always helping with the kids and never shying away from everything that was going on. Whatever his background, this wasn't his first rodeo.

"James!" Olive shouted as she exited Helen's makeshift classroom.

She ran up to him and he bent down, giving her a hug. "How are you doing today, you little munchkin?"

"I'm not a munchkin," Olive said, smiling up at him.

"Sure you are," James said as they walked towards the lunch tables.

He was supposed to eat in the Mess Hall, but

Helen Olger and the others in charge didn't mind him eating with the kids. They always brought over plenty of food anyway.

"What's on the menu today?" James asked Olive as he sat down next to her.

"Sandwiches and chips, like always," Olive said, making a face.

"What? I thought you loved sandwiches."

"It's ham today."

"Oh, well, I bet you won't even know the difference." Olive looked up at him and raised an eyebrow, causing James to laugh. "Fair enough, it's pretty easy to tell the difference, isn't it?"

"Yeah, ham sucks."

"I'll show you a little trick I use when a sandwich isn't very good."

Mark handed out sandwiches, bags of chips, cookies, and juice boxes to all of the kids, including James. He watched the man, noticing how sunken his eyes were. James didn't know his story or why everyone else was looking so much better when he was beginning to look worse. He'd have to ask Mark what was going on and make sure everything was okay. If he was coming unhinged, he didn't want that around the kids, especially Olive.

Felix came over and sat down across from them.

"Hey, Felix," James said.

"Hey, Mr. Andderson," Felix said.

"How many times have I told you, just call me James?"

"I know, but Mr. Wolfe says that saying Mr. and Mrs. is a sign of respect."

"That's true, but after I've given you permission

not to, you don't have to keep doing it."

"Mr. Wolfe is going to teach me to shoot soon, but he said first I should learn how to be a man, and respect is a big part of that."

"I can't argue with his logic, I guess."

"When are you going to teach *me* to shoot?" Olive asked James, poking at her sandwich.

"Soon, but you'll have to keep it a secret. I'm already in trouble with Mrs. Olger for mentioning it the last time. Now, let me show you how to make that sandwich better."

Popping open his bag of Doritos, he lifted the top of his sandwich and lined the inside with the cheesy chips, then put the bread back on top and took a bite.

"See," he said, his mouth full of food. "Just like that."

"Manners, Mr. Andderson," Helen said, walking to the other side of their table.

He looked up, chastised. "Yes, Mrs. Olger."

That was why he'd hated school so much when he was young. And now, even in the middle of the apocalypse, people still wanted him to behave properly in a place of learning. Maybe he would have liked it better back in the day if they'd been allowed to be kids. Then again, he probably still would've gotten in trouble.

Olive giggled as she took the top piece of bread off her sandwich and did the same. She took a bite.

"Better, isn't it?" James asked.

She nodded enthusiastically and took another bite. James ate his sandwich as well, making sure not to talk with his mouth full again. The whole room was mostly silent, with Mrs. Olger watching everyone like a hawk.

"I have something to show you!" Olive said when they'd finished eating. She jumped up from the table and ran over to a stack of boxes turned sideways along the one wall, which created cubbies to hold the kids' school stuff.

"No running, Olive!" Mrs. Olger commanded.

Olive slowed her pace to a fast walk, which was just shy of running, and James could tell Mrs. Olger wanted to say something again. Instead, she shook her head in frustration.

"That girl," she whispered under her breath.

Olive came back, holding a drawing she'd done. She showed it to James, and he was impressed that he could tell what was going on. There was a man in camouflage who was carrying a child in one arm. In the background there were vague, humanoid shapes, and it looked like the man and child were heading towards a cornfield.

"This is you," she said, pointing to the man. "This is your gun, and that's me." She pointed at the child in the man's arms.

"And all this back here?" James asked, pointing to the shapes in the background.

"Those are the zombies chasing us, of course," she said, smiling sweetly, as if being chased by zombies was a normal thing to draw. "It's when you first saved me."

He could easily see that it looked like that night in Burns. "Wow, that's amazing," James said, looking at it more closely. He could even see that the gun resembled an AR-15.

"Thanks," she said, handing it to him. "I did it for

you."

"Thanks, Olive," James said, truly touched. "I'll put it up in our place."

"You mean that old store?" Olive said, giggling. "I hear it's haunted."

"If that's true, we'll scare the ghosts off," James said. "How's Squeezer doing?"

"Great!" Olive exclaimed. "Mrs. Olger let us feed him a mouse the other day. It was so cool!"

"It was pretty sick," Felix said.

"You making sure to keep him company?" James asked.

"Yeah," Olive said. "I hold him every day."

"I'll make sure to tell Connor. He'll be happy to know that," James said. "So what'd you learn today?"

Olive started by telling him how Mrs. Olger was teaching them math, science, English, and history. Then she grew animated when she told him about how Mr. Harkin was teaching them about defensive techniques—what to do around zombies, how to stay quiet, and how to survive in different situations. The way she talked about Neil's teachings confirmed what he'd thought earlier. The man had military experience, and James was glad that someone like that was teaching the kids practical lessons in survival. Olive went on to talk about how she, Felix and another kid, Noah, were the best kids in his class. She beamed when she proudly informed him that Mr. Harkin had told her that she was a smart kid and she'd be able to survive.

James smiled as he watched the little girl next to him talk energetically. One small, seemingly insignificant choice for him to stay and rescue a stranger that night outside the school had brought them to this moment. If James hadn't stopped and risked his life to save her, she wouldn't be here, and the thought of harm coming to her broke his heart. It wasn't surprising to him when he realized he cared for Olive like she was his own daughter. Even though he'd only know her for about two weeks, he'd grown a strong bond with her.

All too soon, Mrs. Olger was telling the kids it was time for afternoon classes.

"You'll come by tomorrow?" Olive asked, looking at him hopefully.

"I won't be able to make it tomorrow," James said, hating to disappoint her. "We have a run, and I'm not sure when we'll be back."

"So you'll come by the next day?"

"I'm not sure, but I promise to as soon as I can."

"Good," Olive said as she gave him a hug.

He held her in his arms, cherishing the feeling. He'd always wanted to be a dad, and even with everything that was going on, he'd found little Olive.

"Now, make sure to pay attention in class, especially Mr. Harkin's," James said as she walked towards the classroom. "You too, Felix."

"I will, sir," Felix said, passing by James.

"Good. See you later, little munchkin," James said.

Olive looked back at him and rolled her eyes. "I'm not a munchkin!"

"Sure you aren't," James said, as she entered the classroom.

He left the building, passing Mark coming in from

outside. The man jumped and looked around nervously when he saw James.

"Hey, Mark," James said. "How you doin'?"

"Good," Mark said, passing by him and entering the community center.

He'd have to keep his eyes on that man. He didn't trust him and was surer than ever that something was going on.

James walked back to their place on the other side of town. Luckily, Coutts was so small that it wasn't a long walk, although the summer sun beating down on him made the few-minute walk almost unbearable. By the time he made it there, he decided he'd have to go visit the neighbors and take a shower before his date later that night.

The date. His first *real* date.

~~~

Tank lay on his cot in the old store they were staying in. While this place didn't resemble a home in any way, he was beginning to think of it like that. Chloe was going to stop by before work, and Connor was out loading their gear into Scourge. Tomorrow was going to be a big day by the sounds of it. They were supposed to lead a group of Marines to the two towns they'd scouted and help them recover the supplies. The three of them prepared in their own way for what lay ahead. Connor prepped all their guns and gear, James went on a date, and Tank lay there, waiting for Chloe to start her shift at the saloon so he could do what *he* did to prepare—drink.

Before leaving the mechanic's shop, Tom had told

him that he had something in mind for Frostmourne and it would only take him a couple of days. Tank was grateful to get anything that even resembled the iconic sword of the Lich King. Just thinking of the sword reminded him of the week the outbreak started. He and his guild were just about to beat the Wrath of the Lich King expansion in WoW. Then he was back at work and that man, John, had come in bleeding from multiple bites. Not until John woke up from the dead did Tank have any idea of what was happening. It didn't take him long to gather his crap and get out of FoCo though. Well, actually it had taken days, and he'd joined with a good group. They were all dead now, other than Chloe. The brothers hadn't even been able to meet Garett, and that sucked, but that was just life now. It was rarely pleasant and usually ended up with someone getting hurt.

As the afternoon stretched on, Tank got off his cot and walked outside, itching for something to do. It was hard to just sit around like he used to. One of the LAPVs like Scourge drove by from the north, heading towards the makeshift helipad. The black-uniformed men watched Tank as they drove by. Those damn people gave him the creeps. Tank and his group still hadn't learned who those men were or what they were doing there. They'd been told to treat them like the military, and that meant to stay out of their way. So he did. But it still irked him that he didn't know. Maybe the brothers were right; something might be a little fishy around there—like all those helicopters coming and going multiple times a day.

He glanced at Scourge. Their vehicle looked

exactly like the rest of those unmarked LAPVs, and it was time to make this beasty their own, officially. He needed to do something to make it stand out, so he started off down the road.

"Where you goin'?" Connor asked, climbing out of Scourge.

"To find that artist here in town," Tank said. "There's somethin' we need to remedy. You done?"

"Just finished," Connor said, stowing his ACR in the passenger seat.

"Let's go," Tank said, walking off.

Connor shut the door and followed. "What'd you have in mind?"

"We need to mark Scourge, make it ours."

"Good idea."

They only had to knock on two doors to get directions to the guy they were looking for. Finally, on their third try, a young Hispanic man with full sleeve and neck tattoos answered the door. He wore a beanie on his head even though it was over eighty degrees out.

"Yeah?" he asked.

"You Angel?" Tank asked.

"Yeah, what ya need?"

"I hear you're a helluva artist."

"The best in town. You need some new ink or somethin' painted?"

"Painted, somethin' on the side of our vehicle."

"I can do that. Meet me at the garage."

He shut the door and they walked around to the side where the garage was. Angel opened the door and they walked in. There was a tattoo chair in one corner with pictures of his previous work. The rest of the walls were covered in layers of graffiti, creating a chaotic collage of sorts. It looked badass. There was a representation of Cthulhu, some video game characters, and other crazy stuff painted on every surface. This guy was talented.

"What ya thinkin'?" Angel asked, standing in the middle of the room as Connor walked over to flip through his book of tattoo designs.

"Not sure, honestly. Somethin' badass," Tank said "Any ideas?"

"You know those black armored rigs that are all around town?"

Angel nodded.

"We have one of those, and I want to make it different than the rest."

"How different?" Angel asked with a look in his eye.

"Enough to stand out. I was thinkin' about an emblem on the side. We don't really have much of a way to pay."

"At this point, I'll do it just to do something."

"Tank," Connor said, "come look at this."

He walked over to Connor and didn't need Connor's finger pointing to the image for him to pick it out immediately from the page. It was perfect!

"Oh, hell yeah!"

8
THE DATE

James left his place a little before seven and walked over to get Alexis for their date. He'd thought about driving, but with the oppressive heat of the day abating, it was actually comfortable to walk, and she didn't live far from their destination. Now that he was actually on his way, he felt some of his anxiousness dissipate. The fresh air really did something to calm his mind. He was still a bundle of nerves, but he wasn't scared like he'd been earlier. It was more of a nervous excitement. At twenty-one, he was finally going on his first date. While it hadn't been his choice to stay single during high school, there hadn't been that many girls to choose from, and he was weird back then. After graduating, he'd decided to continue to wait for the right one to come along, but that hadn't happened until the apocalypse, so here he was.

Before stumbling into Coutts and learning more about what was going on in the nation as a whole, he'd thought the world had ended. Now he'd learned that wasn't quite true. The world may be ending, but it was far from over. The apocalypse hadn't even affected the entire world yet, from what he knew—

just North America.

Turning onto South Avenue where Alexis lived, he reined in his thoughts. His mind was trying to distract him from his nervousness, and he didn't want to be distracted. Whatever the outcome of this night, he wanted to remember it for years to come. Arriving at her house, he took a deep breath and walked up to the front door.

~~~

Alexis left the bathroom and walked into her bedroom where Chloe waited. She only had an hour before James would be there—less than that if he was early, which she guessed he would be. He was too much like her dad, and the thought made her smile. They always said girls went for guys who were most like their fathers.

Chloe sat on Alexis's bed in her bedroom. "You have an outfit picked out?" Chloe asked, going over to the closet.

"I was thinking something like this," Alexis said, pointing to the pair of blue jeans and a green tank top lying on her bed.

"Hmmm," Chloe said as she began to dig through the few clothes in Alexis's small closet.

That first night they'd arrived in Coutts, Chloe had stayed there with Alexis before the leaders figured out the housing situation. That night, Alexis had heard Chloe crying, and she'd gotten up to talk with her. She'd told Alexis everything that had happened to her since the beginning and what she'd had to do to rescue the others. Alexis was horrified when she'd talked about killing that man, Bryce. It was too much like what Ana had done, but after talking with her more, the light bulb clicked. There had been no choice, just like with Ana. It was different, but it was also the same, and now she felt like she understood Ana a little bit better.

Since that night, she and Chloe had become almost inseparable, hanging out during most of their free time. Alexis had even confided in Chloe how she felt about James, and admitting her feelings aloud had been what finally made it real to her. Now here she was, getting ready for a date with the man she had a huge crush on. She was both nervous and excited but also guarded. She'd been down this path before and it'd never worked out. Would this time be any different?

"You're right," Chloe said, sighing. "That's the best you've got."

"It's not that bad," Alexis said. "Cute *and* functional."

"I was just hoping you had something more along the lines of 'shock and awe,'" Chloe said.

"I'm not shocking enough on my own?" Alexis asked, teasing.

"Oh, yeah. He'll probably die from a heart attack as soon as he sees you."

"I hope not. I'm really looking forward to the date."

"Better get dressed. It's already six-thirty."

"Crap!" Alexis said, dressing quickly. She hadn't even done her hair and makeup yet!

~~~

James knocked on the door and waited. The old fight-or-flight instinct flared within him, and he felt the desire to run, but that didn't last as he clamped down on his emotions, taking back control. All of that control shattered a few seconds later, however, when the door opened and he almost went into shock.

Alexis stood in the doorway, and in that moment he truly *saw* her for the first time—not as a friend or someone he needed to protect, not as one of their group, and not even as Emmett's daughter. He saw her for herself, the beautiful woman she was. Her loose brunette hair cascaded down her back and shoulders. There was a smile on her lips, and her hazel eyes glinted in the light. He didn't even register what she was wearing as his eyes locked onto hers and he couldn't look away. He finally admitted to himself how strongly he felt about her. Maybe he *did* already want to spend the rest of his life with her.

"You're beautiful," James said in a whisper, unaware that he'd even spoken.

Her smile widened and his heart threatened to explode out of his chest.

"Thanks," Alexis said. "You look quite handsome as well."

He continued to stare until someone inside the house cleared their throat. Glancing in, he realized for the first time that Chloe was standing in the living room.

"I guess we should be going," James said as he turned and walked down the porch steps with Alexis following.

"You two kids have fun now," Chloe said, giving

James a wink as she closed the door.

"Where are we off to?" Alexis asked.

"Follow me," James said, smiling and motioning for them to walk east on South Avenue.

"Oh, so it's a surprise."

James held out his arm and Alexis took it as they started walking. He was still nervous, but he also felt at ease at the same time. It was such a contradiction that he didn't try to figure it out, and they walked the one block to the Mess Hall in contented silence. James took a deep breath of the summer air and noticed how it mingled with the fruity fragrance of Alexis's hair.

"Interesting choice," Alexis said as they turned for the old diner. "Taking me to the only place that serves dinner. I have to admit I didn't see it coming."

James just smiled and held the door open for her as she let go of his arm and walked inside. He passed her, leading her into the kitchen. The large woman everyone called Cook looked up at them, and James nodded to her. She smiled and pointed towards the back door. He continued through the kitchen and out the back, exiting onto a small patio with a privacy fence around it. In the center of the patio sat a small table with two chairs set up in the shade. A candle sat in the middle of the table next to a vase filled with freshly picked wildflowers. White lights were strung up around the circumference of the patio. Alexis stopped just outside the back door, taking it in as James walked over to the table and pulled out one of the chairs.

"I know it's not much," James said. "I was limited in my options."

"Not much?" Alexis said. "It's perfect."

She walked over to the table and took the chair James was holding for her. After getting Alexis settled, James walked around to the other chair and sat down as one of Cook's helpers came out carrying a pitcher of water.

"Good evening," the young woman said. "My name is Sheri and I'll be your server today. Can I start you off with some water?"

"Yes, please," Alexis said. "And I'll take some lemonade, if you don't mind."

"And I'll have a root beer," James said as Sheri poured their water.

"I'll be right back with those," Sheri said, smiling as she left and throwing a wink at Alexis.

"You know, we worked together," Alexis said after Sheri left.

"I know," James said.

"How'd you pull this off?"

"I was able to work out a deal with Cook."

Alexis hadn't stopped smiling since they'd sat down.

"You really did go to a lot of trouble, didn't you?"

"Eh, a little. But it was well worth it."

"You're so cheesy," Alexis said with a small giggle.

"I try to be."

"So, do you have a special menu planned too?"

"That's also a surprise, but I can tell you it'll start off with a salad."

"With real lettuce?"

"Of course."

"Wow, you really must've worked out a good deal

then."

James smiled mischievously.

Alexis looked around again. "I take it you did all the decorating?"

"It's not like I'd have anyone else do it. I even picked those flowers myself, which just about gave me heat stroke walking around trying to find them all. So how was your first day working at the infirmary?"

"It was lame. They had me watching these old training videos. I knew everything they covered."

"How many more days of that do you have?"

"Today was it. I get the tour tomorrow morning and then I start helping out."

"Well, that's exciting."

"Yeah, but enough about all that. We're on a date and I know hardly anything about your past." She leaned forward. "Where'd you grow up?"

"Born and raised in Alaska, then moved down to Colorado when I was twelve. We stayed there until my brother and I graduated and then moved out to Montana. What about you?"

"Texan, born and raised and proud of it."

"That makes a lot of sense."

"What's that supposed to mean?"

"The slight drawl, knowing how to shoot guns, being tough and independent. Doesn't that pretty much describe all Texans?"

"Yeah, that's a good representation."

Sheri returned, bringing their drinks and salads. "Your meal will be out shortly," she said. "Is there anything else I can get you?"

"I think we're good," Alexis said. "Thanks,

Sheri."

"My pleasure," Sheri said as she left.

They dug into their salads and continued to talk about their pasts. James told her about growing up in Alaska at their wilderness lodge, which was also the final destination on their journey north. He talked about how he and his brother had always been inseparable, how they went on imaginary adventures wielding sticks as swords, and how their mother had homeschooled them. He told her about moving to Colorado and starting public school in the sixth grade, and then about meeting Tank on his first day there and forging the friendship that was still strong today. About guiding in Alaska for his dad's business and how the whole family went north every year. It was hard to talk about his parents at first, but as he continued, it felt good to remember those times. He did have to quickly wipe away a few tears before she noticed.

Sheri brought out the main course—chicken Alfredo with spinach and peppers. She set the meal down in front of them and took their salad bowls.

"How'd you know?" Alexis asked, admiring the food.

"Your dad," James said, picking out his peppers.

"You're a crafty one, James Andderson."

"Thanks. I was going for the 'wow' factor."

"Well, you got it. This is the most effort anyone has ever put into a date for me, especially when they include food they don't like," Alexis said, eyeing his pepper-filled napkin.

"I love chicken Alfredo," James said, then followed her eyes. "Oh, yeah. I don't mind a little of the taste, but they're the one food I hate most."

"Do you mind?" she asked, motioning to the peppers.

"Not at all."

She took his peppers and added them to her plate. "I don't know how you don't like these. They're delicious!"

James shrugged and took a bite. Cook really did know how to make one heck of a meal. "So, what about you? You stay in Texas your whole life?"

"Mostly," Alexis said after swallowing the food in her mouth. "We moved around a few times when I was little, with dad in the Marines. But we came back to Texas because that was home. The small ranch we owned was where my brother and I grew up."

"Your brother?" James said, looking at her in surprise. He hadn't heard anything about Alexis having siblings. But judging by the way Alexis stiffened, he knew those memories held pain. "I'm sorry. You don't have to talk about it."

"No, I want to."

A tear streaked down her cheek and she wiped it away. Then she told him the story about her seven-year-old brother dying in an ATV accident when she was young, the divorce coming in the same year, and her father going on another deployment. It sounded like her mother had been a real piece of work with what she'd pulled to get custody. He could tell Alexis still loved and missed her mom, but there seemed to be a deep resentment as well. Then she talked about her father leaving the Marines so he could be with her while she grew up and having to spend time at each parent's house. Growing up in a separated household was never easy. James didn't know that from experience, but he knew it'd been hard for Tank to grow up like that. By the time she finished telling her story, they were done with their meal and Sheri had taken their plates.

"Dessert?" Sheri asked poking her head out at the perfect time. James wondered if she'd been listening and waiting for Alexis to finish or just had good timing.

"That'd be great," James said as she walked out carrying a tray with two pieces of chocolate cake.

"Wow!" Alexis said as Sheri set her cake down in front of her. "I sure hope you aren't indebted to Cook for your whole life for this."

"Pretty much, but it's okay," James said, taking a piece of cake onto his fork. "A life of slavery for the perfect first date with a beautiful woman—I'll take that any day."

Alexis chuckled, taking a bite. "Mmmm, this is so good," she said. "It's been a while since I've had cake."

James watched Alexis as she ate her cake. He picked at his, eating it slowly. He wasn't a huge fan of chocolate cake, but once again, he knew it was her favorite. She took another bite, savoring the flavor, and he was struck for the hundredth time that night by how beautiful she was. He was intoxicated with the way her cheeks dimpled, her sweet laugh, and, of course, that smile. He finally understood how all the guys in the romantic comedies felt when they first noticed the woman of their dreams. He truly felt like he was in a rom-com with how awkward and weird he was being. However, from what he could tell, she was enjoying the date. He knew *he* was. His head had yet to come down from cloud nine since he'd first seen her earlier in the evening.

"You gonna finish that?" Alexis asked, and he realized he'd been staring at her.

"Uh, no," he said, trying to recover. Hopefully, his eyes had been gazing at something appropriate when he'd gone to La La Land.

"You mind if I do?" she asked, reaching for his half-eaten piece of cake.

"Of course not," James said.

"Not much for desserts, or just chocolate cake?"

"Oh, I love dessert. Actually, I love anything that has sugar in it. Just not a huge fan of chocolate."

"Yet here we are."

"It had to be perfect. I could care less what we were eating tonight. It's the company I was looking forward to."

"And how was the company?" Alexis asked, looking at him with a twinkle in her eyes.

"The best I've ever had," James said honestly, gazing back into hers.

They held each other's gazes for a few seconds. When she finally glanced away to finish eating her cake, he released a breath he didn't even know he'd been holding.

Holy crap, he thought. *This woman...*

"You said something about your first date earlier," Alexis said after finishing her cake. "You mean *our* first date or your first date ever? I don't remember hearing about any girls in your story."

"This is my first date ever."

"You never liked anyone or just didn't find the

right girl?"

"Oh, I liked girls, probably too much. I used to crush really easily, but in high school there weren't many options, and then after... I decided since I'd waited that long, might as well continue to wait for someone special."

Alexis smiled. "That's a good way to look at it."

"What about you? I take it you've done this before?"

"What's that supposed to mean?"

"Just that you're so relaxed. I'm practically sitting in a pool of my own sweat right now."

She laughed that laugh of hers and his heart felt like exploding again. He was surprised he hadn't had a heart attack yet.

"I'm not that experienced. I only had one serious boyfriend in college. He turned out to be a dick and left me for the girl he'd been cheating with for a month."

"That sucks. I'm sorry."

"All water under the bridge. I *would* like to see him one last time and kick him right in the junk though."

James laughed. "When you talk like that, you sound like Emmett."

"I do have a lot more of my father in me than my mother, although I do have some of her, too."

"What was she like?" James asked, taking a chance. He just hoped the memories weren't too painful.

Alexis took a moment. "In the beginning, she was a great mother—loving, caring, supportive. She was always there for my brother and me, but a couple of years before Mason died, things began to change. She wanted dad to stop going off to war, said we needed him here more than his country did. As you can guess, my dad didn't take it well. He was a warrior through and through, and he couldn't give it up that easily. It all came to a head when my brother died. Mom became bitter and angry, and marrying George only made things worse."

"Who's George?"

"Oh, I guess I forgot to mention him. A couple years ago my mom remarried a guy named George. I never liked him. He was a sorry excuse for a man."

There was something in her voice when she talked about George that let James know there was more to the story than what she was telling him.

"What happened to him?" James asked.

"Dad shot him the day this all started. George had been bitten and turned. He was actually the first infected we'd seen. As you can imagine, mom didn't take it well."

"It didn't shock you when your dad killed a person right in front of you?"

"A little. I knew he'd do it. Heck, he'd been doing it for a living. The whole situation was shocking, really, and so I just added it to the rest of everything that was going on. Things happened so fast, I didn't have time to think about it much. Now it just seems so long ago."

"Do you think about all that now that things have slowed down?"

"Yeah, it's like it's all catching up with me. You?"

James hesitated. "Yeah, it's all coming back."

Saying it out loud made everything come up to the

surface—his parents' deaths, all the people he'd killed or helped kill, all the others he'd lost. An image of the beaten bodies of his parents flashed through his mind, followed by Felicia's head cradled in his arms, blood smeared on her face and her eyes pleading with him. He'd barely known her and yet her death had hit him hard. And Mila was dead, too. He hadn't even crushed on her. She'd just been nice and helped out with Olive, yet they were all dead, and the ones who weren't soon would be. It was a never-ending cycle.

Suddenly, he was standing in a room, covered in blood. Fourteen children were kneeling around something in the middle of the floor. He moved closer to them, realizing they weren't kids anymore; they were zombies. The small creatures tore chunks of flesh from a corpse lying there. One of them moved and he got a look at the body. It was Alexis, her bloody hair matted to her cheeks and a look of absolute terror on her dead face. He stumbled back, trying to escape from the horror. He tripped over something in the doorway and turned to see that it was the corpse of his brother with half of his face eaten off. Tank and Chloe lay out in the hall, holding each other in death's embrace, their stomachs torn open and intestines leaking out onto the carpet.

He screamed.

"James!" Alexis yelled from far away with fear in her voice.

His eyes shot open and he sat up abruptly, looking around. He was outside, not in a room, and there were no bodies, no zombies. Alexis was kneeling next to him where he lay on the ground, a shocked expression on her face.

"What the hell was that?" she asked, resting a hand on his arm.

It had happened again; he'd had another episode. Those were supposed to be gone. He was supposed to be healed. It'd been well over a week since the last one, and he'd thought it would be the last. Why had he had one now of all times? It wasn't like he was still out in the world, his sanity fraying. He was safe here, and it shouldn't have happened again.

"James," Alexis said, "answer me!"

He was too ashamed to look at her. Instead, he stood up and took a step towards the gate at the back of the patio.

"Where are you going?" she asked.

"I have to leave," James said, opening the gate and slipping out before she could say another word.

9
MEETING

Emmett strolled toward HQ, enjoying the warm evening air. The climate up there wasn't much different than what he was used to, just a little drier than east Texas. It was odd to think that he'd never be going back to where he'd grown up. He'd spent most of his adult life overseas, living on various bases, and that had been fine with him at the time. But he'd always told himself that when he got out of the service he'd move back to the same area he'd grown up in, which he had. Now he'd never get to see that country again. Would this town ever feel like home? Should they even stay? This place was as safe as any and under the protection of the government. As long as the military was there, he'd stay. It was what was best for Alexis.

His daughter was on a date that night and he still didn't know what he thought about that. James was a good guy, much better than that idiot she'd dated back in college, but was he good enough for his daughter? James would be able to protect her; he'd seen that himself. On one hand, it would be good for his daughter to settle down with someone, to be able to live a somewhat normal life again. But on the other hand, it could be devastating if James broke her heart by leaving her or dying. The caveat in all this was that he didn't have a say in the matter. This was beyond his control, and he dismissed the thoughts. If his daughter was happy, he'd be happy. There were other things to worry about.

As he entered the building, he couldn't help his mind drifting to Ana. Where was she now? Was she safe? He hoped so. It'd been hard not to go back out after her once they'd arrived in Coutts. In the end, he decided he couldn't leave his daughter alone, and if Alexis was right, Ana didn't want to be found anyway. What exactly had happened at the Reclaimer's compound? Alexis had told him the story a couple of times, but he didn't understand why Ana would want to be on her own. It was ultimately her choice, but he wished she'd stayed with them. He'd grown quite attached to her rather quickly.

Going up the stairs, he walked into the conference room. Both Cpt. Miller and Cpt. Sanders where already seated at the large table.

"Evening, Emmett," Cpt. Saul Miller said

Cpt. Sanders just nodded.

"Evening, Saul," Emmett said, sitting down.

This was the first official meeting they'd invited him to. It felt good to be in these situations again, surrounded by people he could rely on. It was the opposite of how he felt traveling with the rest of the survivors from Burns. Over the next five minutes, a couple of military and a few civilian personnel showed up. Emmett recognized some of the faces in the assembly. The night before, he'd been in a private meeting with the two captains and the man in charge,

Colonel Briggs. They'd asked him questions and done an unofficial job interview before deciding he'd be an asset to their meetings, being able to provide a unique perspective. Emmett and his group had spent the most time out there, surviving in a hostile world.

"Is everyone here?" Cpt. Miller asked once they were seated.

"Yes," said a woman sitting in the corner with a laptop. She'd be taking notes on the meeting, more than likely. This wasn't strictly a military meeting but a gathering of all the leaders in town.

"Anything new to report, Sharon?" Cpt. Miller asked the same woman.

"The power plant is running at seventy-five percent," Sharon said. "That's only two percent down from last week. The food supplies are slowly decreasing, but if the run tomorrow goes as planned, we'll be good for another ten days at this population. Only a few infected have made it to the fences over the last couple of nights, and they were all disposed of with little effort. In fact, I have nothing negative to report."

"Finally, a good week," Cpt. Miller said. "Anyone have any comments before we move on?"

"I put an order in for more pharmaceuticals and various medical supplies," said a man with black hair and hard eyes.

"Yes, Dr. Hart," Cpt. Miller said. "Sharon gave me your list, which I passed on to Cpt. Sanders for the run tomorrow. But I have to ask how you're going through so many drugs when hardly any people are going to the infirmary. We just restocked it last week."

"With all due respect, Cpt. Miller," Dr. Hart said, his voice portraying the opposite, "you aren't aware of the people coming and going day to day who have a common cold and other minor ailments. We have limited supplies, and every time Joe Blow comes in with a stuffy nose, those supplies dwindle."

"Very well," Cpt. Miller said, looking at Cpt. Sanders.

"I'll get your drugs," Cpt. Sanders said.

"Thank you," Dr. Hart said.

"Anything else?" Cpt. Miller asked.

Emmett looked around at the men and women who were gathered in the room. It was an odd assortment—military leaders, a doctor, a cook, a mechanic, a man in one of those black uniforms, and a few others. It had to be a very unique situation for the military to divvy out power to all these civilians, but it spoke volumes that maybe they wanted this place to seem normal.

"The helicopters," Cook stated. "They're beginnin' to worry people with how they come and go, bringin' and takin' people."

"Those are none of your concern," Cpt. Sanders said, coldly. "It's military business."

"What Cpt. Sanders is trying to say," Cpt. Miller said, "is that they're doing what they've always been doing—bringing in key survivors from the surrounding areas and taking out key survivors to secure locations where they're needed. It's nothing for people to fear."

"Just tellin' ya what I've been hearin'," Cook said.

"Thank you for informing us. Now, if there's nothing else..." Cpt. Miller paused and then continued. "Cpt. Sanders, are your men ready for the run tomorrow?"

"Yes, they are," Cpt. Sanders said. "Although I'm not sure about the validity of your sources."

"They're reliable," Cpt. Miller said.

"They just got here and could be leading my men into a trap," Cpt. Sander said.

"They went through a rigorous testing process, and they passed," Cpt. Miller said. "Plus, Emmett Wolfe vouches for them."

"While I trust Mr. Wolfe," Cpt. Sander said, not glancing at Emmett, "I won't wager my men's lives on his vouching for them. Why didn't we send a military escort with them?"

"It was unnecessary and a waste of manpower. We only have so many trained men at our disposal," Cpt. Miller said.

"We still should have sent at least one soldier with them to verify," Cpt. Sanders said.

"Duly noted," Cpt. Miller said. "Now, I was thinking they could accompany you to show you exactly where they found the supplies. James drew a crude map, but it would be more effective if they went with you."

"No," Cpt. Sanders said. "I won't babysit those three and put even more of my men in danger."

"You'd rather fumble around looking for the supplies?" Emmett asked.

"Yes," Cpt. Sanders said, looking at him. "I'd rather that than take three untrained men into the field with me. Everyone seems to think that just because a catastrophe has hit, the way of the world has changed. It hasn't."

"I happen to agree with the captain," Dr. Hart said. "And that brings me to my next concern."

"No," Cpt. Miller said before the man could talk. "You'll take the help you were given and be grateful for it."

"With all due respect—" Dr. Hart began, but Cpt. Miller cut him off.

"It's nonnegotiable," Cpt. Miller said. "You asked for all Vindex guards and you were given them with no military involvement. You ask for more supplies on every run and you're given that. But this isn't up for debate. Col. Briggs himself approved this, and no matter how much we let everyone in on the running of this town, it's first and foremost a military outpost and we're in charge. You'd do well to remember that."

Emmett hadn't seen Saul that worked up since he'd arrived. It reminded him of years ago when Saul hadn't been stuck behind a desk job. It was good to see he hadn't lost all his fire.

The large, red-bearded man in a black Kryptek uniform stared daggers at Emmett from across the table. He was the one in charge of the rest of those mercenaries working for the Vindex Corporation. Emmett hadn't learned much about them and didn't know why they were there, but it seemed they were working for the government as extra protection. Why this man would be staring at him like that, Emmett didn't know, but he stared right back anyway.

Dr. Hart fumed but said nothing else and the meeting continued. They were briefly updated on how the rest of the country was faring, which wasn't too bad. The east coast had been hit the least. Whole cities were still standing, quarantined off. The west coast had been like that early on, but the latest reports showed them slowly losing cities they'd thought were secure, and they couldn't figure out how. Even though there'd been no breaches in their security, all of a sudden the infection would show up in the middle of a city and begin to spread. The Canadians weren't faring much better, and earlier in the day they'd gotten word that Calgary had fallen in the same way the west coast cities had. Most of the people in the meeting didn't take that information well, but it was music to Emmett's ears. He'd been hearing rumors that the country was better off than they'd thought, but this was the first official confirmation he'd gotten. While he hated to hear that more towns were falling to the infection, it was all better than he'd hoped.

Cook talked in more detail about food supplies and how well the eating system at the Mess Hall was working. The mechanic, Tom, informed them about the new pieces of fencing and the modifications his men were making to their current perimeter. The more people talked, the more Emmett realized this was the exact place they needed to be. It was the real deal. Even though the military was in charge, everyone had their own parts to play, and it made the place feel less like a military base and more like a town under military protection. This place was as safe as any could be. It was small but well defended and had a lot of talented people keen on keeping it afloat.

The meeting concluded and everyone dispersed. Emmett was about to walk out when Saul motioned him towards his office. Emmett walked down the hall and into the office while Saul finished talking with Sharon. After a couple of minutes, Saul walked into the room and slouched into his chair with a prolonged sigh.

"Scotch?" Saul asked, opening one of the drawers in his desk and pulling out the bottle and a glass.

"No," Emmett said. "You know I don't drink."

"I know," Saul said, "but I figured I'd ask. This whole situation can cause even the likes of you to need a stiff drink."

He poured some of the amber liquid into the glass and took a sip, nursing it. Letting out another sigh, he leaned forward, looking Emmett directly in the eyes.

"What do you think?" Saul asked.

"I think you have one hell of a town here," Emmett said.

"Thanks, that was one of the best meetings we've had. These people are glad we're here, but sometimes they forget the stakes. Our entire survival is at risk."

"The doctor doesn't want Alexis working in the infirmary, does he?"

"No, he doesn't. But I pulled in a favor with the colonel."

"Thank you, Saul."

"Don't mention it. It's the least I can do after all the times you saved my ass."

"That did happen a lot."

"More so than I care to admit."

They both chuckled, remembering the good old days.

"How much do you trust James, Connor, and Allen?"

"Allen?" Emmett asked.

"Oh, he goes by Tank, right?"

"Huh, so that's his name. I don't know much about him, but he seems to be a good man."

"And what about the brothers?"

"I trust them with my life and the life of my daughter."

"That says a lot."

"It does. We've all been through the grinder out there, and I've been highly impressed by how they've handled it. While I don't know much about Allen, they seem to work well as a team. I still stand by my recommendation."

"Good, because I have a situation. I'd normally send Marines, but we'll be shorthanded with Cpt. Sanders going out tomorrow. I'm worried about these people you faced. They may still be out there, and I don't want to take too many away from the defense of this place. That's our first priority. Do you think those three can handle a real mission?"

"Yes. They're just as dependable as anyone inside these walls, if not more so. The only thing they lack is actual training, but out there that doesn't matter so much. They're survivors."

"Good. I need them to look into something."

10
THE EPISODE

James walked down the alley with no direction in mind. He just knew he had to get away. He didn't know where or what he was running from, but he had to go. The problem was, where could he go? There was no escaping his own mind.

"James," Alexis called out, jogging up to him.

"Alexis, please," James said.

"What? You think we're done just because you had one of your episodes?"

"How do you…?"

"Chloe told me, but that doesn't matter."

"Really?" James said, looking her in the face and raising his voice. "I can't go a day without my mind replaying all the death I've seen. The images won't leave my head, and I have to relive them every time I have one of those episodes. And now that we aren't on the road, all of it's coming back to haunt me. I hardly sleep and I'm constantly reminded of the people I've lost."

He wanted to say more. The anger was raging inside him, trying in vain to cover the pain and loss, but before he could speak, Alexis stepped closer to him and stared into his eyes.

"You think you're the only one who's hurting? James, I lost my mom and then was captured and almost fed to zombies. Then I watched my best friend shoot someone who was going to kill me. I can't get that image out of my head!" Tears were beginning to brim in her eyes. "I close my eyes to sleep at night, but I can't, because I keep seeing Evan's brains being blown out the side of his head. I don't feel safe here—not with the fence, not with all the people. I just keep thinking that at any moment they're going to turn on us, or Jezz is going to get in here and kill me. You weren't there, and you didn't see that look in her eyes."

Tears streaked down her cheeks as James stood there, stunned at the show of emotion and the realization that he wasn't alone in his struggle.

He wasn't alone.

Alexis was trying to deal with what she'd been through as well. Without thinking, he pulled her into his arms and they embraced. She began to cry on his shoulder and he couldn't stop his own tears. He cried for his parents and Felicia and Mila and all the people they'd lost. He cried for his brother who he knew was hurting in his own way, and Alexis who was as broken as he was, but most importantly, he cried for himself. He'd lost something since all this began—a piece he'd never get back. He'd killed, stolen, and fought for every mile they'd traveled, and he'd do it all again if he had to, but he'd lost his innocence along the way. He was a broken man in need of healing.

The sun neared the horizon and he took a step back, drying his tears off on his shirt. He looked into

Alexis's face and wiped tears mixed with mascara from her cheeks. Even in this state, she was still the most beautiful woman he'd ever seen. He wanted to say something profound, to comfort her and let her know how much her opening up had helped him, but he could find no words to express the depth of his feelings.

"Thank you," James said, simply.

"You're welcome," Alexis said, wiping the remaining tears from her chin.

"Wanna go for a walk?" James asked, holding out his hand.

"I'd love that," Alexis said, taking James's hand as they walked through town towards the western fence.

They walked in silence, content just to be with each other. James had bared his heart to someone he was still getting to know, and he rarely even did that with people he'd known for years. Yet, it felt right.

They passed by where James was staying, and all the inside lights were off. Connor and Tank must be up at the saloon again. Scourge was missing though, which was weird. They usually didn't drive there.

"How is it, staying in an abandoned store?" Alexis asked, breaking the silence and trying to lighten the mood.

"Better than out on the road, that's for sure," James said.

"Yeah," she said, but the tone in her voice and the faraway look in her eyes gave him pause. "Do you ever miss it?"

"Miss what? My life before all this?"

"No, being out on the road. Not knowing what

might happen or when."

"Yes," James said, "and no. It's hard to explain. It's almost like I'm *used* to being out there, constantly on edge."

On the road, he had to always be ready for anything, and it was as exhausting as it was exhilarating. In here, on the other hand, he felt safe, and somehow that put him more on edge. He was expecting things to go wrong at any second, knowing the good times wouldn't last. Whether it was tonight, tomorrow, or in a week, something was bound to happen and this whole town would go up in flames.

"I'm glad it's not just me," Alexis said. "I almost had myself convinced I was crazy."

"No, it's hard to let your guard down after all you've been through."

Alexis shivered. "I still have nightmares about that night. If you guys hadn't shown up…"

James nodded. He could only imagine the feeling of hopelessness she must've felt then and again a few days later to get captured by someone even worse. She'd been through more than he had, and even he had nightmares. She had a rare inner strength to have gone through all that and still continue on. Most people would end up like Margaret, who hadn't spoken in days. She barely ate and barely slept. Something in Margaret's mind had broken back when they'd been taken by the Reclaimers, and he didn't think she'd ever recover.

"That's all in the past now," James said. "We've survived, somehow."

"We've been blessed," Alexis said.

"Blessed?"

"God's been protecting us," Alexis stated matter-of-factly.

"I didn't know you were a Christian."

"I grew up one and just recently found my faith again."

James smiled. "Well, good for you."

"What do you believe, James Andderson?"

"I believe Jesus died for my sins and I've been called to live my life to the fullest, following the path He sets before me."

"And how do you think all of this fits into that?"

James took a few moments to try and figure out how to put it into words. "I honestly don't have any idea. I just take it all on faith and move on with my life, trying the best I can. If I think too much about it, I just come up with doubts."

Alexis nodded. "It's hard to reconcile all we've been through. The important part is that we got through it and survived. That has to count for something."

She didn't say anything about the ones who *hadn't* survived, but he knew it was on both their minds. Why should they survive all this when others hadn't? People always died—good people, people who deserved to live. It was just the way of the world. That hadn't changed. It was just the scale on which it was happening that gave him pause.

"What about the people you've killed?" Alexis asked.

Even though he could hear something in her voice that told him she wasn't accusing him, the question still felt like a blow to his gut. He stopped, and she looked back at him, a deep pain in her eyes. It seemed like she wasn't asking a simple question and that more hinged on his answer than just what he thought. People's faces flashed through the back of his mind—people he'd killed. He didn't know how many that was and couldn't even count them if he wanted to.

They'd given him no choice; he knew that. If he wanted to save those he loved, help strangers, and protect his own life, he'd had to do it. And he'd done it without hesitation, but the more he killed, the easier it became. Now that they weren't busy focusing on survival, the questions and doubts nagged at his mind. Had he really *had* to kill them? Was it wrong that he had? He'd spilled blood, and he knew it wouldn't be the last.

Alexis watched him as he stood there, trying to sort through his thoughts and feelings. "I'm sorry," she said, turning from him. "I just... don't understand how she could've done what she did."

"You mean Ana?" James said, walking up to her.

His feelings were a whirlwind of chaos. He'd been excited about how well the date was going earlier, but now all this? Between his episode and these questions they couldn't possibly answer, the night was taking a turn for the worse, and he knew he couldn't stop it. She needed to be able to work through all this, just like he did.

"Yeah," Alexis said. "How could she do it? Ana said it was to save us—to save me—but I don't want to live with that. I feel like it's my fault they're dead."

Tears were brimming in her eyes again.

"It's not your fault," James said. "Ana made the

choice, and whether it was right or wrong, it was hers to make, and it created an opportunity for you to escape. She probably saw it as sacrificing a few to save the rest. That's how I would've looked at it."

"Would you have done it?"

Her eyes pleaded with him. He almost responded immediately and instinctively, but he stopped and really thought about it instead. Would he have killed Mila and Evan to save Alexis? Connor? Olive? He knew the answer, no matter how hard it was to admit.

"Yes," James said, knowing it wasn't the answer she wanted.

She turned and started walking the way they'd been going. James followed her as the sun began to set before them.

They arrived at the end of the street to the bench James had *borrowed* from someone's backyard earlier. Alexis stopped, but he walked up and sat down on it, and she joined him shortly after. Despite the high fence in front of them, they had a decent view of the sunset through the top six feet of the double-layer chain link. The bottom four feet was a solid block that made it possible for the guards to take cover if they were being shot at.

The sun painted the sky in hues of orange and pink as the temperature started to drop. Alexis moved closer to him and he reached over, putting his arm around her as she rested her head on his shoulder. It almost shocked him how forward he was being with her. He should've been more nervous, but he wasn't, and he wouldn't let himself be. Their dinner had been perfect, and he felt like he'd known her for a long time already. They continued to watch as the sun slowly disappeared behind the horizon and the light faded. They sat on the bench, enjoying each other's company.

"I don't like what she did," Alexis began, "but maybe she didn't have a choice. Not really. It still hurts though. She was the closest thing I had to a friend in all this, and when she did that I saw a part of her I hadn't seen before. It scared me. That wasn't the Ana I knew. I think that's what shocked me the most."

"It's hard sometimes," James said, "to know what we're all capable of until the time comes for us to step up. Look at Chloe. I never would've guessed that she could kill Bryce. I know she didn't want to do it, but she did, and saved our lives in the process. If she hadn't acted, there might not have been another opportunity and we would've been in one of those graves the next morning."

"It's just hard to think about making that choice. Would *I* be able to do it to save the ones I love? Or would I do nothing and inadvertently be the cause of their death and have to live with the knowledge that I could've saved them if only I'd acted."

"You can't do that to yourself. You can't wonder what you would've done in that situation. We have to move on, leave the past in the past and look to the future."

"Saying that for yourself as well?"

James chuckled. "Yeah, I think I'm the one who needs to hear that the most."

He looked down at her as her head rested on his shoulder, and it was as clear as day to him. His heart had found a home. This was it—what he'd been waiting all those years for. He knew this was the woman he wanted to spend the rest of his life with. The revelation should've shocked him, but deep down he'd already known. He wasn't sure when he'd first realized. Had it been when he'd seen her helping the survivors from Burns over a week ago, dropping zombies with style, or earlier while having dinner? But it didn't matter; the fact was, he wanted to marry this woman in his arms.

His parents had known early on that they wanted to get married and they'd accomplished that in under a year. It wasn't that uncommon. Not that he was going to ask her now. He needed to see how she felt, and there were other things to worry about. He pushed the thoughts aside and came back to the present. This moment was too good to miss out on.

She glanced up at him and he smiled.

"You're so beautiful," James said as he gazed down at her.

Her eyes were so tender and her lips so inviting. He shocked himself by leaning down, his lips meeting hers.

11
PREY

Max sat in a copse of cultivated trees, whittling on a stick. This one was turning out to be a simple spiral design, like someone would hang in their window. Next to him, lying on the ground and aiming a large-caliber rifle with high-powered scope, was Zeke. He was watching the fenced-in city of Coutts as the sun set behind them. A spotting scope was set up in front of Max, but he wasn't bothered with looking through it. Zeke would watch for them, so he carved on a stick. Finishing the spiral design, he tossed it to the side. One of the curls was uneven so it wasn't worth keeping. He picked up a larger stick and began to work on it.

"Will you quit that?" Zeke said in his heavy Russian accent. Even after weeks of being around the man, Max still had trouble understanding him sometimes. This wasn't one of those times.

"Nope," Max said in his deep voice.

Max outweighed the man by a hundred pounds and stood over eight inches taller, but there was no doubt in Max's mind that he couldn't take him. Zeke was a killer, a trained assassin, from what he'd overheard, and someone who'd adapted to this lifestyle long before the world went to hell. Max thought back to before all this. After his second stint in the pen for breaking and entering, he'd finally got out and cleaned up. He'd even gotten a legitimate job at a UPS warehouse, and things had begun to look up.

Then came the day when he'd gone in to work and beaten his boss to death with a fire extinguisher.

He'd run from the scene, not knowing his boss had actually been infected. All he knew was that the man had attacked him and he fought back. Then he ran. He wasn't going back to jail. It was good that he'd already decided to leave Casper, because it got bad there quickly.

"I see movement," Zeke said. Max didn't even look up. "False alarm, just another guard on rotation."

Zeke had been calling out that kind of stuff all evening, like Max would know what that meant or even care. He'd never been in the military or anything like that. Hell, the only time he'd used a gun before was holding up a gas station. He hadn't even known how to shoot it. That had changed quickly after he met Jezz. He'd found a nice group around Sheridan, decent people who were just trying to survive, and after a few days on his own he'd been happy to join. Then *she'd* come in, looking all wild-eyed. The next day their leader and half of the guards were gone, all stabbed to death. She'd walked into the common room and commanded the rest of them to follow her or die.

Instantly, a few of the ones Max didn't like—the types he used to run with—joined her, leaving the others with little choice. He'd joined her, too, and it'd saved him. The ones who hesitated a moment longer were gunned down by her new goons on her orders. Then she instructed them about what it meant to "reclaim" someone's soul, and how to send it back to the earth—a fancy way to say "kill them." Now here he was, one of her top men. How had things gotten this out of control? He'd just wanted to survive, which he was doing, but at what cost?

Shaking his head, he looked down at what his hands had been working on while his mind wandered. His mind did that sometimes, but he hated when it went to his past. It made him feel like he shouldn't be doing what he was doing, but it was too late for that now. There was nothing else for him but to survive.

An intricate eagle totem sat in his hands. How long had his mind been wandering?

"I see movement behind the fence," Zeke said.

Max pocketed the totem. It was a good one. When he got back, he'd see if Jezz liked it. She hadn't liked any of the rest, but maybe this one...

"It's a couple. They just sat down on a bench," Zeke said, glancing at him out of the corner of his eye. "Get your big ass up to that scope!"

The dangerous growl in his voice had Max moving without thought. He had to survive this. Scooting up to look through the spotting scope, he adjusted the focus so he could see.

"Where?" Max asked, eyeing the fence.

"Where the fence dips in towards town, right at the 90."

Max looked back through the scope, moving it to the right and then to the left, realizing he was going the wrong way. All of this tactical, sitting-around stuff was the worst. He just wanted to be back at their new base sitting on a couch, maybe taking a quick nap. They'd been up since early that morning, getting here and moving into position. A nap would be nice. Maybe a soda, too. It was always nice when they got a soda or a candy bar. Since they'd recruited more Reclaimers after the last had been wiped out, they'd had to start rationing food again. Jezz would kill him if she realized he was sneaking a Twix every once in a while. Well maybe not kill. He was one of her favorites, after all, but she would teach him a lesson.

"Have you found them yet, you imbecile?" Zeke asked.

Max flinched at Zeke's tone, continuing to scan the scope to the right. There was the dip in the fence and... there! Just past the corner were two people on a bench. Judging by how close they were sitting, they looked like they were a couple. It was hard to tell through the fence if he recognized them, but... Yes, that was her—Alexis. Jezz had taken a liking to her. Not like she had to Ana though.

"That's her," Max said. "One of them."

"Perfect," Zeke said, making some adjustments on his scope.

Max didn't know the first thing about a high-powered scope like that with all those knobs, but he'd seen enough movies to know that it could shoot a long way. Zeke seemed to know what he was doing, and Max didn't doubt it. How far away were they? Half a mile?

"How far are we?" Max asked.

"One thousand and fifty-eight yards," Zeke said,

taking his hand away from the scope and cupping the stock with it.

That was an oddly specific distance, but he guessed that at that distance, every foot mattered. Zeke looked comfortable, almost like he could take a nap right there. Max wished he could be like that— comfortable out here, leaning against one of the tree trunks. Glancing into the scope again, he noticed the couple on the bench was kissing now. A pang went through his heart and he wished that could be him. He'd always wanted to have a family, but the women he'd been with had never lasted long and he couldn't figure out why. Did Zeke really have to kill these two now? Was that what they were even there for?

"You're not going to kill them, are you?" Max asked.

"Of course not," Zeke said. "At this distance, the bullet would disintegrate when it hit the metal fence. We're just here to confirm it's them."

"We've done that, so can we go?" Max asked, just wanting to get back to his warm bed.

"No. To properly hunt your prey, you need to know your prey," Zeke said in a cold voice that made Max shiver. This man was almost as bad as Jezz sometimes—almost.

12
THE KISS

The whole world fell away when their lips touched. It was just him and her, and nothing else existed or mattered. The kiss lasted only a few moments, but it felt both like an eternity and the blink of an eye all at once. Their lips parted and his smile was so wide that it hurt his face. She giggled.

"That good?" Alexis asked.

"Wow," James said. It was all he *could* say. His mind was fuzzy, and if she hadn't been holding onto him, he swore he would've floated into the darkening sky. "Wow."

"Boys," she said with another giggle.

The rest of the evening passed in a blur of happy feelings, their earlier conversation long forgotten. Nothing could compare to the euphoria he felt. When it was dark, he walked Alexis back to her house. They talked some along the way but nothing deep or painful; they both wanted the night to end on a high note. Outside her door, she stopped and they shared another short kiss.

"I could get used to that," James said when their lips parted.

"Me too," Alexis said, the porch light making her

eyes glitter.

"I hope I didn't ruin the date with my episode and all that," James said. "I didn't mean to walk away, I just…"

"No, you didn't ruin it. In fact, that made it better. It was authentic, and in that one moment I was able to get to know you better than our whole conversation before it. Tonight was perfect. Thank you."

"No, thank *you*," James said with a wink.

"You're such a dork."

He smiled. "Goodnight, Alexis."

"Goodnight, James."

He watched her as she opened the door and went inside. She stole one last glance at him as the door closed. Standing paralyzed for a few moments, he began to practically skip back towards his place. Actually, he did start jogging for a few steps before his side began to ache and he stopped. Both of his wounds had been healing well now that they had proper medical care and he'd been taking it easy for a week. They did still bother him, however—mainly his side. It'd closed up but was still tender.

Arriving at their place in record time, he noticed again that all the lights were off. They must still be up at the saloon. Why not go celebrate tonight? It was only ten so James walked to the saloon.

Inside, Connor and Tank sat at their normal table with Chloe waiting on them. By the looks of things, they were taking it easy. That was good since they had a big day tomorrow.

"Jamesy boy!" Tank hollered as James made his way to them.

"How'd the date go?" Connor asked as James sat down, a massive grin on his face.

"That well, eh?" Tank asked. "Gonna give us them details?"

He did, starting with the dinner, which they had him skip through. When he got to the episode, he left that part out. His brother would be pissed if he knew he'd had another one. He just told them they'd both opened up about struggling with stuff. Then he told them about the walk, sitting on the bench, and finally the kiss.

"Well, hell," Tank said. "*You* kissed *her*?"

"Yep," James said.

"Chloe!" Tank yelled. "We need a round of shots for James here. He just kissed a girl for the first time!"

James was too ecstatic to be embarrassed at the dozen or so heads turning towards him. It was true and he wasn't ashamed of it, even if it had taken twenty-one years. Chloe came over and dropped off their shots, smiling the whole time.

"She's been waiting for that for a while now, ya know," Chloe said. "I'm just glad it didn't stay as awkward as it was at first tonight."

"Oh, shut up," James said, still smiling. "It wasn't *that* bad."

"It was," Chloe said over her shoulder as she walked away.

"Well, buddy," Tank said, "this toast is for you! Welcome to the world of a real man."

The three of them tipped their shots back, and James felt the burning liquid go down his gullet. He'd have to be careful tonight to not drink too much or tomorrow would be miserable.

"Wait," Tank said. "Didn't you have your first kiss back in Colorado?"

"That doesn't even come close to counting," James said, indignant. "She just randomly stuck her tongue in my mouth! I was in the middle of talking with her."

Tank laughed. "I don't know…"

"You shut up, too," James said.

He glanced at his brother. Connor was staring off into the distance. There were things going on inside his head that James couldn't even begin to understand. He felt bad for his brother. His issues rarely allowed him any peace, even for one night. Connor just needed to drink a little more.

"Chloe," James said, as she walked by, "let's get another round."

"Sure," she said, walking back to the bar.

"Damn," Tank said. "Your balls really did drop tonight. Congrats man!"

James couldn't even pretend to be mad at him. Tonight was just too perfect.

Chloe brought them another round.

"What are we toasting now?" James said.

"Bro, we don't have to toast *every* time we take a shot," Connor said.

"I usually agree with you, but we do have another reason to toast tonight," Tank said, a grin on his face. "I took your advice. Chloe and I are officially dating!"

The last part he said loudly and Chloe looked over from the bar, laughing. One of the regular patrons a couple of tables over grumbled something.

"That's right, Lincoln," Tank said to the man. "She's officially mine, so keep your hands off!"

"Whatever," the old man, Lincoln, replied, waving a hand at him. "I don't know how a guy like you got with a lady like that."

"It's all about the moves, my man," Tank said.

That got a laugh out of the patrons within earshot and a scowl from Chloe. The scowl didn't reach her eyes, however. They truly liked each other, James realized. He thought it'd just been about sex at first and maybe it had, but now it'd blossomed into a real relationship. Tank deserved someone special, and James liked Chloe. She was a good match for his best friend—supportive, but she didn't take any crap.

"Another round for the lovebirds," Lincoln said to Chloe. "On me!"

"Thank ya, ya old bastard," Tank said with a laugh.

"You better watch it. I may be old, but I'll still kick yer ass!"

They laughed and Chloe brought them another round. They toasted to the Wolf Pack next, a tradition every time they had shots—well, a tradition James liked to indulge every time they had shots. He liked to make sure each shot had an appropriate toast, but after a couple more rounds even he forgot to toast. They continued to drink late into the night.

13
SUNBURST

Post-outbreak day 19

James woke up with a headache and immediately knew he'd overdone it the night before. He'd even warned himself to be careful not to do this, yet here he was. He never could keep up with his brother when it came to drinking, let alone Tank. Leaning up, his head swam, but after a little food and a lot of water, he should be feeling mostly back to normal.

Damn alcohol, he thought. *More like damn lack of self-control. Oh well, what's done is done.*

Then he remembered why he'd been celebrating and a smile broke out on his face. He'd been on his first date and had his first kiss with the most amazing woman he'd ever known. Sitting on the edge of his cot, he stared at the wall in befuddlement. It hadn't been just a dream; it'd really happened. What a night!

Climbing out of his cot, he dressed and noticed Connor was already up and outside. Going through all the pouches on his plate carrier and pack, James reorganized a few of the items. This only took five minutes since they ran their kits similarly. He set his decked-out ACR on the bed, along with his tactical belt, suppressed .22 Beretta handgun, plate carrier, combat helmet, and small backpack. One last glance and he was content that everything was all set.

Connor came inside. "Tank up yet?"

"Yeah," Tank said, rolling over. "Don't really want to get up, but I'm awake."

"Ten minutes until food," Connor said.

"I'll be ready," Tank said, sitting up.

In ten minutes they were all ready and loading their gear into Scourge.

"What is that?" James said, stepping out the front door and pointing to their LAPV.

"Just a little upgrade," Tank said.

The front doors on each side of the vehicle now sported an emblem painted in gray. It looked like three wolf heads, one facing out and the other two facing each side.

"That's kick-ass!" James said, taking a closer look. "What is it?"

"Angel, the artist in town, said it was his version of Cerberus," Tank said.

"It looks more like wolf heads than dogs," James said.

"Exactly," Tank said. "I thought it was fittin'— three separate heads workin' as one."

"It sums up the Wolf Pack perfectly," James said.

"Plus, it just looks awesome," Connor said as he finished loading up.

"Well done," James said, climbing in as Tank started the rig.

"Thanks. I wanted something to distinguish Scourge from the rest of the LAPVs."

He pulled out and headed to the Mess Hall where

they quickly ate and then drove over to HQ. There were a half dozen various military vehicles running outside, with soldiers moving all around. They pulled up to an open parking spot and jumped out, walking over to where Emmett stood next to the man who must've been Cpt. Sanders.

"Morning, boys," Emmett said.

"Mornin', sir," James said. "They heading out to get those supplies?"

"Yes, sir," Emmett said.

"Where do you want us, sir?" Connor asked, looking to Cpt. Sanders.

"Head upstairs and talk to Cpt. Miller," Cpt. Sanders said, not even looking at them. "He's on babysitting duty, not me."

"Excuse me?" Tank said.

"I'm in charge of real soldiers and Marines, not three boys playing army," Cpt. Sanders said as he walked off, then barked orders at a group of soldiers standing next to one of the Humvees.

Tank opened his mouth, probably to yell something at the captain, but Connor elbowed him in the side. Tank glanced at him and then mumbled, "Dick," under his breath.

"What was that about?" James asked Emmett.

"Cpt. Sanders doesn't like it that civilians are helping out with military duties and doesn't think they need the help. He thinks they have everything under control without us."

"What do you think?" Connor asked.

Emmett looked at them. "I think they could use all the help they can get. Even though they're in contact with other bases in the states, I don't think they fully realize how bad it is out there."

"How is it, really?" James asked.

Emmett paused before answering. "I've been in one of their meetings and I'm not at liberty to speak, but I will say this: more cities have fallen and the infected are growing in number every day. It's better than we originally feared, but how long it'll stay that way, I don't know."

"Is it safe here?" Connor asked.

Emmett nodded. "The safest place right now."

"Emmett!" Cpt. Sanders hollered from inside one of the Humvees.

"I'll see you tonight," Emmett said, walking off. "Stay frosty out there."

"Yes, sir," Connor said.

"Well, that's bullshit," Tank said.

"I'm starting to think they just want to keep us busy so we'll stay out of their hair," James said.

"That might not be far from the truth," Connor said. "But to be fair, they do have it well under control."

"True," James said. "And we *are* untrained."

"Still," Tank said, "that guy didn't need to be an ass about it."

"Let's head up and see what Cpt. Miller has for us today," James said, leading the way through the glass doors and up the stairs. They knocked once on the captain's door and were ushered inside.

"Morning, gentlemen," Cpt. Miller said. "I have another scouting mission for you today. You ready?"

"Yes, sir," Connor said.

"One of our birds saw activity down by Sunburst, in the US Customs building east of town."

"What kind of activity?" Tank asked.

"There were some vehicles there that weren't there before, and we have reason to believe there may be survivors inside."

"Why send us?" James asked.

"Most of our men are heading north today and the rest need to stay here to protect the town. We figured you could head down there and check it out."

"If they're friendlies?" Connor asked.

"Invite them back and we'll interview them."

"If not?" James asked.

"You survived out there against the odds. I think you know what to do if they're hostile."

"Yes, sir," Connor said.

"If we don't see you back here by tonight, we'll assume something went wrong and send a team out to check on you in the morning."

"Good," Connor said. "Anything else, sir?"

"That's it."

"Then we'll be on our way," Connor said, standing.

"Good luck, gentlemen, and be careful out there."

"We will," James said as they left the room.

As they exited the building, they noticed that all of the military personnel had already left, their taillights shining in the predawn light as they headed north. The three of them piled into Scourge and Tank started it up. Pulling out, they headed south towards Sunburst. *Remember We Die* by Gemini Syndrome played through the speakers as they drove back through the narrow channel of vehicles that guarded the border. Now that James had stayed in Coutts for a while, he appreciated the security that wall of vehicles provided, especially since this was their first time heading south since they'd arrived.

"I like the captain," Connor said.

"I do, too," James said. "I trust our military. Just not so sure about our government."

"You do know our government controls the military," Tank said.

"I do," James said. "But the military could be acting on orders, just doing their jobs, and still not know what's truly going on."

"Yep," Connor said.

"I can see that," Tank said. "What I'm still wonderin' is who those people in the black uniforms are. Black ops? Private contractors? Or maybe somethin' more sinister."

"That's a very good point," James said. "I don't trust them at all."

"They did let us keep Scourge," Connor said.

"But why?" Tank asked.

"Maybe Emmett really went to bat for us and Cpt. Miller gave them no choice," James said.

"That's assumin' they follow orders," Tank said.

"They have to at least pretend to follow orders, or they wouldn't be in town," Connor said.

"Yeah, I guess that seems legit," Tank said. "But I still don't trust 'em."

"I'm not sure who I trust," Connor said.

"But you do trust Cpt. Miller?" James asked.

"He seems honest," Connor said.

"What about this mission?" Tank said. "Sound like a trap to anyone else?"

"Could be," James said. "The few Reclaimers that survived are out here somewhere, including Jezz."

"You hear what Alexis said about her?" Tank asked.

"She talked about her last night," James said. "That woman sounds like the most unhinged person we've met so far."

"And a psychopath," Tank said.

"Yeah, if the woman is as crazy as Alexis claims," James said, "I wouldn't be surprised if she wants revenge. There's no telling when or where she might turn up and how many of them there'll be."

"We need to make sure to watch ourselves out here," Connor said.

"Already plan on it," James said.

"How we gonna play this?" Tank asked.

"I'd like to be able to scout the building," Connor said. "But…"

"It's open as hell out here," Tank said.

"Anywhere we stop to scout the survivors, they'll be able to see us if they're paying attention," James said.

"Roger," Connor said.

"Then we shock-n-awe again," Tank said.

"Go right in with Scourge and have someone on top with the SAW," Connor said.

"But we drive around a bit before going in," James said. "Hopefully, they'll come out."

"If there's even anyone there," Connor said.

"And if they don't shoot at us right away," Tank said.

"I hate all these unknowns," James said.

"Semper Gumby," Connor said.

"Always flexible," Tank translated. "And if anyone is gonna shoot the SAW this time, it's me.

Jamesy Boy, you wanna drive?"

"Do Dall sheep love the mountains?" James asked, smiling.

"I don't know," Tank said. "You're the damn hunting guide."

"Of course they do!" James said.

"Then why are you asking me?" Tank asked.

"It was a rhetorical question to..." James trailed off after seeing Tank's smile. "Oh, just shut up and pull over."

Tank started laughing as he pulled over on I-15.

14
SECRETS

Alexis made her way through the front door of the infirmary. The black-uniformed guards out front had been even more brisk than the last time. First, they asked to see her ID, then they wanted to go through her purse, and they even made her leave her gun belt with them at the gate. She'd been reluctant to do so but reminded herself that the entire place was surrounded by heavy-duty fencing. Thankfully, they hadn't checked her whole body and found the knife she kept concealed on her lower leg, a habit her dad had taught her—always have a weapon on hand.

Her excitement about her date with James the night before was clashing with her nervousness at finally starting her actual job.

"Good morning, Ms. Wolfe," Dr. Nelson said with a smile as he walked into the lobby.

"Morning, Dr. Nelson," Alexis said.

"Remember, call me Henry."

"Okay, and I'm Alexis."

"Fair enough, Alexis. You ready to start working today?"

"Definitely."

"Good, then follow me and I'll give you the grand

tour," Henry said, walking down a hallway to their left.

There were three doors down the hall. The first one led to a large conference room and the second led to a small classroom with an outside door. The last door at the end of the hall was locked tight with a keypad next to it. Henry explained the first two rooms and turned to leave.

"What about that last door?" Alexis asked.

"Oh, that," Henry said, turning around. "Dr. Hart keeps all the pharmaceuticals under lock and key in that room."

"Is that all that's in there?"

"There's also a door that leads to the basement, but we don't use that. Supposedly, it's full of mold and rats."

"What do I do if I need to get something from inside?"

"Dr. Hart has the code and only he goes in there. If he wants you to get something from inside, he'll give you the code, but even *I* don't know it."

He continued on, but Alexis took a longer look at the door. She then jogged to catch up with Henry as he escorted her to the stairs in the main lobby. After climbing to the second floor, he continued the tour. The two doors to their left were Dr. Hart's and Henry's offices. There was a cubby with a desk next to the farthest room where Alexis's "office" would be. To their right was a long hallway with four rooms on each side. These were all examination rooms. Apparently, they weren't usually very busy since they typically only used the first four rooms and rarely the back.

"And that's it," Henry said as they exited the first examination room.

"I see you're showing our newest assistant around, Dr. Nelson," said a man with black hair and a stern smile as he walked out of the office closest to the stairs. This must be Dr. Hart.

Alexis immediately disliked the man. He reminded her of Father Ahaz, with the same stern look and holier-than-thou tone in his voice like she was a mere mortal and he was far above her. No, she didn't like him at all. There was also something about him that seemed familiar, as if she'd met him before, or maybe he resembled someone she knew.

"We just completed the tour," Henry said.

"In that case," Dr. Hart said. "Ms. Wolfe, I have a job for you."

He brushed past them into the exam room they'd just left, and she begrudgingly followed.

"I assume you recognize most of the items in here?" Dr. Hart asked.

"Of course," Alexis said, trying to hold back her sudden anger. Who did this man think he was?

"Good," Dr. Hart said. "Restock the supplies in all of the exam rooms. Then, when you're done with that, organize the supply closet. I hear it's a mess."

Without even waiting for her to respond, he walked out of the room, heading straight for his office. She had to use all of her self-control not to flip him off, and she wondered where this sudden anger was coming from. Yes, he reminded her of Father Ahaz, but that didn't mean he was a bad guy. He just had one of those personalities that always rubbed her the wrong way.

"Sorry about that," Henry said. "Dr. Hart is a very... brisk man. But he's not all bad, and you'll get used to working with him."

"I'm sure," Alexis said. "Do you have a notepad or something I can take stock with?"

"Yeah, there's a tablet at your desk. I'll show you."

They exited the room and Henry led her over to her new office area. It contained a simple metal desk with a computer sitting on top and an office chair behind it. She'd be tucked into a corner next to Henry's office with a view of the hallway, stairs, and both office doors. It wasn't a bad location since no one could come and go without her seeing them— another of her dad's habits that had worn off on her.

"If you need anything else, I'll be in here," Henry said, walking to his office.

"Thanks, Henry," Alexis said.

"No problem," Henry said as he closed the door behind him.

Time to get to work, Alexis thought, grabbing the tablet and walking back into the first exam room.

A couple of hours later, she had taken stock of all the rooms. The first two rooms on either side of the hallway needed the most, and surprisingly, the far right room needed supplies, too. It looked like it'd been recently used, which wasn't necessarily odd. It was just Henry's comment about not using the far rooms that had gotten her thinking. A small part of her wondered if she was just being paranoid because of all she'd been through, but she shoved those thoughts aside. Descending the stairs, she entered the first room to the left, next to the staircase. Boxes of various medical supplies were scattered around the floor and on the shelves.

"He wasn't kidding about it being a mess," she muttered to herself as she began to look around for the items she needed.

Her work was interrupted as the front doors to the infirmary opened and voices carried to her. Instinctively, she quickly stood up and turned the light off, casting the room into darkness. The door to the storage room was open a crack, letting a shaft of light in. She walked up to it as two men in black uniforms moved down the hall towards the locked door housing the pharmaceuticals. They were pushing a small cart with a sheet over it, hiding the contents. Stopping outside the door, they looked around and she shied back a little. Content that they weren't being watched, one of the men entered a code into the keypad. Alexis was too far away to actually see what the code was as they opened the door and entered.

Inside the room, there were a couple of shelves with various pharmaceuticals on them. There was also a third uniformed man standing against the far wall next to a newer-looking metal door. The door was closing behind the men with the cart, and she caught one last glimpse as the third man opened the door leading to the basement and white light poured out.

She waited for a few minutes to make sure they didn't come back out and then opened the storage room door fully and turned the light back on. She returned to her task but kept one eye on the hallway, waiting for the men to come out. After twenty minutes, they still hadn't, so she gathered her supplies and went back upstairs to finish her job.

Maybe her mistrust of Dr. Hart was well founded. If he had the code to get in there, he must know what was going on. What were they hiding?

15
HELPING HAND

Tank stood on the seat in Scourge, his head poking out of the hatch on top. Finally, he was the one who was going to mow down some undead or hostiles with his SAW, although he couldn't help cringing at the thought of James driving. He had to remind himself that James was as good a driver as he was. It was just that this rig was like Tank's baby, and he didn't like other people driving his baby. It was his precious. He chuckled a little to himself; he was starting to sound like Gollum.

His mirth faded as they crested a high point in the landscape and the town of Sunburst came into view. He adjusted himself and checked his SAW. Everything was ready to rock and roll.

"I see the town," Tank called to the brothers below.

"Roger that," Connor said. "I got eyes on it, too."

"He said the building was east of town," James said. "Keep an eye on that area."

Tank looked to the east, now able to see the building they were heading to as it became distinguishable from the rest of the landscape. It was a large building with a red metal roof. A few vehicles sat in the parking lot, but he didn't see any movement of either undead or survivors. There was a chance that there were people staying there who might not have seen Scourge yet, but once they drove closer, they'd know. James slowed just before Exit 389, the customs building only a few hundred yards to their left. There was still no movement.

"I don't see anythin'," Tank said.

"I see nothing from down here either," James said.

"Stick with the plan and be ready," Connor said, hoisting his rifle.

The windows in Scourge didn't roll down, so if they got into any trouble, Tank would be on his own, which simply meant more fun for him. The thought made him smile, even though he knew it was to cover his nerves.

James turned off the interstate and drove onto the road leading to the target building. They closed in on it and Tank kept a sharp eye peeled. It seemed as if the survivors may have left since he still saw no sign of anyone. Arriving at the building, James took the driveway leading to the parking lot.

"Drive around it a few times," Connor said. "See if we can get 'em to come out."

"Got it," James said. "Watch yourself up there."

"Oh, I am," Tank said.

Tank's eyes flicked to movement by one of the vehicles, but it was just a yellow plastic bag that was stuck in a window, blowing in the wind. They did an entire circuit around the building and then a second one. If anyone was there, they were staying hidden inside.

"Now what?" James asked as they pulled to a stop

in the parking lot.

Tank ducked back in. "Not sure."

"We have to check it out," Connor said.

"Yeah, I guess you're right," James said.

"Well, hell," Tank said. "Nothin' like goin' into a buildin' potentially full of hostiles."

"We'll do this carefully," Connor as James turned the rig off.

"Let's check and see what doors are unlocked," James said.

"Be ready for anythin'," Tank said.

Tank picked up his helmet, turning the headset on. Emmett had finally shown them how to use these, and they'd sure come in handy today, especially if they had to split up. Climbing out, he grabbed his daypack and the brothers followed suit. James tossed the keys to Tank, who pocketed them.

"Can you hear me?" Connor whispered into his headset.

"Gotcha," Tank said.

"Loud and clear," James said.

"I'll take point," Connor said. "Tank, you follow behind me and be ready with that SAW."

"I'll get our six," James said.

Connor led and Tank followed, going to the nearest door. It was locked, so they moved towards the back of the building, checking the next door, which was locked as well. Arriving at the back door, Connor checked it while Tank covered him.

"Unlocked," Connor whispered.

"Let's check the rest," James said.

They moved on, checking the rest of the building. All of the other doors were locked. They couldn't see what was inside the building because all the window shades were down. The front doors were glass and Tank could see through those, but everything inside looked as he'd expect. Should the need arise, these doors could serve as an alternative exit since they could shoot through the glass if they had to. After checking the entire perimeter of the building, Tank jumped into Scourge and moved it closer to the unlocked back door.

"We ready?" Connor said, looking at the other two.

"Let's do this," James said, and Tank nodded.

Connor posted up beside the door and Tank took his stance, ready to open it at Connor's signal. James hung behind, watching their backs and ready to come in after them. Connor nodded and Tank opened the door. Tank slipped in after Connor, gun up and ready. The interior was dark and Tank quickly clicked the flashlight attached to his SAW. Connor already had his on as he crouched partway into the room behind the cover of some boxes. Tank edged up to Connor as James closed the door behind them, plunging them into darkness.

The room was large and mainly unfurnished. It looked like a storage room. There were two closed doors on each side of the room, and there was a set of double doors at the far end that would lead into the main part of the building.

"Let's check these doors," James said, "then move in farther."

"Roger," Connor said, moving off to the first door.

Tank followed him, the three of them staying tight but not too close together.

"It's locked," Connor said, starting to move away. After just a step, he went back to the door and pressed the side of his helmet against it. "I hear something in there."

Tank moved up to do the same. Low groans could be heard from inside.

"Undead," Tank said.

"Someone must've trapped them in there and locked the door," James said.

"That means someone *has* been here," Tank said.

"Proceed with caution," Connor said, moving to the door on the other side of the room.

The other three doors were the same—locked with undead groaning from inside.

"This is weird," Tank said.

"There have to be a lot of zombies in here for them to fill four rooms," James said.

Looking at the floor, it seemed like the undead had been in there for a while before someone had locked them in the rooms. Maybe a group of survivors had just stayed there for the night, but why not pick a building they didn't have to clear? Unless this was one of the clearest buildings in the area.

"They could still be here," Connor said.

"We'll know soon," James said.

Tank continued to follow Connor as he walked through the room, head swinging from side to side in search of threats. They were closing in on the double doors when Connor looked down sharply. A few loud pops sounded behind them like firecrackers going off. Tank swung around quickly. The four doors containing all the undead swung open, the locks and handles blown off.

"What the hell!" Tank said.

Smoke settled around the doors as the undead began to pour out. Tank brought his SAW up and began to fire on them, taking down one, two, and then three in quick succession, but he might as well have been trying to plug a torpedo hole in a ship with a cork as they continued to pour from the doorways.

"There's too many!" James shouted.

"In here!" Connor yelled, ducking into the room they were heading for.

Tank shot one more and then followed the brothers through the double doors. As soon as Tank was in, Connor shoved a piece of rebar through the handles of the doors. A curse from James caused Tank to glance back and see him pulling and then pushing on the door leading out, to no avail. Connor swung the ACR at his side into his hands and aimed at the entrance with Tank. The undead slammed against the metal, forcing the double doors to open slightly before the rebar stopped them. The groaning was frantic as a few arms reached through the gap, trying to get to them. James fired a few rounds into the door behind them and then cursed again.

"Something has it barricaded," James said.

"Ya got this?" Tank asked Connor, who nodded.

Tank turned around to investigate the small room they were trapped in. It seemed that this was the entryway between the main part of the building and the back room. The only exits were the one they'd come through and the one James was currently trying to kick open. There were no windows or other openings they could escape through. They were effectively trapped in there. Something on the wall next to the barricaded door caught Tank's eye. Walking up to the yellow sheet of paper taped to the wall, he let out a low curse. He recognized the handwriting.

"Guys," Tank said, standing next to the paper.

James quit kicking the door and walked over to him. He began reading the note aloud, but Tank already knew what it said and his stomach sank.

"Fret not, my dears," James read out loud. "We will be there shortly to lend a helping hand. J."

Tank cursed.

16
SAFETY

Emmett walked down Second Street toward the Mess Hall for lunch. He'd just come from a meeting with Saul, who needed him to take a leadership role to help out with the day-to-day running of the town. The job was too much for one man, so he wanted Emmett to take over the scouting runs, working with James, Connor, and Tank. Saul was going to make them the official scouting team if their current mission was a success, which would free up quite a bit of their military resources that were normally allocated to those runs. The boys would report to Emmett, who would then report to Saul, who would give Emmett their next orders. He could even go with them if he chose to oversee the runs. He wanted to accept the position. It would finally be something to do, whereas up until then, he'd just been trying to find things to keep himself busy.

They'd be sent out on runs four to five times a week to look for supplies, survivors, or anything else they needed to keep the town running smoothly. Basically, they'd be glorified errand boys, but he knew they wouldn't mind. It might also help them establish roots in the town and convince them to stay.

He could see what the brothers intended, always keeping their gear packed and not getting too attached to anyone outside their group. They planned to leave and continue their way north. He couldn't fault them; they had a plan and wanted to see it through to the end. But this place could be a home for them all. It was secure and run by good people who knew what they were doing. Most importantly, Alexis was safe and she could have a life here—a real life, not like what they'd have out on the road, trying to get to Alaska. He had no doubt that it would be safe in Alaska, but he wasn't sure they'd ever make it.

Arriving at the Mess Hall, Emmett walked through the doors. It was clever of Saul to set up the schedule like he had, with different people eating at different times. That way, there wasn't a huge rush for meals with everyone in town trying to eat at the same time. Walking up to the serving line, Emmett took a plate and waited to be dished up. After he'd gone through the whole line, his plate was mostly full, and he walked over to his usual table with a view of both entrances. Like clockwork, Troy walked over to join him as he did every day.

"What do you want today?" Emmett asked.

"I haven't seen Alexis working here the last couple days," Troy said, sitting down across the table from him.

"Good deduction," Emmett said, taking a bite of his food.

"She's not working here anymore?" Troy asked.

"Another good deduction," Emmett said after he'd swallowed.

"Where's she working now?" Troy asked, ignoring his own plate of food.

Emmett continued to eat, pointedly ignoring Troy. After a minute, Troy got the hint and started eating his own food as well. The kid was annoying, and he just couldn't take a hint. He'd been dogging Alexis ever since they'd arrived, and yet, as far as Emmett knew, she hadn't returned any of his interest. But still, he persisted. It was a worthy quality, just highly misplaced in this situation. His time would be much better spent dedicated to whatever job he was supposed to be doing in town.

"Sheri said something about Alexis being on a date last night," Troy said, "but I think she was confused."

"Nope, she was right," Emmett said, finishing his food.

"What?"

"You heard me," Emmett said, standing up. "You have yourself a good day now, Troy."

Emmett walked off, returning his tray to the pile of other dirty dishes by the kitchen door. He left, sparing Troy a brief glance. The kid sat at the table looking utterly dejected. How Troy hadn't known that Alexis didn't return his feelings was beyond Emmett. Well, he knew now. Emmett figured he should've felt a little bad for being so blunt with the boy, but he just couldn't bring himself to feel that way. Troy had been pestering him every day they'd been there, asking about his daughter, so he didn't feel bad for what he'd done. He didn't want his daughter to date someone like Troy anyway. He wasn't all bad, but he was still too much of a kid. He had yet to grow up, and the apocalypse wasn't helping.

Leaving the Mess Hall behind, Emmett strolled around town. The afternoon heat barely affected him. Actually, he found it pleasant. He didn't have any destination in mind; he just needed to walk and think. He'd learned long ago that his mind worked better when he moved. It wasn't uncommon for him to pace at home when he was trying to figure something out.

Alexis was happy here, and it was truly a safe haven for survivors—not like the last time when they'd been like sheep being led to slaughter. Yet a small part of him wondered if he'd been duped again. He didn't think so. He knew Saul and the way their government worked, and however strict and sometimes secretive they were, they had the best interest of the country—or at least what was left of it—at heart. There was no doubt in his mind that Saul would give his life to protect everyone inside these walls, and that meant Emmett could trust him. He would follow his lead, just like in the old days.

Now that Alexis and James had gone on a date, she would want to go with the brothers if they decided to leave. He needed to persuade them to stay, to show them that they were all better off here. James would eventually come around because the closer he grew to Alexis, the more protective he would be. He'd want her best interest, just like Emmett, and that would be enough to convince him to stay. Tank seemed like he was already willing to stay, so Emmett wasn't worried about him. That left Connor, who'd be the hardest to convince. Emmett saw a lot of himself in Connor—the untrusting and stern part of him that had come out after the divorce. Connor was suffering in his own way, just like he had been all those years ago. But he knew if James and Tank decided to stay, that would be enough for Connor. He wouldn't leave his brothers; he'd been wired that way. It was a part of who he was as a warrior.

Emmett continued to walk around town, nodding to those he knew, and quickly realized that he wouldn't have to convince anyone to stay. If things kept progressing the way they were, they'd all want to stay soon enough. And in the end, he knew he couldn't have done much to change their minds. They were too similar to him—stubborn and determined to finish what they started. But Emmett truly believed this place was safe, that this was their home. He had to believe it because if this town that was under the protection of the military wasn't a secure and safe place for his daughter, nowhere would be.

17
BITTEN

James finished reading the note and Connor glanced back at his brother.

"Jezz," Connor said.

"Those bastards," Tank said.

"How the hell did they know we were gonna be here?" James asked.

"I don't know," Connor said, "but we need to get out."

"How?" James asked.

"We'll fight our way out if we have to," Connor said.

"I'll look for another way," Tank said.

"I'll keep workin' on this door," James said.

"Make it quick," Connor said. "These doors won't hold 'em for long. There's too many."

Connor let his ACR swing to his side as he drew his tomahawk. He approached the double doors and could see dozens of zombies in the room beyond, pressing against the doors. A few had their arms reaching through, and their heads were within reach. He drove the pointed spike of his tomahawk into the closest one's head, causing it to slump to the floor. Another one pushed into its spot and he drove the spike into that one's head as well. Soon, he had a small pile of bodies lying outside the door and the others were unable to reach the gap. Metal screeched as the rebar started to bend and the doors shuttered on their hinges.

"We need to move quickly," Connor said.

"The damn door won't budge," James said from the other side of the room.

"And there's no other way out," Tank said.

"Then we shoot our way out," Connor said, sheathing his tomahawk.

"Can we just shoot 'em all through the gap and the windows in the doors?" James asked.

"I don't see why not," Connor said, "but we don't have much time. The rebar is bending."

"Then let's make use of it," James said.

Connor aimed through the gap, sighting on one of the zombie's heads. With a single pull of the trigger, its face blew out the back of its skull and it dropped to the ground. His brother fired through the window next to him, but his shot missed its mark because of blasting through the thick glass. Connor fired again, taking down another one. Even though they used suppressors, the noise from their shots could easily be heard through the doors. The zombies began a frenzied push, knowing their meal was just on the other side. With a sickening groan, the rebar bent, giving way for the doors to burst open.

"Take 'em down!" Tank yelled, letting loose with his fully automatic SAW.

Zombies dropped as some of Tank's rounds found heads, while others punched through torsos, necks, and other appendages in a spray of blood. Connor began to fire wildly, aiming more quickly and losing some of his accuracy. Blood and flesh flew in a crimson shower around the three of them.

"Aim for the ones on the left," James called out. "Once it's clear, we take off that way!"

His brother was right. They weren't going to be able to drop all the zombies before they got to them. They had to create an opening and get out while they could. Tank's bullets ripped through the zombies on the left side, creating a small path.

"Go, go, go!" Connor said.

Tank took off through the small gap between the rest of the zombies and the wall. Connor followed behind him, with James bringing up the rear. They moved quickly but it wasn't enough. Tank stopped in the middle of the room. Connor slowed behind him as more zombies came at them from all sides. Tank fired at the ones towards the exit while Connor and James kept the rest of them at bay. They only had a couple of seconds before they'd be overrun.

"In here!" James said from behind, motioning them into a room.

Connor glanced back, noticing they had worked their way towards one of the rooms where the zombies had been locked up. He continued to fire as he backed towards the doorway, Tank in front of him to the left. Glass shattered behind him and he assumed James had broken through the window.

"C'mon, Tank!" Connor yelled.

Tank turned and started towards him. Connor spun around and ran across the room towards the window James was hopping through. In front of him, James turned around once outside and aimed back through the window, covering their retreat. Tank cursed loudly behind Connor and James's face fell. Connor quickly whirled around, watching a zombie sink its teeth into Tank's shoulder. He swatted at the thing, but its hands gripped his upper arms. Connor quickly drew his tomahawk and ran up, slamming it into the zombie's head. It released Tank, who stumbled forward into the room. Connor grabbed the door and slammed it shut into a zombie's face. The door wouldn't stay closed; the lock and handle had been blown off. He pushed against the door, straining to keep it closed as more zombies piled up outside, their arms reaching through the crack.

"Get out, now!" Connor said.

"When you open the door, I'll cover you," James told Connor.

Tank hopped out the window and turned around, ready to cover Connor. James nodded, and Connor let go of the door and ran towards the window. He could hear zombies stumbling into the room behind him, mere inches away. He didn't look back. He lunged out the window as James and Tank opened fire.

"Get to Scourge!" Connor yelled, spinning to face the zombies.

James and Tank ran away from the window, sprinting towards the rig. Connor fired at the few zombies that had made it to the open window. After James and Tank had a good lead, he followed.

Tank had been bitten! What were they going to do? They couldn't amputate a shoulder.

He's not going to survive this. Connor thought. *No! He has to, I can't lose him.*

They arrived at the rig and Tank jumped into the

driver's seat while James got in the back. As Tank started the engine, Connor ran around the front and climbed inside. As soon as his door shut, Tank took off across the parking lot, heading towards the road that led to the interstate.

"How bad's your shoulder?" James asked, leaning forward to look at it.

"I'm not sure," Tank said, worry in his voice. "I must be in shock because I don't really feel it."

Connor looked over at Tank's right shoulder where the zombie had bitten him. Touching the wound, his fingers came away bloody. Some was dark and congealed but most was bright red. The zombie's teeth had shredded Tank's uniform, but he couldn't see the wound because there was too much blood.

Connor cursed.

"That bad?" Tank asked.

"I can't see through your shirt and vest," Connor said, "but there's quite a bit of blood."

"Well boys, been one hell of a ride, but we've all gotta die sometime."

"Stop it, bro," James said. "We just need to get you back. They may be able to do something."

"Yeah, like put a bullet in my brain," Tank said.

"If it comes to that, I'll make sure you go out right," Connor said.

"Thanks, brother," Tank said. "You boys know I love ya, right?"

"Course we do," James said, his eyes beginning to tear. "Let's just get back."

"Yeah," Tank said, his face ashen.

He pressed on the gas and Scourge sped up. They

were all silent, just sharing each other's company. Connor couldn't wrap his mind around it. Tank couldn't be infected. He just couldn't. Their parents and now Tank? The world really was set against them.

You better not let him die, Connor said, glancing towards the heavens, *or I'll never forgive you.*

Soon the border came into view and Tank slowed as they went through the wall of vehicles. He looked worse than before, but not as much as Connor would've expected. Tank pulled to a stop at the gate, and the guards came over to both windows.

"We need to get to the infirmary," Connor said, opening his door.

"What happened?" one of the guards asked.

"Tank was bitten," James said from the back seat.

The guards raised their rifles and Connor quickly shut his door. If they started shooting, Tank would ram through the gates.

"Get Cpt. Miller," Connor shouted from inside.

"We just want to get him to the infirmary," James said.

The guards looked at each other. Luckily, they were both Marines and not the men dressed in black.

"Don't move," one of the guards said.

"We won't," Tank said, taking his hand from the steering wheel. "Just make it quick."

One guard moved off and the other lowered his rifle.

"That almost got bloody," Tank said.

"It still might," Connor said.

18
BLOOD FOR BLOOD

Zeke rode in the passenger seat of Jezz's black SUV. The woman herself was behind the wheel, driving like a maniac. It was how she always drove. Their scouts had reported that one of those black armored vehicles had approached the US Customs building. Their ploy had worked and now they'd be able to get some answers. He hoped it would be those three imbeciles. Then he'd finally be able to get his payback and settle the debt between them. He needed blood.

The SUV swerved to a stop at the front of the building and Zeke jumped out, his tactical AK-47 to his shoulder. There should be no way anybody could get out of the trap, but that didn't mean he was going in recklessly. Three other vehicles pulled in behind Jezz's and the rest of their group jumped out. He was still surprised they'd been able to gather twenty-two new killers who would follow Jezz. She hadn't given them much choice, but there'd still been a choice, and all had followed her.

Pulling the key from his pocket, he unlocked the front doors and entered, rifle to his shoulder as twelve others followed behind. The rest would stay at the back with Jezz and Max. The room looked just as they'd left it, and he walked to the door leading into the back. Two large filing cabinets had been pushed against the locked door, and there were now a few bullet holes in them. He motioned to a couple of the others to move them while he kept his gun trained on the door. They tried to do it quietly, but it was impossible, and the filing cabinets scraped against the floor as they were moved. Once they were out of the way, he motioned to another man to open the door. The people trapped inside would be stupid to attack them. He nodded, and the man flung the door open.

Infected poured out.

Zeke opened fire, dropping two before the rest could react. The two Reclaimers closest to the door didn't stand a chance as dozens of the things stumbled out. They were taken down in a swarm of rotting flesh and gnashing teeth, screaming as blood poured from their bodies. Zeke backed up while firing, dropping more. Most of the other Reclaimers had been smart enough to move, not staying close to the door. After the initial men had gone down, the advance of the horde slowed and they were able to pick them all off. Less than a minute later, two dozen infected and two Reclaimers lay on the ground, unmoving. He could hear more groans in the back room.

"Move to the back," Zeke said.

Three of the others moved without question. Jezz had instilled in them that there was a strict pecking order—her, then Zeke and Max. All of the rest were nothing but pawns, and they took to their role with fervor. She had a way of scaring people into submission. He followed the three as they moved into the back room where a few infected were scattered around, and they quickly took them down. A large group of them came out of the closest room to the left. He opened fire and the rest of the Reclaimers did as well.

After five minutes, Zeke had checked the entire building. It was clear, and he knew what'd happened. Those three *had* been stuck in the room. Their trap had worked perfectly, but they'd underestimated not only their opponents but the rebar holding the doors in place. It had bent and they'd fought their way out, exiting through the window in one of the rooms. He wasn't sure he could call them imbeciles any longer. No matter how much he hated to admit it, they were turning out to be extremely resourceful. Not all of it was luck, after all. They did have some skill, and they kept proving themselves harder to contain. He walked out to Jezz, who was waiting outside with her guards and Max.

"I see by your face that things did not go well," Jezz stated in her cold voice.

"No," Zeke said, handing her the note that had been on the wall.

One of them had taken the time in the middle of the trap to write a reply: *Not today, bitch. T.* If Zeke had been one of the men guarding Jezz right then, he'd be afraid for his life. But he wasn't, and when she killed one of them in anger, it only made the rest all the more devoted.

"Your trap did not work as you said, Russian," Jezz said, looking up at him.

Those eyes held a cold fury. Zeke couldn't help

himself as an involuntary shiver ran up his spine. He was scared of nothing in this world, but she was by far the thing that made him most uneasy. She was a wild card, and while he didn't think she'd ever attack him, there was always a possibility with her.

"No," Zeke said. "It did not."

"Very well," Jezz said. "We will just have to try something different. Where are Damian and Habb?"

"Dead," Zeke said. "They left infected in the room, surprising us when we opened the door."

Jezz took a deep breath, closing her eyes and reaching for the knife sheathed behind her back. She was on the edge of an explosion, and when that happened, somebody died. Surprisingly, after a few deep breaths she opened her eyes again.

"They continue to best us," Jezz said. "We will not give them another chance."

19
WE'VE ALL GOTTA DIE

James stood in one of the makeshift examination rooms in nothing but his underwear. At least they'd let him keep those on when they sprayed him down with that chemical shower. In addition to the discomfort of being almost naked, his ear was throbbing. Normally, his ear didn't bother him much unless it was agitated, like now.

After the guard had returned with Cpt. Miller, they'd immediately quarantined the three of them. They weren't taking any chances and James understood. One infected person inside the fence and the whole place could fall. He didn't know what was happening to Tank, and that was what frustrated him the most. He wanted to be with his friend at the end.

Hopefully this isn't the end, James thought. *Lord, heal him.*

After standing for a few minutes in his wet underwear, he decided to sit down on the chair in the middle of the room. The bite hadn't seemed bad, and Tank hadn't gotten much worse as they drove. Those were all good signs, but he couldn't get past the fact that he'd seen the zombie's teeth sink *into* his shoulder. Maybe...

His thought was interrupted as the door opened and Alexis walked into the room. Immediately, his face turned a bright shade of red. He'd forgotten she was working there.

"Hey, James," Alexis said, a mischievous smile on her face.

"Umm, hi," James said, sitting straight up and crossing his hands in his lap.

James just stared at her as she did her best to keep from giggling. He was an adult in a life-or-death situation with his best friend possibly dying in the room next to him, and yet he was so embarrassed that he could barely think. He didn't know what to say, didn't know how to act. He was naked in front of the girl he liked. Well, practically naked. This was like one of those dreams—no, more like one of those *nightmares*.

"Mr. Andderson, I'm Dr. Nelson," said a man walking into the room and offering his hand. James shook it, and it lessened some of his embarrassment to know somebody else was in the room. "I have good news. Your brother and friend are okay, and so are you."

"Tank's okay?" James asked, shocked.

"The plate carrier Tank was wearing stopped the infected's teeth from sinking into his flesh," Dr. Nelson said. "It bruised him but didn't break the skin. We're going to keep him overnight just to make sure, but I'm confident in my assessment that he's not infected."

"You're serious," James said, a smile beginning to grow on his face. "What about the blood?"

"It must've been from the infected's mouth. It wasn't Tank's, even though some of it was fresh."

"Praise God," James said.

"Indeed," Dr. Nelson said. "He was extremely lucky. Just another inch closer to his neck and it would've missed his vest."

"Yeah, luck," James said. "What about my brother and me?"

"You're good to go whenever you're ready."

"Can I get some clothes?"

"Of course. Alexis, could you grab those?"

"Yes, Dr. Nelson," Alexis said, giving James one last look before turning and walking out the door.

James let out a sigh of relief.

"I didn't realize you two were seeing each other," Dr. Nelson said.

"Yes, sir. We had our first date last night," James said.

"I see it went well."

"It did."

"Good for you. Alexis seems like a good girl. Reminds me a lot of my wife."

The way he said it gave James pause. "She didn't make it?"

"No."

James could see pain in the man's eyes and wondered what it must be like to lose someone so close. Losing his parents had been bad enough and he hoped never to feel that again, but he knew he would.

Alexis returned a little while later, begrudgingly giving him his clothes, and then left. He dressed and exited the room, meeting his brother in the hall.

"You hear about Tank?" James asked.

"Yeah," Connor said.

"You two can see him if you'd like," Dr. Nelson said. "He's down at the end of the hall."

"Thanks," James said.

They walked down the hall. It was evident which room Tank was in since two guards were standing outside. They didn't stop James as he walked into the room and Connor followed behind him. Tank was in a typical hospital bed with one of those gowns on and his left hand cuffed to the rail.

"They aren't takin' any chances," Tank said as the brothers walked up.

"Holy crap, man," James said. "That was too close. I thought…"

"The doc said I got lucky." Tank said, smiling.

"More like blessed," James said.

"Glad you're okay," Connor said.

"Me too," Tank said.

"Sounds like they're gonna keep you in here overnight, just to make sure," James said.

"Yeah, I don't mind," Tank said, "as long as they feed me."

"We'll stay, too," Connor said.

"You don't have to do that," Tank said.

"Of course we do," James said. "We're brothers."

"Plus, if you do turn…" Connor let the rest go unsaid.

They all knew what would need to be done. They'd made a pact back when they were captured by Bryce that if any of them turned, one of the others would finish them off. There would be no waiting and putting others in danger. They had each other's backs, even at the end.

"We could take shifts," James said. "That way, we'll all be rested for tomorrow."

"What's tomorrow?" Tank asked.

"We need to sit down and seriously think about what our plan is," James said. "The Reclaimers know we're here, and it's only a matter of time before they find their way inside."

"We take the fight to them," Connor said.

"Or we leave, soon. We could have a huge head start before they even realized it."

"Ya think bein' out on the road with 'em is safer than in here?" Tank asked.

"Maybe not," James said, "but we have to do something."

"I agree," Tank said, "but runnin' ain't it."

"We don't have many other options," James said.

"We'll figure it out," Connor said.

"Right," James said. "For now, we just need to rest and be ready for whatever comes next."

Tank glanced at the clock on the wall. "No wonder I'm starvin'," he said. "It's almost seven o'clock."

"You want some food?" James asked.

"That'd be nice."

"I'll go see what I can do," James said, turning to his brother. "You got first watch?"

"I got it," Connor said.

"Rest up, brother," James said to Tank. "I'll be back with some food soon."

"Hey," Tank said, looking at James as he began to leave the room, "tell Chloe I'll come see her in the mornin'. I don't want her to see me like this."

"I will," James said, exiting the room and heading towards the staircase.

How could Tank not see that their best bet was to leave? James didn't want to be out on the road with the Reclaimers either, but they didn't have much choice. Without any idea of where they were, it would be near impossible for them to hunt the Reclaimers down, and he wasn't going to just sit here and wait for them to find some way to get in. Those people were resourceful. They'd find a way to attack them in here; he was sure of it. Turning the corner out of the hallway towards the stairs, he practically ran into Emmett, who was just coming up.

"You guys okay?" Emmett asked.

"Yes, sir," James said. "It was a close one though."

"What happened?" Emmett asked.

"The Reclaimers," James said. "They set a trap in the customs building Cpt. Miller wanted us to check."

"How'd you know it was a trap?"

James chuckled. "It sure as hell wasn't an accident. There was a tripwire rigged to some explosives on four doors containing dozens of zombies. The wire was set so we'd have a safe room to barricade in, and there was another note from Jezz in the room."

Emmett cursed. "How could they have known you'd be there?"

"That's the question, isn't it? Maybe they didn't, but they knew someone would come to investigate. The trap could've been set for anyone from Coutts."

"They could be looking for information about the town."

"I need to report to Cpt. Miller," James said.

"No need. He put me in charge of you guys and any other scouting parties we send out."

"Sweet. It'll be easier working with someone we trust."

"Indeed, but you can trust Cpt. Miller. He's one of the good guys."

"I'll take your word for it."

"Anything else to report?"

"Just that Tank was bitten, but it didn't pierce his vest so he'll be okay. They're keeping him overnight, and we're going to keep a watch on him personally."

"Good. Being a leader means always being there for your men. It's one of the keys to a good team."

"Yes, sir."

"Anything else?"

"Sir," James said and then hesitated.

"Speak your mind, James. I'm your friend first."

A question had been nagging at the back of his mind ever since they'd been sent on this little scouting mission. He didn't think it was true, but he had to ask. He needed to hear it from someone he trusted.

"The mission," James said. "You don't think Cpt. Miller or someone else set us up, do you?"

Emmett didn't answer right away, which James respected. At least he was thinking about it. "Saul didn't know and wouldn't do that, I can promise you that. But someone else brought him the information. I don't think anyone knew, but I can't tell you for sure. I wouldn't worry about it either way. It was probably just coincidence."

"Good. That's what I was hoping you'd say."

"Anything else?"

"No, sir."

"Get yourself some rest tonight. You three had a long day."

"Yes, sir."

"And James, I can tell by how Alexis is acting that last night went well. Make sure you continue to take care of her."

"I will."

"Good." Emmett turned and walked back down the stairs.

James stood there for a few moments. It felt good to know that Emmett didn't suspect anything, and he knew now that Cpt. Miller could be trusted. Emmett had alleviated most of his fears, but there was still a small part of him that wondered what else could be going on. He started down the stairs but stopped, realizing he didn't know if the guards outside would let him back through the gate if he left. He walked over to the desk in the corner where Alexis sat looking at something on her desk.

"Hello, Alexis," James said, unable to stop the smile that spread on his lips when he looked at her.

"Hey, James," Alexis said, looking up at him from her tablet. "You feeling better now with your pants on?"

James chuckled. "Much better. I didn't think you'd still be here. It's getting late."

"I wanted to finish the inventory I started earlier before I was interrupted by you guys coming in here all bloody and covered in gore."

"Sorry about that. We had a little trouble this morning."

The mirth left her eyes as she stood up and walked

around the desk to stand in front of him. "You're okay, right?" she asked, concerned.

"Yeah," James said, emotions surging within him.

In the moment, all he'd cared about was survival, about getting out alive. After that, he'd been too concerned with Tank to really think about how close they'd come to death. It'd been easy to keep a tough face then, but standing here looking into those hazel eyes, he could feel his resolve waning. He felt like wrapping Alexis in his arms and just letting all his emotions out.

Not here, he scolded himself. He had to stay strong… for now.

"I was worried about you," Alexis said, taking his hand in hers.

"I know. I was, too," James said, reveling in her touch. "Can we talk about this later tonight? In private?" He glanced at the open door to Dr. Nelson's office.

"Sure, I'll be done shortly," Alexis said, giving his hand a squeeze before she released it.

"Thanks," James said, leaning in and giving her a small kiss on the cheek.

Smiling, she walked back behind her desk, and James walked into the doctor's office. Dr. Nelson sat at his desk, looking at some papers on a clipboard. The name on the top read *Hook, Allen.*

"Mr. Andderson," Dr. Nelson said, looking up, "how may I help you?"

"I wanted to go out and get some food," James said, "but I'm not sure if they'll let me back in."

"No need to go out," Dr. Nelson said. "I can radio the Mess Hall and have them bring some food."

"I'd really like to get out for a bit."

"I see. I'll get you a guest pass that'll be valid for twenty-four hours."

"That'd be perfect."

Dr. Nelson opened a drawer on his desk and pulled out a clip-on plastic badge. He scanned it with a small device that was hooked up to his computer and then typed in some information. Once he was done, he handed it to James.

"This'll only work for you."

"Thanks, I appreciate it."

"Don't mention it. And if you need anything else, I'll be here all night, regularly checking on your friend."

"We plan to stay with him too, if that's okay."

"I don't mind."

"Thanks again," James said, turning and leaving the room.

Alexis was standing by her desk when he walked out. "Walk a girl home?" she asked.

"Of course," James said, smiling.

They took the stairs. He noticed that she glanced down a hallway at a door set at the back. He wanted to ask her about it but decided to save it for later. They exited the building, the cool evening air a relief from the heat earlier in the day. Checking out with the guards, James told them he'd be back soon. Outside the gate, James took Alexis's hand in his as they walked down the driveway towards her house.

20
CHANGE OF PLANS

Alexis walked hand in hand with James and felt more at peace than she had in a long time. Their date the night before had been on her mind all day, and she kept thinking back to when he'd broken down after his episode. That had been the best part of the whole night. The vulnerability he'd shown had allowed her to see his heart, and it made her feel even closer to him. They'd shared something then, and she imagined they both had a small piece of each other's hearts now. The kiss had been the icing on the cake, but the deep conversation after sharing that moment together had *been* the cake.

She smiled, it'd been the best night she'd had, maybe ever. That might be a little exaggerated, but at the moment she felt it was true. And now, with him holding her hand and them walking side by side in the cool night air, she felt better than ever. Love really was intoxicating.

Wait, love? something said in her mind.

They crossed the street, approaching her house. She needed to distract her mind from the crazy thoughts she had swirling around in it.

"So what happened?" Alexis asked.

James hesitated for a few moments but then told her the story about how they'd been sent to investigate the US Customs building and about the trap set by the Reclaimers and their mad dash to get out. She shivered at the thought, knowing Jezz was out there right now, hunting them. She'd known that the woman would want to "reclaim" them even more now, but she hadn't figured she'd find them so easily. They could've gone anywhere. Yet, they'd continued their trek north, so it hadn't been hard for Jezz to follow the main route and find them there. Maybe they shouldn't have stayed so long. Not that it mattered now; they couldn't leave with the Reclaimers out there somewhere.

"I haven't felt hopelessness like that since this all started," James said, stopping outside of Alexis's house. "Not even when we were captured by Bryce."

He gazed past her to something unseen, the emotions plain on his face.

"It's okay," Alexis said, pulling him into a hug. "You made it out, and you're safe now."

He chuckled as a couple of tears streaked from his eyes. "I thought I was supposed to be the one who comforted and protected you."

"A relationship is more of a partnership," Alexis said. "One is strong when the other is weak."

"Makes sense," James said, wiping the tears from his cheeks. "So we *are* in a relationship?"

"I assumed," Alexis said. "From the kiss and all."

"I mean I want to be. I just don't know how to do all this stuff."

"Good, because I want to be, too."

She leaned forward and kissed him. The moment

was cut short when Alexis's front door opened, causing James to jump back. He relaxed instantly, seeing who it was.

"How's Tank?" Chloe asked, eyes red.

"He's going to be okay," Alexis said, climbing the steps and hugging her.

"I didn't know what was going on," Chloe said as a sob escaped her throat. "All I heard was that he'd been bitten."

"I'm so sorry," Alexis said. "I should've gotten word to you."

"So he's going to be fine?" Chloe asked.

"Yeah, the teeth didn't penetrate through his vest," Alexis said. "He has a nice bruise and they're keeping him overnight to make sure he doesn't turn, but Dr. Nelson thinks he'll be okay."

"I need to go see him," Chloe said, stepping back from Alexis and wiping her eyes.

James opened his mouth but Alexis spoke first. "Security is tight. I don't think they'll let you in."

"I'm getting food and then going back," James said. "I can take a message to him."

"Can't you take me in with you?" Chloe asked.

"I don't think so. The doctor said the badge will only work to get me in."

"Okay," Chloe said, taking a deep breath. "Okay, if he's going to be fine then I can wait and see him tomorrow. Tell him that he needs to come see me as soon as he gets out, whatever time it is. Tell him I'm thinking about him."

"I will," James said.

"Don't you have work tonight?" Alexis asked.

"Yes," Chloe said, taking another deep breath.

"Let's get you freshened up," Alexis said, looking down at James.

"We can catch up later," James said, smiling at her. "I've taken too long getting food anyway. See ya later."

He walked off towards the Mess Hall and she watched him go. Yes, she did have strong feelings for him. She ushered Chloe inside so she could help get her ready for work and fill her in on more of what'd happened.

~~~

James left the Mess Hall carrying two grocery bags full of hot food. Cook hadn't even hesitated to pack up some food for him to bring back; however, she had threatened him about bringing the dishes back, but he'd been planning on that anyway. He really did owe her even more now and would have to make good on their next run.

If we even go on another run, James thought.

He was tired of delaying their journey there. They'd wasted over a week and could probably have been at their lodge in Alaska right now. This place was secure, sure, but it wasn't safe—not like the lodge would be with their own community. Only in Alaska would they truly be as safe as they could be.

The air was even cooler than when he'd left the infirmary earlier and the wind had begun to pick up. He looked up at the dark clouds in the sky, a streak of lightning flashing in the distance. A storm was coming tonight.

Security was seriously tight at the infirmary. They

patted him down and even checked inside all the food containers. Luckily for him, Cook had given them plastic silverware; otherwise they probably would've taken that. After scanning his badge and asking him some questions, they finally let him through. He understood them wanting to keep people contained in there in case they were infected, but why would they be so concerned about who came in? What could someone really do by getting in there?

Shrugging it off, he went inside and up the stairs to Tank's room. The guards outside gave him a brief glance but didn't search him again. The ones at the gate had probably already radioed ahead.

"What the hell took ya so long?" Tank asked as James opened the door.

"The damn guards at the gate had to practically strip-search me," James said.

"Sure," Connor said, skeptically. "That's why."

"I can tell by your smile that it wasn't the guards that kept ya," Tank said. "It was a certain lady."

"Maybe," James said.

Setting the bags down on the counter, he served up three plates of spaghetti with garlic bread. Connor came over and took his plate, and James brought one to Tank.

"Thanks, bro," Tank said.

James walked over to one of the chairs against the wall and sat down. Fortunately, the chain on Tank's handcuff was long enough that he was able to eat freely. They weren't trying to keep him immobile, just making it difficult for him to get loose if he turned.

"I saw Chloe," James said between bites. "She

said she was thinking about you and to come see her as soon as you get out."

"Did she try to come see me?" Tank asked.

"Yeah, but Alexis talked her out of it. Plus, I don't think she could've gotten past security."

"It's really that tight?" Connor asked.

"Yes, they had to pat me down, and they looked in all the food."

"Really?" Connor said.

"Ya think they're hidin' somethin'?"

"I don't know," James said. "Could just be to keep potential threats inside."

"Then why is it so hard to *get* inside?" Connor asked.

James shrugged, finishing his spaghetti. Once they were done, he rinsed off the dishes in the sink and put them back in the bag.

"I think we should talk about what we're going to do," Connor said.

"Might as well. We have nuthin' better to do," Tank said.

"Okay," James said, sighing. "You know what I think."

"That we should leave," Connor said. "But that's not the right call, not while they're out there."

"What else is there?" James asked.

"We continue with what we've been doin'," Tank said.

"We can look for them when we go out. Next time will be different if we're ready," Connor said.

"And once we find them?" James asked.

"We kill 'em all," Connor said. "End them for good."

"It's a whole lot better than runnin'," Tank said.

"What if we can't find them?" James asked. "Or what if the next trap actually works? We barely made it out of the last one."

"We won't let them trap us again," Connor said. "I would've seen that tripwire if I'd been looking for it."

"And if they just shoot an RPG at us when we're in the rig?" James asked.

"I don't think they have that kind of munitions anymore," Connor said.

"But if they do?" James said, standing up. "They've beaten us at almost every turn."

"Except when we almost wiped 'em out," Tank said.

"But we didn't," James said. "They almost killed me, and that one almost shot Connor."

"We ain't runnin'," Tank said more forcefully. "And we ain't just gonna sit here either, so where does that leave us?"

"I don't know, but we have to be more careful out there," James said.

"We agree," Connor said. "But we have to do something, and running isn't the right call. You should know that. We don't run from anything."

"Well, just for once, maybe it wouldn't end with everyone we know dead!" James yelled. "All we've done is fight, and look at where it's gotten us. We were all almost killed today. Our parents are dead, along with most of the people we started out with. If we keep going down this path the way we have been, there'll be no one left to get to Alaska!"

"Precisely," Tank said. "Maybe we shouldn't try

and get to Alaska anymore. Once the Reclaimers are gone, we can stay here."

"Are you kidding me?" James said, throwing his hands into the air. "You really think this place is safe and that it's all it seems to be?"

"Don't be stupid," Tank said. "Just because you have a hard time trustin' people doesn't mean this whole place is one giant conspiracy."

"*I* have trust issues?" James said, pointing a finger at his chest.

"Enough," Connor said. "Your bickering is ridiculous."

"And I bet you agree with Tank," James said, his voice rising. "You're my brother, and you're supposed to have my back."

"Get off it," Connor growled at him. "We're *all* brothers here. This has nothing to do with having each other's backs. It's about making the right call that doesn't end with all of us dead."

James shook his head, walking to the door. "You'll see. This whole place will come crashing down on our heads, and then where will we be?"

James slammed the door behind him and stormed out into the hall, ignoring the looks from the two guards.

21
THE COST OF SURVIVAL

James pushed out the front doors and stomped around to the side of the building. Why couldn't they see that they needed to leave? It was the only way they could survive this. He wanted to scream at them, to scream at the sky. If they pursued the Reclaimers, it would end in death. Even if the Reclaimers didn't kill them, he'd have to kill again. He'd have to end someone else's life, and he didn't want to do that anymore.

Every time he took someone's life, a small piece of him died, and he didn't like who he was becoming. He thought back to a few days before when they'd seen the smoke on their first run. Sure, it could've been the Reclaimers. It could've been another trap. In fact, that seemed even more likely now. Yet, he still felt they should've checked it. Someone could've needed help, and they'd just turned a blind eye. That was exactly what he *wasn't* supposed to do. It wasn't who he wanted to be, but in the moment it'd been exactly what he'd wanted to do, just like the ones who'd passed by the injured Samaritan on the road to Jericho. He'd hardened his heart and ignored the calling deep within.

He was straying down a dark path, and he didn't

know if he'd ever be able to turn back from it. It wasn't a path he wanted to walk but one that had been forced on him by their circumstances. The apocalypse left them with few choices, and if they wanted to survive, that would entail the taking of lives. Even if the lives he took were evil, it was still someone's life. He'd been raised and taught to honor life, to protect those who couldn't protect themselves, but never to kill. Connor had been trained to kill, and his mindset was already like that before the Corps, but not James. In the past, James had known he could do what needed to be done in self-defense, but not everything they'd done had been in self-defense. They'd hunted down human beings and killed them.

It was taking a toll on him, and he realized now that he'd never be the same. Was that for better or worse? Was it making him into something he needed to be or something he shouldn't be? Would he ever be able to live the life God had set out before him with who he was becoming? Did that even matter anymore? Question after question piled up in his mind and he sank down onto one of the swings behind the infirmary. There was a whole playground back there, and the sign out front indicated this had been a school at one time. Not anymore. It had been a place of learning, and now it was an infirmary—a place of pain and death. But its purpose was not to *cause* pain or death. Its purpose was to heal those who were in pain. He was in pain, so shouldn't this be the place where he came for healing? Yet, it wasn't that kind of pain. It was a deep pain buried in his heart and soul.

Lightning flashed across the sky. He'd

experienced loss in the last few weeks unlike any he'd faced before. His whole life had been torn away, including most of the people in it. There was no going back to what once was. His mind strayed down a familiar path, thinking about his parents, Felicia, Mila, Peter, and all the others. His vision began to tunnel as images of children's gutted bodies flashed in the back of his mind.

Not again, he thought, desperately, trying to hold on.

But he could feel himself slipping. He fell to his knees, face to the sky.

"Why, God?" James cried at the heavens as small raindrops began to fall on his face. "How could you let this happen?"

Everything he'd once known was gone, overshadowed by this consuming urge to survive and protect what he still had left—his brother, Alexis, Tank, Olive. The images in his mind continued to slowly rise to the surface as he fought to stay in the present. God had healed him of this already, so why was it continuing to happen? Then it hit him. He couldn't run from this, just like they couldn't run from the Reclaimers. He knew that. They'd just hunt them down and kill the rest of the people he cared about. But he didn't want to shed more blood. It was tearing him apart and he didn't know how to reconcile it. He was breaking inside.

No, I'm already broken.

He lost control and his mind flashed dark. He was standing in a room with fresh blood covering every surface. Fourteen little bodies were spread around in various states of decay. Lightning flashed in his vision and then he was in the gray Dodge, driving through a storm north of Sheridan. Bullets slammed into the truck and he glanced over to see one smash into Mike's neck, his blood spraying onto the windshield. Mike looked at him with accusation in his eyes. Lightning flashed again and the thunder crashed against his body. He was standing outside the barn at the Reclaimers' base with Mila's body lying in the pool of light cast by the outside lamp. Her lifeless eyes stared up at him, a silent scream on her lips. Then her face shifted and her hair changed to blonde, and he was kneeling on the ground with Felicia's head in his hands, the bullet hole in her head that *he* had put there. Another flash of light and he stood over the beaten and bloodied body of his father, crimson pooling in the hay around him. James could *feel* the disappointment emanating from his father's body. Blackness. His mother's body, disfigured and beaten, lay on the cold hard cement. She was splayed in a broken heap. Blood covered most of her and the rest was bruised from the abuse she'd been through in her final hours. He'd failed them all, and he would fail the rest.

In the midst of the darkness consuming him, there was a small prick of light. Something tickled the back of his mind, something his mom had said at the end.

"Don't let this moment define you. Keep your faith. Promise me."

The words rang in his head. Even in all her pain, she hadn't been worried about herself. She knew where she was going and that it was much better than this place. Instead, she was worried about them and what their parents' deaths would do to them. She'd known it would send them down a dark path, and she'd made sure her last words were of encouragement.

The memories and images faded from his mind and he found himself lying in the mud, cold rain pouring down from the sky.

James curled into a ball and wept.

22
QUICK TO FORGET

Connor exited the infirmary, stopping on the top step under the overhang of the roof. Rain poured down as lightning flashed across the sky. His brother had been out here for hours and it was now dark. Connor knew he shouldn't be worried. Nothing could happen to James within the fence, but he was anyway. He'd thought that being here and settling into a normal routine would help James deal with what was going on inside him, but it almost seemed like it was getting worse. Connor had always had an easier time keeping his emotions inside, but James tended to wear his on his sleeve. He knew his brother was hurting and it scared him that he didn't know how to help. But how could he help?

Connor was dealing with the same crap, but he just pushed it deeper whenever it came up. The difference was that he could contain it without any side effects, while his brother was manifesting these episodes. James had seemed convinced that he was past them, and yet Connor had a feeling that wasn't the case. Something had happened in the last few days that had shaken his brother to the very core. James'd had another episode, he just knew it.

After scanning in front of the building, Connor stepped out into the rain. He pulled his coat tighter and flipped the hood up, heading towards the back of the building. He was confident James wouldn't leave the grounds. He'd stay close for Tank, even if he was pissed at him. Going around the side, Connor looked at the back lawn. There was a small playground and a set of swings, but he didn't see James. Where would he have gone? Lightning flashed, illuminating the playground and something on the ground by the swing set. He walked over to get a better look.

"Oh, brother," Connor whispered.

James sat on the ground, his back against one of the poles of the swing set. His legs were pulled up to his chest and his head was bowed. It was the exact picture of someone who was defeated. Anger rose up in Connor. How could his brother be this weak? Why couldn't he just pull himself together? If he didn't do something about this, it would defeat him entirely. He stood only a few feet away from his brother, and James showed no sign that he even knew he was there. James needed to toughen up. This wasn't the way to deal with all of this.

Is holding it all inside any better? said a part of his mind.

He was not his brother and his brother was not him. However similar they were and no matter how strong their bond, they weren't the same. They both had their own strengths and weaknesses. James had always felt more, while Connor had been able to push through all the obstacles, shoving his own feelings down. They would eventually burst through the walls containing them, but that didn't happen often. As he stood above James, the anger faded, replaced by a deep compassion for his brother. James was doing the best he could, and maybe this was the better way to handle it. Or maybe not.

Connor walked closer and sat down in the mud next to his brother, putting an arm around his shoulders. James looked over, tears mixing with the raindrops on his face. His eyes were pleading, like he was hoping Connor could fix all this.

"How are we supposed to keep going?" James asked in a whisper.

"We just do," Connor said.

"But how?" James asked again.

"I just shove it all down and continue forward, but that's never worked for you."

"Then what works for me?"

Connor shrugged. "That's something you have to figure out."

James was silent for a while. "I had another episode."

"I know."

"I had one last night, too."

"I could tell."

"Why didn't you say anything?"

"What good would it do? I see now that you have no control, so saying something won't help."

"I thought I was healed. I *knew* I was healed."

"James, you've always been quick to trust, quick to have faith. I've envied that about you. But you're also always quick to forget. Just because you had another couple episodes doesn't mean you weren't healed."

"But if I was healed, I shouldn't be having them."

"Maybe, or maybe it just means you have the power to stop them from happening now."

"I couldn't stop these."

"Couldn't you?" Connor said, and James looked at him like he was crazy. "I'm just saying maybe there was something you could've done."

"Like what?"

"Did you try praying?" Connor asked.

"I… well, no."

"Try that next time. It may help. Remember, the Bible says that God won't allow us to be tempted beyond what we can handle. He'll always give us a way to overcome it. Maybe this is the same."

"Maybe," James said, taking a deep breath and shivering.

Connor stood up, offering his hand to his brother. James took it and pulled himself to his feet, giving his brother a hug.

"You got this, bro," Connor said. "You'll figure it out. I know you will."

"Thanks," James said as they separated. "I love you, Connor."

"I love you, too," Connor said. "Now let's get the hell inside and get some dry clothes on."

"That'd be nice," James said. "And maybe finish off some of those leftovers."

"You may have to fight Tank for those."

James chuckled and Connor could tell that a weight had been lifted from his shoulders. Whether he'd just needed to cry in the rain and let it all out or Connor had helped him realize some things, he was feeling better now, which helped Connor feel better, too.

23
FINALLY LIVING

Post-outbreak day 20

Tank exited the infirmary, James and Connor by his side. Dr. Nelson had just released him with a clean bill of health—he wasn't infected. He couldn't lie, not even to himself. Last night had been a long one. He kept waking up after having vivid nightmares about turning and eating the people he cared about the most. The sun rose over the clouds in front of him and he stared at it in wonder. Was it just him, or was this the most beautiful sunrise ever? A little over twelve hours ago he hadn't been sure he was going to survive to see another sunrise.

He walked down the steps and the brothers followed him. Connor had come back with James last night a couple hours after James left. He'd apologized for the outburst, but Tank knew there was more to it. James was going through some serious shit, and he couldn't fault him for it. They'd stayed up late into the night, talking about how they should proceed. It'd come down to the fact that until the Reclaimers were dealt with, they couldn't leave safely, but that brought up another question. How would they deal with the Reclaimers? They all knew Jezz would try something again soon and they'd need to be prepared. But they didn't know what she'd try or when, or how many others she had with her. They were fairly confident after talking to Emmett and the others that they'd taken out all but a few of them. Had she recruited more? They exited the gate and the guards took James's badge he'd used the night before.

Emmett stood at the end of the driveway to the infirmary. "How you boys feelin' this morning?" he asked.

"Good," James said.

"Much better than last night," Tank said.

"Glad to see you're okay," Emmett said to Tank. "I'm sure James already told you, but Cpt. Miller put me in charge of the scouting runs. As it stands now, you're the only three we plan to send out until we've trained a few others. With that being said, after the events of yesterday we're giving you guys the day off. Meet me at HQ in Cpt. Miller's office at 1700 tonight and we can go over the plans for the next few days."

"Roger that," Connor said.

"How did the supply run north go?" James asked.

"They were able to recover everything you found with little problem, although there were quite a few tangos in Milk River."

"Told ya," Tank said.

"They were able to clean a lot of them out."

"What about the Reclaimers?" Connor asked.

"Cpt. Miller is working on a plan. Cpt. Sanders didn't think they were much of a threat, but I convinced him otherwise. You'll have to watch your backs out there."

"We plan to," Connor said.

"That's all for now," Emmett said. "You boys enjoy your day off and don't get into too much trouble."

"Never," Tank said, smiling.

"Thanks, Emmett," James said.

"You three deserve it. You're becoming a huge asset to the community, like I told them you would be. Keep making me proud," Emmett said with a fatherly smile.

"Yes, sir," the three of them said in unison and continued on their way.

Tank wondered why he was feeling so warm and fuzzy inside but then realized it was because his real dad had never said anything like that to him. It was probably that, coupled with the fact that he was just happy to be alive today. He'd never come so close to death. In fact, he should've been dead. Glancing at the sky, he said a quick thanks to whoever was listening. Someone had been watching out for him yesterday, that was for sure.

Once they hit North Avenue, the brothers turned left for their place while Tank took a right and headed to Chloe's.

He glanced at his watch. It was only six, still early in the morning. Chloe would be sound asleep. Was he sure he wanted to wake her again? The last time had almost been more frightening than getting bitten by that undead. Eh, what the hell? She'd told him to stop by so he'd stop by. He really wanted to see her anyway. There'd been a lot of time to think last night, and he'd come to a few realizations. He was tired of being alone, and it was time to let someone in. Even though that very well might end in him getting his heart ripped out, he'd rather go to the grave with a broken heart than knowing he hadn't let himself fully love or be loved.

Ugh, even thinking like that made him sick.

Walking into the house Chloe shared with some of the other survivors, he quietly snuck into her room. She was asleep, curled in a ball in the middle of the bed with half the blankets thrown off. She was such a cute mess. Taking his shoes off, he crawled onto the bed next to her. Without even waking, she moved to him, curling up against his side. There was a half used box of tissues on her nightstand with several used ones on the floor. She must really care about him. He closed his eyes and began to slowly stroke her hair. After a few minutes, he fell asleep.

A few hours later, he opened his eyes and saw Chloe sitting up, watching him. She smiled.

"Mornin', sleepyhead," Chloe said as Tank stretched.

"Mornin', beautiful," Tank said.

She leaned down and kissed him, and he lost himself in the touch of their lips. It was unlike anything he'd felt before.

After a while she pulled away. "I was afraid I'd lost you," she whispered, tears forming in her eyes.

"I was, too," Tank said, feeling a surge of emotion. None of this was normal for him. He usually saved the emotions for when he was alone and had consumed massive amounts of alcohol. Sitting up, he pulled her into his arms as she started

BAD COMPANY

to cry softly.

"I've lost too much already," Chloe said, her head nuzzled into his shoulder.

"I know," Tank said. "I couldn't stop thinkin' last night about how if I died it wouldn't just affect me."

"No, it wouldn't."

"Most of my life I've felt like only a few people cared about me. Then when my mom died, it was even harder for me to let people in."

"It's easier to keep people away, thinking you won't get hurt, but you end up hurting yourself when you do that."

"Tell me about it."

Sitting there with his arms wrapped around someone he truly cared about, he realized just how lonely a life he'd been living for the last couple of years. Sure, he had the brothers, but that wasn't the same as this. The brothers knew him, but they didn't know everything he went through. That's not how that sort of friendship worked. This was different. He wanted to tell her everything about himself, to let her truly in. It'd been years since he'd done that, and even his last couple of girlfriends hadn't really known him. It wasn't their fault—he just hadn't let them in. Today, he wanted to change that.

"What's on your mind?" Chloe asked, able to read his silence.

"Just thinkin'," Tank said.

"About?"

"How hard all this is."

"You mean the end of the world?"

"Amongst other things."

"Well, what else… is it *us*?"

"No, just opening up to people in general."

"Why do you think that is?"

"Prolly cus my past..." Tank said, trailing off.

She looked at him expectantly. He knew she wanted him to keep going, but it wasn't that easy. This was all so foreign to him. He never did this, but that thought gave him the push he needed. This *wasn't* what he would normally do, and that was why he was going to do it now. It was time to change things.

Tank sighed.

"My dad left me and my mom when I was seven," he said. "He'd never really been there for me, but at least he'd been around. Then he left and I didn't see him again until he reached out to me in college. I told him I didn't ever want to see him again, and I never did."

"What'd you and your mom do after that?" Chloe asked.

"We moved to a small town in southwestern Colorado where I started middle school. My mom remarried and my stepdad was good to me, but it wasn't the same. I knew he wasn't my real dad, and I put too much into tryin' to find acceptance from him. That never worked. Then, years later when my mom died, it left me feelin' hollow inside. My stepdad took it even harder and we've barely talked this past year. The only people I still had were James and Connor, and they were always off to who knows where while I was stuck in Fort Collins. I don't think I was truly livin' these last couple years, just survivin', so when the apocalypse happened, I used it as a new start. I turned somethin' terrible into somethin' hopeful."

"Do you still feel that way?"

"I'm livin' again, and I feel like I finally have a place. We're doin' somethin' good for this community, actually helpin'. Then yesterday it almost ended for me." Tank paused, gathering his thoughts. "I was scared. I thought I was done. I just couldn't stop thinkin' about all the things I wish I would've done different in my life. How I would've *lived* different."

"You are living differently." Chloe reached up and rested her hand on his cheek. "I don't know your dad or your stepdad, but I know they would be proud of who you've become."

"Maybe my stepdad, but not my real dad. He was an asshole and wouldn't have cared."

"Was?"

"Oh, he's dead by now, I'm sure." At her questioning look he continued. "He was a lazy bastard livin' in the middle of Denver, and it was hit hard. No way he survived."

"How does that make you feel?"

"Pullin' some psychological crap on me now?"

"No, really. How does it make you feel? You lost your mom, now your real dad, and maybe even your stepdad."

"I'm glad my mom didn't have to live through this, although I wish somethin' fierce she was still here. My stepdad is probably still alive; at least I hope he is. And I could care less about my real dad. Hell, I'm glad he's dead."

Even as he said the words he knew his anger was just covering up his pain. It was a lie. Even though he hated his dad, he was still his dad. And since when had he become so honest with himself without alcohol?

"That's not true," Tank said with less anger than before.

"I know."

"I miss him. I've missed him for years, but now that he's truly gone, I can't help but wonder if I should've reconnected with him when he reached out. It's too late for all that now, and I'm not gonna dwell on things I can't change. I'm gonna focus on the things I *can* change."

"Like this?" Chloe asked, smiling. "Opening up to me?"

"I had to do it with someone, and there's no one else I'd rather share it with than you. Wow, that was cheesy."

"Well, I liked it," Chloe said, pulling him into a deep kiss.

So this was what it felt like to be emotionally intimate. It felt good. He was free to be himself around her—all of himself, not just part. His near-death experience had made him realize that he couldn't continue living a half-life or he was no better than the damned undead. After all these years, he owed it to himself and those he cared about. He knew Chloe truly cared. He didn't know how he knew; he just did. There was a break in their passionate kiss and Tank pulled back, looking Chloe in the eyes. She looked up at him, a half smile on her luscious lips and a twinkle in her dark brown eyes.

"My name's Allen, by the way," Tank said, staring into her eyes. "Allen Don Hook."

24
ADOPTING AN INTROVERT

James and his brother sat on their cots in the old store. He couldn't stop thinking about the night before. His latest episode had been different in that he'd been aware of what was going on around him. It hadn't been as all-consuming as the others. His brother's words repeated over and over in his mind. Had he been healed and he just needed to believe it? Did he have the capacity to reach out for help and resist when an episode hit him? Why hadn't he prayed? When he was going through all that, he'd felt alone, yet he knew he hadn't been. He had his brother, his best friend and now his girlfriend, plus Jesus was always with him. He knew that, but why was it so hard to believe and reach out for help in the moment?

Connor sat across from him on his bunk, cleaning his ACR. James knew his brother was hurting as well, but it didn't affect him the same. Connor was there for him, but was James really there for his brother? He'd been so consumed with what he was going through that he had yet to think about how his little brother was dealing with all this. And he was pretty sure Connor wasn't faring much better.

"How are you doing, bro?" James asked, beginning to tear down his own ACR.

While he didn't love cleaning guns like his brother did, he did enjoy it, especially when he wanted to keep his hands busy and let his mind work on things like trying to figure out what was going on with him, how to fix it, and what the hell they were supposed to do.

"Good," Connor replied automatically.

"No, I mean really, how are you doing?"

Connor looked up at him. "You really wanna do this?"

"We need to work through some of this or it'll consume us."

"Consume you maybe. I'm doin' fine."

"Connor, we both know you can deal with this stuff better, but I still know you're struggling."

"Of course I am. Our parents are dead, all our friends and family but Tank are gone, and life will never be the same. How do you think I'm feelin'?"

"Kinda like how I am, I'd guess."

"Yeah, kinda like that."

"So," James said, knowing he was pushing him. "How *are* you feeling?"

Connor growled, setting aside the lower receiver of his rifle. "I feel like the world is ending, like God has abandoned us to live a macabre, goat-rope of a life, and like we're the ones who killed our parents by not getting there in time. That's how I feel."

"Do you really think God has abandoned us?"

"Yes! I *know* he hasn't, but it sure as hell feels that way! What else would explain all this?"

"I don't know, but we can't lose our faith. We

can't let our past define our future."

"Now you sound like Mom," Connor said bitterly.

"Do you remember what she said to us before she died?"

"Yeah."

"Then you know we can't keep going down the path we're on and still honor our parents' sacrifices. They may not have died actively protecting us, but their deaths can be more than a tragedy. We can continue in a way that would make them proud."

"They're dead, James. Gone forever."

"Dead, yes, but they're not gone! If you believe they're really gone then why is this life worth living if nothing comes after?"

"I've been askin' myself that same question."

"You're questioning everything?"

"Yes. How can all this make sense with what we've always believed?"

"The same way it did before. Nothing has changed. People have been persecuted for centuries, tragedies have happened, mass murder has taken place. It's no different now than it was then."

"But *our* parents, James. Our parents are dead, brutally murdered."

"Yes, and Jesus was beaten and hung on a cross."

Connor chuckled. "This is completely different."

"Yes, it is. But pain and death are nothing new. It's as old as the Fall."

Connor sighed, picking up his rifle and starting to clean it again. James took it as a sign that the conversation was over. He wanted to keep going, but he knew it was done.

"Know that I'm here for you, brother," James said,

going back to cleaning his rifle as well, "just like you were there for me last night. I got your six."

He finished with his rifle and then went on to clean the blood from his plate carrier. Someone had cleaned their uniforms last night but hadn't messed with their kits. He washed it off and then hung it outside in the sun to dry. All of the magazines and equipment from it lay out on his cot, as he refilled the spent magazines they'd used yesterday. There was something therapeutic about the mundane task of taking care of the things that helped him survive each day.

"Should we have tried to bury them?" Connor asked after a few minutes of silence.

"Mom and Dad?" James asked.

"Yeah."

"How? We didn't have time with dad because we had to try and rescue mom. Then what were we going to do, bury her in the yard of the courthouse or tote their bodies with us? Our bodies are nothing but earthly vessels. We'll do something to honor and remember them once we get to Alaska."

"Like a memorial."

"Exactly. We'll do it for everyone we've lost."

Connor nodded and went back to refilling his magazines. James had gotten through to him on some small level at least. He might not ever admit it, but James knew. There was still hope. He had to constantly remind himself of that, but it was true. It had to be true, or what else was there?

The brothers went and grabbed lunch in the Mess Hall. James noticed Troy glaring at him as he exited the building, but he didn't think anything of it. The guy must be having a bad day. After lunch, they returned to their place. Tank and Chloe were sitting out front on the bench under the awning.

"Afternoon," Tank said to them as they walked up.

"Afternoon to you, too," James said, smiling. Tank was in fine form today. "How are you doin' Chloe?"

"Much better today," she said, smiling at Tank.

"I bet," Connor said.

James noticed Tank's vest was hanging outside to dry as well. He'd probably gotten his gun cleaned and gear together, too. It was a habit they were quickly falling into—taking care of their gear in their downtime.

"Where's Scourge?" James asked, noticing their armored vehicle was missing.

"Gettin' an upgraded paint job," Tank said.

"Oh, sweet," James said.

"I was just talking with *Tank*," Chloe said. The way she said his name was weird, like she was putting more emphasis on it than necessary. "You ever see that Mr. Smith guy who interviewed us the first night we were here?"

"Actually, I haven't," James said. "I'd forgotten all about him."

"I hadn't noticed him around either," Chloe said.

"Probably took one of those out of here," Connor said, pointing to the horizon as the familiar drum of a helicopter met their ears. James was so used to the choppers coming and going that he hardly registered them anymore.

"We still don't know what they're doin' with those, do we?" Tank asked.

"Nope," Connor said.

"You ever wonder how the outbreak started?" Chloe asked.

"Yeah," James said. "But then I realized I'll probably never know, so I just ignore it."

"I still think it has somethin' to do with those men in the black uniforms," Tank said. "I don't trust 'em."

"Me neither," Connor said.

James shrugged. "They let us keep our gear and Scourge, so who cares?"

"I just hate it when people keep secrets," Connor said. "Why hide it even now?"

"Cus the world ain't endin'," Tank said. "At least that's what they think."

"I still can't believe they think they can get ahead of this," James said.

"They must know something we don't," Connor said.

"Now that makes sense," James said. "Never considered that."

"See, they *are* hidin' somethin'," Tank said.

"Why don't you just go ask them?" Chloe asked.

"That's a horrible idea," Connor said.

"If they want it hidden, they sure as hell won't like it when people come around askin' questions," Tank said.

"Do you think they'd kill people to keep it hidden?" Chloe asked.

"Societies and governments have been doin' just that for years," Tank said. "Wouldn't be any different now."

"If anything, it'd be easier," Connor said. "Laws are hard to uphold with everything that's going on."

"Plus, they could cover it up easily by claiming said person was infected or something," James said.

"Wow," Chloe said.

"Now, onto better topics," Tank said. "I've been thinkin'."

"Oh, no," James said. "Here we go again."

"STFU," Tank said. "It's a damn good idea. Even Chloe likes it."

"I said it was dorky," Chloe corrected. "And kinda cute."

"Oh, so your idea's cute?" James asked.

"You're askin' for it," Tank said.

"What is it?" Connor asked.

"Tattoos," Tank said.

"Great idea," Connor said.

James nodded. "But of what?"

"Similar to what's on Scourge," Tank said.

"That's genius," Connor said.

"I have to admit," James said, "that *is* a pretty good idea."

"Precisely, so just shut it next time," Tank said.

Chloe laughed and they all smiled. It felt good to have normal moments like this. It reminded them of the times before and that there could still be life in the midst of all the death and killing.

This is what I fight and kill to protect, James thought. *I can't lose sight of that.*

"So how did you all meet?" Chloe asked. "I know it was in school, but how exactly?"

"It was our first day of middle school," James said, "and my first day of public school."

"Jamesy boy was homeschooled up until that point," Tank said. "It's why he's still so damn weird."

"Tank was just standing there, a little ways apart from the crowd," James said. "So I walked up and asked if he wanted to be friends."

"Just like that?" Chloe asked.

"Yep," James said. "I didn't realize I'd adopted my first introvert that day."

Chloe laughed. "You two are complete opposites."

"I tried to run," Tank said, "but he was relentless."

James chuckled. That was pretty much exactly how it had gone. Yet through all the years, they'd stayed good friends, even when they wanted to kill each other.

"Then, a year later when Connor came to school," Tank said, "he and I hit it off, too. And now here we are."

"Years and a whole lifetime later," Connor said.

"That's pretty cool," Chloe said. "Anticlimactic, but cute."

"So, the only problem with the tattoos," James said, "is where do we get 'em?"

"You just let me handle that," Tank said. "Your adopted introvert has it all figured out."

25
LET SLEEPING DOGS LIE

Alexis sat in the dark in the supply closet again. It was organized, but she still had to finish inventorying everything there, plus the new stuff that had come in the day before. She was taking her sweet time, glancing out the cracked door at the hallway beyond. It was around the same time as it had been the day before when she'd seen the two guards bring in the cart. Hopefully, she'd get another look at what they were doing in there. A pair of her dad's binoculars sat next to her. The guards had asked why she needed to bring them in, and she'd lied and said that Henry wanted to see them because they were the new Leupold 8x32s.

A few minutes later, she heard the front doors open and stood up, setting her tablet on the shelf. Gripping the binoculars in her hands, she watched as two black-uniformed men came into view, pushing a cart just like the last one. They stopped at the door, glancing around again. One looked at the supply closet door she was hiding behind, but the other lifted his hand to push the buttons on the keypad. She brought the binoculars to her eyes. The second man moved, blocking her view. The door clicked open and she continued to watch as it swung inward.

This time there wasn't another guard inside the room. Everything else was at it had been though, with drugs stacked on shelving in the room. The two men wheeled the cart in and the door closed behind them. She hadn't seen what they'd typed into the keypad, but she knew now that something strange was going on. It was a mystery she had to figure out, one way or another. As long as something unknown was going on, her mind wouldn't let her rest. She just kept thinking back to the last time an entire town had hidden a dark secret.

After turning the light back on and opening the door fully, she went back to work. Thirty minutes passed and still the men hadn't come out.

"Ms. Wolfe," Dr. Hart called from upstairs, "can you come into my office, please?"

She sighed in exasperation. She wanted to be here when those men came back out. Grabbing her tablet, she finished counting the last of the gauze and replaced the box on the shelf. Upstairs, Dr. Hart had the door to his office open, which was a rare occasion from what she'd seen in the last couple of days. She walked inside, tablet under her arm. Once again she thought how much he reminded her of someone. Maybe it was just the similarities to Father Ahaz, which would also explain her paranoia about the secret door to the basement.

"Yes, Dr. Hart?" Alexis asked.

"How goes the inventory?" Dr. Hart asked, barely looking up from his computer screen.

"Almost done. I'm having to sort through everything that came in yesterday."

"Did they deliver what we were low on?"

"I'm not sure. It seems like there was plenty of everything."

"Is that so? Hmmm, my inventory must've been out of date. Well, carry on and bring me the list when you're done."

"I will."

Alexis turned and left his office. Descending the stairs, she heard the front door open, and she rushed down the last few steps. There was no one inside the lobby, but someone had just left. Looking through the glass front doors, she noticed two men in black uniforms leaving the building without a cart. She'd just missed them, it seemed. What a frustrating coincidence.

Alexis went back to work inventorying the rest of the supplies and finished before noon. Exiting the supply closet, she closed the door all but a crack and went upstairs to Dr. Nelson's office.

"Come in," he said as she knocked on the door.

"I'm going out for lunch," Alexis said as she opened the door, sticking her head in.

"Sounds good," Dr. Nelson said. "Be back in thirty minutes."

"Yes, sir."

"And could you grab something for Dr. Hart and myself while you're out?"

"I can do that."

"Thank you."

She shut his door and left the building, walking out to the gate. Once she was through, she noticed James standing at the end of the driveway, waiting for her. Seeing him made her smile.

"Afternoon, Miss," James said, holding out his arm. "May I escort you to your destination?"

"You're such a dork," Alexis said, taking his arm in hers. "But yes, you may."

He leaned in and gave her a kiss before they started on their way to the Mess Hall. It was weird how comfortable she felt around him, almost like when she'd gone on vacation in Europe during her senior year of high school. She'd met a girl over there who was also from the States, and by the end of the week they were best friends. They'd stayed in touch through the years, but it still seemed odd how quickly they'd become close. Perhaps two people in a foreign setting who shared a common bond created closeness. She and James had been sharing in this struggle for over two weeks now, and the apocalypse was as foreign a setting as there could be.

"How's work today?" James asked as they walked.

"Good," Alexis responded. "Been doing inventory for the past two days, so I'll be glad once that's done. How are you today? You seem tired."

"I am, physically and mentally."

"I can imagine. That would've been nerve-racking yesterday."

"It was, and everything just seems to keep piling up. It feels like there's a weight on my shoulders. After our talk the other night, I felt some of that weight lift, but it's back now."

"Do you keep surrendering it? Or are you trying to do it all on your own?"

"It's not like I'm *trying* to."

"But you are. We weren't meant to do this on our

own. We're meant to ask for help."

"You sound like my mom."

"Your mother was a wise woman then."

"She was."

After a few moments of silence, she spoke up. "Do you ever get the feeling these people are hiding something from us?"

"What people?" James asked.

"The people in charge, like there's more going on here than they're telling us."

"You too?" James said, and she glanced at him. "We were just having this conversation. We all feel the same to some extent."

"Good, because there's a room in the infirmary. It's locked, and inside there's a door leading to a basement that's sometimes guarded."

"What's in the basement?"

"I don't know. Henry said they didn't have anything down there."

"Who's Henry?"

"Dr. Nelson."

"Oh, okay. That *is* a little suspicious. Who're the guards?"

"I don't know them, but it's those men who wear the black uniforms."

"Them again? This is starting to get like one of those movies with the mysterious organization operating in creepy basements."

"I'm not joking about this. They're hiding something. I know they are."

"I believe you, and I think so, too. But I say let sleeping dogs lie. They haven't put us in any danger yet, so we'll just stay out of their business."

"But what if they do put us in danger? What if something really bad is going on? Like in Safe Haven?"

James opened his mouth to respond but shut it again. "I guess there could be, but that wouldn't make any sense. There has to be more to it."

"I agree, and I want to find out what it is."

James stopped outside the front of the Mess Hall. "Just be careful. Sometimes people will do anything to keep secrets hidden, and I don't want you getting hurt."

"I can handle myself."

"I know," James said, taking her hand in his. "I just don't want anything to happen to you."

"I'll be careful," Alexis said, kissing him on the cheek. She turned and walked towards the front doors but stopped when James didn't follow. "Going to see Olive?"

"Yeah," James said, glancing at his watch. "She'll be out on break in a couple of minutes."

"I'll see you after work then?" Alexis asked, walking back to him.

"I'll be there," James said, smiling as he gave her a quick kiss. "Remember, don't do anything stupid."

"I won't, *dad*," Alexis said.

James chuckled. "See you tonight."

"Bye," Alexis said as she walked through the doors to the Mess Hall.

She didn't plan on doing anything stupid, and she would be careful, although her definition of those words was probably vastly different than James's.

~~~

James sat at the table in the cafeteria and commons area of the school. Olive sat across from him. She'd been able to pick up that something had happened the moment he'd sat down, and she hadn't let him rest until he'd told her the full story. After he finished, she regarded him with a look in those blue eyes that belied her age.

"That's because I was praying you guys would make it back safe," Olive said matter-of-factly.

"Oh really?" James said, smiling.

"Yep, I told God he couldn't take you away from me," Olive said. "And he won't if he knows what's good for him."

James burst out laughing, which drew a look from Mrs. Olger. Olive was one special girl. Her strength and tenacity were inspiring in someone so young. Here she was only eight years old, having seen more death than most adults, and yet she was helping him stay strong and not the other way around. Kids sure were something else.

"Well, thank you," James said. "We can use all the prayers we can get."

"I know," Olive said, smiling.

"So what'd you learn the last couple days?"

"Mostly boring stuff," Olive said, and then her eyes lit up. "We did learn how to make snares to catch animals if we have to survive in the woods. That was fun. Eli was a squirrel and Mr. Harkin caught him in a snare. It was funny. He also taught us how to make a fire and a shelter. Tomorrow morning we're going outside to make our own!"

"That does sound awesome," James said. "I'm

glad Mr. Harkin is teaching you all that stuff."

"Me too," Olive said.

"Five minutes, students," Mrs. Olger said.

"Is she always such a teacher?" James asked.

"No, only during the day. At night she's more like a mom."

"How do you like living here?"

"It's okay. Feels almost like a summer camp, like it's going to end soon. It doesn't feel like home." Her eyes misted a little. "I miss having a home."

James reached over and took her little hand in his. "Don't worry. You'll have a home soon, I promise."

Olive nodded, wiping her eyes. The door to the building opened and she looked to see who had walked in.

"You seein' Squeezer today?" Olive asked as Connor sat down next to James.

"Yeah," Connor said.

"I'll go get him," Olive said, running off into the classroom.

"No running!" Mrs. Olger called out after her.

Mark walked out from one of the rooms in the back, looking wide-eyed and sweaty. James watched him as he walked unsteadily down the hallway and into the main room. He almost collided with Olive as she came out with Squeezer in her hands.

"Oh, sorry, Mr. Trall," Olive said, moving past him.

"Watch where you're going," Mark snapped at her.

James began to stand but his brother put a hand on his shoulder. He looked over at Connor, who just shook his head, mouthing "later." Olive came up next to Connor and handed him the snake.

"Thanks," Connor said, looking down at the ball python. "How's he been?"

"Good," Olive said. "We found a real cage for him and everything. Last week we fed him a mouse, and it was so cool." She continued to tell Connor how Squeezer had bitten the mouse and then wrapped his body around it until it died, but James only half listened. He was watching Mark walk past them and out the front door. The man didn't look healthy. Something was going on with him, and they needed to find out what. The last thing they needed was him dying in here and the potential threat of him coming back.

James still wasn't sure if that would happen. He'd have to be bitten or scratched by a zombie, right? That's how it was in all the movies, well other than *The Walking Dead*. Yet, hadn't they seen people turn without being bitten? Or had they all been infected before dying? Could someone be partially infected and not turn right away? Was it transferred just in the infected's blood and saliva getting in someone's bloodstream? Or was there more to all this? There was just so little they knew, and he was beginning to realize they *did* need to know more, because until then, they wouldn't know exactly what they were facing. There'd come a time when they couldn't just keep shooting their way out of every situation.

"James?" Olive asked.

He looked up. "Sorry, I was thinking. What'd you say?"

"I have to go back to class."

"Oh, okay," James said, standing up and giving

her a hug. "Learn stuff today. I'll be back soon."

"I will." She smiled. "I'm praying for you, so you'll be okay."

"Thanks, little munchkin."

She giggled, taking Squeezer from Connor, and then bounded off into the classroom. James watched her go with a full heart.

"You ready, bro?" Connor asked as James stood there, watching the empty hallway.

"Yeah, let's go see if we can find Mark," James said, following his brother out the door.

"He looked like crap," Connor said.

"I'm worried he might be sick."

Outside, James looked around. Mark couldn't have gotten far in the last couple of minutes. He started down the street but stopped after a hundred yards. In a small alleyway between buildings, two feet stuck out from around the corner of the building. James pointed and Connor nodded as they started down the alley. Connor's hand immediately went to the handgun holstered on his hip. Around the back side of the building, Mark was laying on the ground.

"Hey, man," James said. "You okay?"

Mark didn't respond so James knelt down next to him, checking his pulse. He was alive. Noticing something lying beside him, James picked it up and showed it to his brother.

"Drugs," Connor said, looking at the syringe. "That explains it."

"Where would he get these?" James asked.

"He must've gotten 'em from someone or had 'em the whole time."

"We need to tell Cpt. Miller so he can do

something about it," James said. "I don't want the kids staying with a druggy."

"I just don't know how someone could do that."

"It's probably the only way he knows to cope with all this, but it doesn't matter. Something has to be done."

"Yeah."

"I'll go tell Cpt. Miller," James said. "Then we're meeting for tattoos, right?"

"That's the plan. I'll grab Tank and meet you there."

"Speaking of, does he seem weird to you today, like actually happy?"

"He does. We'll have to ask him about it later."

"Good, just wanted to make sure it wasn't just me."

"Nope," Connor said.

"What should we do with Mark?"

"Just leave him. They can figure out what to do with him. He'll probably be out for a while."

Connor left, heading back to their place while James went to HQ to inform Cpt. Miller. He felt a little bad about turning Mark in. He was probably just doing the only thing he knew that helped him, but all James had to do was think of Olive and determination replaced those feelings. He'd do whatever he needed to do to protect her, even from someone who was just unhinged by the state of the world.

26
A SWORD AND A PROMISE

Alexis sat behind her desk, hoping she'd get another excuse to go down to the supply closet. She knew being careful was necessary, but it was hard to just sit there and not see what was going on. She *had* to find out what was happening, even if it wasn't something sinister. Although, if they were going to these lengths to make sure they weren't found out, it was probably something less than reputable.

Now that she'd restocked all the rooms, organized the supply closet, and taken a complete inventory, there wasn't much for her to do, so she spent the afternoon arranging the inventory on the tablet in a way that made it easy to find the different items. While she did that, she discreetly watched the two doctors. She didn't know if they were in on all this secret stuff, but she was planning to find out.

Henry left his office a few times throughout the day but rarely left the second floor. He'd just go into the restroom at the end of the hall and then go back to his office. Dr. Hart, on the other hand, left his office fewer times, but every time he did, he went downstairs. Granted, there was also a restroom down there, but why not use the one up there like Henry did? Also, Henry kept his door closed sometimes, but Dr. Hart never left his door open and even went so far as to lock it when he left, even if just for a few minutes. That by itself was suspicious, not to mention the general vibe he gave off.

Just as she was thinking this, Dr. Hart exited his office and went downstairs in a rush, not taking the time to lock his office. She knew this was her best chance to gather some details. Standing, she walked over to the door but stopped short of going in when she heard people talking downstairs. It sounded like they were discussing something in harsh whispers. She slipped into his office before her courage could falter. Immediately, she went to his desk and started looking through the drawers without moving anything. There were the normal office supplies in most of the drawers, but at the back of one was an old keycard. It looked like the clip that attached it to the doctor's lab coat had been broken. If her hunch was correct, this would get her into the basement. She snatched up the keycard, moving some of the papers inside to cover where it had been. If she was lucky, he wouldn't even know it was gone. She quickly exited the office and shut the door behind her. She turned as Dr. Hart came up the steps, followed by two guards dragging one of the survivors from her group—Mark.

"What happened?" she asked quickly, hoping Dr. Hart hadn't seen her coming out of his office.

"Down there," Dr. Hart said, ignoring her question and pointing down the hall. "Last door on the right."

The guards moved forward between her and the doctor, and she used the brief cover to slip the keycard into her back pocket.

"Dr. Nelson," Dr. Hart said, "we have a new patient. Would you go prep him, Ms. Wolfe?"

"Yes, sir," Alexis said, glad to have an excuse to be away from the man.

Following the guards, she heard Henry come out of his office.

"What happened?" he asked Dr. Hart.

"Narcotics," Dr. Hart responded. "See if you can figure out where he got them. We don't need this in our town."

"Okay," Henry said.

The two men took Mark into the last exam room and handcuffed him to the bed, just like they had Tank the night before. How had Mark found drugs and why would he take them? He didn't seem like that kind of man. She remembered when he'd shared his story in the pole barn. He'd talked about going to jail, but she didn't know why. Was it drug use? After he'd gotten out, he'd turned his life around and volunteered at the church. He'd been helping out with VBS when the outbreak happened. He had an older daughter who was still alive in California with his ex-wife. As far as Alexis knew, he hadn't lost anyone close to him in the early days. He'd been one of the few who'd really opened up to the rest of them, sharing his entire life story. What had pushed him to do this?

After they'd handcuffed him to the bed, the two men walked out past Alexis.

"Be careful when he wakes up," one of the men said to her. "We don't know what he took."

Alexis looked at him, shocked that he'd spoken.

Usually these guys were the equivalent of a stone when it came to speaking or showing any sign of emotion. He was a little older than her, with light blue eyes and short blonde hair. There was a permanent smile on his face, which was probably why his nametag read "Smiles."

"Thanks," Alexis said as the other man grabbed Smiles and pulled him along.

He gave her a quick wink, then turned and followed the other man down the hall past Henry. Maybe they weren't all bad.

"How is he?" Henry asked, walking in.

"Unconscious," Alexis said, setting some items on a tray.

"Let's check his vitals."

~~~

James was the last one. He'd wanted to watch the others get their tattoos first so he could see how it went before he got his. Connor had "persevere" tattooed on his left forearm from when he'd gotten out of the Marines, but Tank and James didn't have any tattoos yet. Tank had gone first, followed by Connor, and now James sat in the chair, excited but also anxious. He'd watched his brother's reaction and could tell that getting the tattoo hadn't felt good. And if Connor reacted like that, it'd probably hurt him a little more—not that the pain scared him. He just didn't know what to expect.

"You ready?" Angel asked.

"Yep," James said, taking a deep breath.

It was worse than he'd thought but also not as bad

at the same time. Within thirty minutes, Angel was wiping the blood from James's hand with a green soap mixture.

"What'd ya think?" Angel asked.

"That looks awesome," James said, climbing out of the chair and looking down at the back of his right hand.

"Hands in boys," Tank said.

They put their fists together, all three of their tattoos showing. They each had the wolf-like, three-headed Cerberus tattooed on the backs of their dominant hands, but had incorporated their own twists to the tats. On Tank's, the three heads each had a spiked collar with a broken chain attached and pieces of shattered chains around the whole tattoo. Connor's had an American flag flying behind the whole thing. James had a simple wooden cross rising behind his. The tattoos were similar, yet completely unique, just like the members of the Wolf Pack itself.

"That's badass," James said, looking at the tops of their hands.

"We're cool like that," Tank said.

"Hell yeah," Connor said.

"If you guys are done ogling each other," Angel said, laughing, "I'll show you the upgrade I did to your truck."

Angel took them outside the garage to where Scourge was sitting in his driveway. James gawked at the sight. Before, Scourge only had the gray Cerberus emblem on the front doors—like their tattoos only with more detail. Now, behind the three heads were streaks of red, white, and blue going all the way to the rear of the rig. Around the front tires and up on the hood there were loose chains that looked like the vehicle had broken free from being chained down, and there were flames streaking out behind the back tires. It was all a little over the top, making the vehicle look like something from a video game.

"It's perfect!" James exclaimed.

"Dude," Tank said, a huge smile on his face, "this is friggin' sick!"

"Well done," Connor said.

"How long did it take you to do this?" James asked.

"All day," Angel said, a satisfied smile on his face. "I drew it up the last time Tank was in here. The plain emblem on the door was just sad. It needed a little *somethin'* more."

"We're gonna be killin' undead in style!" Tank said.

"Hell yeah," James said.

"We can't pay for this," Connor said.

"No need," Angel said. "I haven't been able to work on somethin' like this before. It was worth it just to put my mark on it."

"You did one helluva job," Tank said.

Walking around to the other side of Scourge, James saw that he'd painted the same thing on both sides. There was no way they'd get their rig confused with the other LAPVs now. After they were through gawking, Angel took them back inside and gave them each a piece of paper with directions on how to properly care for their new tattoos. They'd need to make sure to wash them and treated them like an open wound for the first few days, plus lotion the crap out of them. It wouldn't be easy considering how things were now, but it would be worth it. It wasn't just about them getting the tattoos together— although that was a big part—and it wasn't even about the tattoos themselves or what they stood for. It was about living. It was about finding those small moments that kept them rooted in who they were. And it was about them remembering to live each moment as if it were their last, because it very well could be.

James realized all this on the way back to their place, and things began to fall together. He remembered something else he'd realized while chained to the front of the Hummer. He wasn't in control. This was all beyond him, and he just had to trust and hope that there was more to life than killing and death. Why he needed to constantly be reminded of this every few days, he didn't know, but just like on that hilltop, he began to feel better when he decided to let go and trust. Maybe that's what it was with his episodes as well. He might be stuck with them forever, but he had to remember they couldn't be something that controlled him and got people killed. They were just something he had to live with now and accept as part of reality.

Then again, all this might just be his mind's way of trying to subconsciously cope with everything that was going on. But he wouldn't worry about that. He'd do what he'd been doing with his faith for years. He'd set the questions aside and just trust.

~~~

Alexis sat in the exam room, watching Mark's

breathing as he lay on the hospital bed. He was alive, fairly healthy, and definitely high on something, but he should be fine once he woke. If he was lucky, this was a onetime deal and he wouldn't have to go through any intense withdrawals. She was glad she'd been able to help with both Tank and now Mark. It made her feel like she was in the right place when she was able to help people. That was why she'd first decided to be a paramedic—to help others because she hadn't been able to help her own brother.

That was a long time ago and she'd recovered from Mason's death, but that didn't mean it was all water under the bridge. That single moment in her life had rippling effects that could be felt all the way to the present. It'd been the driving factor behind the divorce, although she knew now that it had been inevitable. All of these things had pushed her to be who she was today, and she felt that she was honoring her brother's memory by not letting his death be in vain.

Mark stirred, mumbling something under his breath. Alexis stuck her head out of the exam room door, calling for the doctor. A minute later, Dr. Hart walked into the room.

"He's beginning to wake up," Alexis said.

"Then we'll ask him some question when he does," Dr. Hart said, sitting down in a chair and wheeling it over to the bed.

Mark's eyes opened and he looked around the room. "Where am I?" he asked.

"You're in the infirmary, Mr. Trall," Dr. Hart said.

"What?" Mark said, sounding frantic. "Why?"

"Because you were found passed out in an

alleyway," Dr. Hart said, "with a syringe of narcotics."

Mark closed his eyes.

"Do you know what it is you took?" Dr. Hart asked.

"No," Mark said.

"So it wasn't yours?"

"No."

"Explain."

"It was from Randy's stash. I didn't realize how strong it was."

"Randy?" Dr. Hart asked.

"He was one of the men from their original group," Alexis said.

"What happened to him?" Dr. Hart asked.

"He... died," Alexis said.

"More like your dad murdered him," Mark said with an edge to his voice.

"Yeah, he did," Alexis said, "right after he shot your leader."

"I see," Dr. Hart said.

"It just never ends," Mark said. "And there'll be more and more and more. It won't ever stop."

"Is that why you took the drugs?"

"Yes. There's no escaping our fate."

"Are there more drugs?"

"No," Mark said in a rush.

"I don't believe you."

Mark glanced between Alexis and Dr. Hart with a pleading look on his face. "I just want to escape from all this. Is that so bad?"

"By itself, no," Dr. Hart said. "But when you put the rest of us in danger, it is."

"Then let me leave," Mark said. "I'll take everything with me."

"Why would you want to?" Alexis asked.

"It was so much easier when we were on the move," Mark said. "I can't stand pretending like everything's okay. It's not okay! The world is ending outside these walls."

"It's not," Dr. Hart said. "There are still quite a few safe cities like this one. You just experienced the worst of it."

"That's crap," Mark said. "I bet the rest of the country looks just like what we've been through."

"Why would they lie?" Dr. Hart asked.

"To keep people hopeful," Mark said.

He had a good point. What if the rest of the country *was* like what they'd been through? The people in charge said the government was still intact and the east and west coasts were better off, but what if that was all a lie to keep them blissfully unaware? That would be something they would want to keep hidden at all costs. What if whatever was in the basement had something to do with that—something that showed they were all being lied to?

"You can believe what you wish," Dr. Hart said. "All I need to know is where the drugs are."

"I need those!" Mark said.

"Then I'll have the soldiers confiscate all of your belongings and keep you here, or you can tell me and go free."

"I need those," Mark said in a whisper.

"So be it," Dr. Hart said as he stood up and walked to the door. "You'll stay here until we find them. Time to go, Ms. Wolfe."

Alexis looked once more at Mark's pleading eyes and walked from the room.

~~~

Tank walked down Third Street towards the mechanic shop. He didn't know if Tom would be done with his sword yet, but he might as well check this evening before he went up to the saloon. James said they all should get together tonight since Chloe didn't have to work. Just thinking about tonight made him realize more fully that they really might be able to make a life for themselves here—going out on runs during the day and then coming back and being safe at night. Yesterday had been a close call and there would always be the possibility of going out and never coming back, but being on the road was worse. There was only one problem they had to take care of—the Reclaimers.

The shop door was open even though it was after dinner. They probably worked long days there trying to strengthen the defenses of the town. The trailer that had been loaded with fencing was now gone. Were they double-layering the fencing around the town or taking it somewhere else? Walking into the shop, he saw Greg working on one of the Humvees. Greg glanced up as Tank walked in and nodded, going back to work. Tank didn't know the guy well, but he'd seen him around a few times. There were various other men and women working on vehicles and other projects. Spotting Tom at the back of the shop, he walked over to him.

"Hey, Tom," Tank said.

Tom grunted, working on attaching some sort of blade to the rim of a wheel. That would be awesome to have on Scourge. They would be able to mow down so many undead with those, taking their legs off at the knees, although it wouldn't kill them unless they made a second pass. After Tank just stood there for a few minutes, Tom put the blade aside and looked up at him.

"What'd ya want, kid?" Tom asked.

"I wanted to see if Frostmourne was done yet," Tank said.

"It is," Tom said. "You caught me at a bad time. Those Vindex asshats want these blades attached to the rims of their vehicles, only it's not as simple as just welding them on."

"Vindex?" Tank asked.

"You know," Tom said, "all those men driving around in those armored rigs."

"Who are they?"

"Some private contracting group hired by the government to help out with security and such. At least that's the only explanation I can come up with."

"So you're not sure why they're here?"

"Nah, and I don't care. The more guns we have protecting us, the better."

"Do you know anything else about them?"

"Why are you so interested?"

"Just curious."

"The large man with the big red beard is their leader. He goes by some silly name that I can never remember. That's all I know. Now, you want your sword?"

"Hell yeah."

JOSHUA C CHADD

"Follow me," Tom said, heading towards an office in the back of the large room.

Tank followed Tom as he stopped beside a table with a large sword laying on it. It was Frostmourne, and it looked almost exactly like the one in the game—the hilt with the demon head on it and the jagged blade near the base narrowing out at the tip. The thing looked completely badass. Tank bent down, taking a closer look. The detail was exquisite, from the runes etched into the blade to the demon's horns wrapped around the crossguard. But the closer he looked, the more he realized there were a few differences. The crossguard was less bulky and was scaled down in size, not as enormous as the replica. The pommel had also been changed to a short point, and the grip was simply wrapped in leather and missing the metal ridges.

"Wow," Tank whispered. "How did you get this done in a couple days?"

"Are you kiddin' me?" Tom asked. "That'd be impossible."

"Then how?"

"It was gonna be Jared's birthday present this year…" Tom took a deep breath, composing himself. "I was gonna throw it away until you came into my shop."

"I can't take this."

"You sure as hell will, and you'll honor my boy by using it to make the world a better place for when you have your own children."

Tank was stunned by Tom's sudden intensity and the emotion in his voice. If he took this sword, it wouldn't be a small thing. He'd be making a promise to Tom *and* honoring his son's death. Why did everything always have to be complicated like this?

"I'll take it and do my best to honor your son's memory."

"Good. Now, some things you should know. The blade is custom-ordered carbon steel and will be able to stand up to a beating. It's the same design as the original sword, but the whole thing is scaled down, which makes it shorter and a lot lighter. That way it'll be much easier to wield. The hilt is all stainless steel, but I downsized the whole design there even more, dropping over a pound of useless weight. I also sharpened those small blades going off on either side above the crossguard and added a glass breaker to the pommel."

"Wow," Tank said when Tom finished.

"I'll show you how to properly sharpen and care for it, but just remember, it's not a toy. It's a weapon."

"And I'll treat it as such," Tank said.

An hour later, he left the shop with the sword in a custom leather sheath and a bag full of the items he'd need to take care of the blade—a whetstone, oil, rag, and such. Tom had him swing it a few times and he was amazed. It was *way* lighter than the replica he'd used back in Fort Collins. This one was also much sharper and a whole lot easier to wield—a real instrument of death. He should be ecstatic right now, but what Tom had said earlier about making the world a better place was in the forefront of his mind. Up until that point, it'd been all about staying alive until the next day. He had those he loved and he'd protect them, but what Tom had told him to do was taking that to the next level. Could he live the kind of life that inspired others? Was he selfless enough that he'd truly give his life for another?

He didn't really know.

~~~

James waited outside the gate to the infirmary. The rest of the gang was up at the Bootlegger Saloon already. He couldn't help the nervous butterflies that rose in his stomach at the thought of seeing Alexis again. True, he'd seen her just a few hours ago, but he was still excited. He'd never had a girlfriend before and certainly not someone like her. At a little after six-thirty, Alexis walked out of the front doors with Dr. Nelson. James felt a brief pang of jealousy, but he shook his head, knowing that was foolish. Those thoughts completely left his mind a moment later when Alexis saw him and her face lit up with a smile. There was nothing to be jealous of. Stopping at the gate, they checked out with the guards and Alexis collected her gun belt.

"Hey, James," Alexis said as she walked up to him.

"Hey," he said, wrapping his arms around her in a hug.

"I'll see you tomorrow," Dr. Nelson said, heading off towards the Mess Hall.

"See ya," Alexis said to Dr. Nelson and then turned back to James. "I was hoping you'd be here."

"Of course," James said as they walked across the street towards her house. "I want to spend every second I can with you."

"You're such a romantic."

James shrugged. "Everyone's at the saloon. I figured we could all get together tonight and have dinner up there."

"That's a good idea. I just need to change."

Ten minutes later, they were walking hand-in-hand towards the saloon on the northwest side of town.

"Wait, is that a tattoo?" Alexis said, grabbing James's right hand.

"Oh, yeah," James said, showing her.

"That's so dorky," Alexis said with a chuckle. Then she looked at his face. "Not in a bad way. It looks awesome. It's just totally dorky, which is how you are. So it's fitting."

"Oh," James said, recovering.

He hadn't realized how such a small comment from her could make him feel so... intensely. He usually prided himself on not caring what other people thought. Not with her, apparently.

"All three of you get them?" Alexis asked.

"Yeah, but they're all a little different."

"That's sweet. So, my day was exciting. Mark was admitted to the infirmary. Did you know he was taking drugs?"

"Actually, Connor and I are the ones who found him passed out in an alley."

"I was wondering how he got caught."

"Why was he taking them?"

"I think all this is a little too much for him. He kept talking about wanting to have an escape from reality. I don't think he can handle everything he's been through."

"I guess that makes sense. Where did he get 'em?"

"They were Randy's."

"He must've gone through Randy's stuff when he died. I didn't even think about checking for that."

"It's not your fault."

"I know, but still. I just wonder how long he's been on them, and we let him stay with the kids."

"Well, at least we found out before he hurt anyone, himself included."

"Yeah, and I'll make sure to talk to Cpt. Miller so he gets moved somewhere else."

"I think that's wise. What'd you do with your day off?"

"Cleaned and prepped our gear, got tattoos, and just got done talking to your dad about our runs for the rest of the week."

"I thought you reported to Cpt. Miller."

"We did, but he put your dad in charge of all the runs so we report to him now, which is nice. It's a lot more relaxing, and I know your dad won't steer us wrong."

"Good, I'm glad dad got a job. He's just been making himself look busy, but now he actually has something to do."

"He's also training some of the other survivors on how to make runs so we can have a rotating schedule."

"It seems like everyone is putting roots down."

They arrived at the saloon.

"How do you feel about that?" James asked, pausing outside the door.

"I'm not sure. I want to feel safe here, I really do, but something is holding me back, and until I get past that, this place won't feel like home."

"I agree. You didn't do anything to get into the basement today did you?"

"Nope," Alexis said. "I told you, I'll be careful."

"Good."

"You're the one we should be worried about," Alexis said and stepped closer to him. "You're the one going out on runs."

She gave him a quick kiss and then slipped inside, leaving him standing outside the door. Smiling, he shook his head and entered the saloon. Connor, Tank, and Chloe sat at their usual table in the corner, and there were to-go boxes stacked in the middle. Alexis was already with their friends, sitting down next to Chloe, which left a seat open between his brother and his girlfriend. Three of the people he cared about most sat at that table, and he couldn't help but smile.

Enjoy each moment like it's my last, he thought. *I can do that.*

He walked over and sat down.

"I see you finally decided to show up," Tank said.

"Emmett's not coming?" Connor asked.

"He said he had work to do tonight," James said. "He may show up later."

"Can we eat then?" Chloe asked. "I think I'm about to turn into a zombie over here."

They all laughed as Tank passed out the Styrofoam boxes.

"Cook said we owe her at least two dozen cans of Coke now," Tank said.

"I figured," James said, taking a bite of his food.

"Tell James what you told me," Connor said, looking at Tank.

"So you know those men in the black uniforms?" Tank asked and James nodded. "They're mercenaries working for a company called Vindex Corporation. Tom, the guy in charge of the mechanic shop, said that he thought the government hired them as extra muscle."

"Really?" James asked. "Any idea why they were outside of Sheridan too?"

"Nope," Tank said. "But maybe they're all over the country tryin' to help."

"You think so?" Alexis asked.

"No," Connor said. "There's more to them, but at least we know who they are now."

"I wonder why they're the only ones guarding the infirmary," Alexis said.

Tank shrugged. "Oh, and check this out," he said, pulling Frostmourne out of the sheath draped over the back of his chair.

"That's sick," James said. "How did he make *that* in a couple days?"

"He's been working on it for a year," Tank said, sheathing it after a look from Durt, the owner, and bartender that night.

"Really?" James asked.

"It's a long story. I'll explain later," Tank said. "For now, we need a round of drinks!"

"Just two for me tonight," James said.

"You overdo it the last time?" Alexis asked.

"Just a little," James said.

She laughed.

Durt came over and took their order, returning a minute later with their drinks.

"To us," Tank said. "The world may be goin' to

226

hell, but at least we're all together!"

"Cheers!"

James took a large gulp of his Captain and Coke, and then set it down, glancing over at Alexis. She was having a hushed conversation with Chloe, a smile on her face. His heart soared. How, at the end of all things, had he found someone like this? It was truly amazing how everything had worked out. Looking at his friends gathered around him, he realized maybe God did have a plan in all of this.

27
RED WIRE, BLUE WIRE

Max whittled on a small piece of sagebrush. He liked how the wood smelled, and it helped put him at ease. It was the only time he was at ease anymore. When he'd first joined with Jezz, it had mainly been out of self-preservation. She made him do things he hated, but some small part of him also liked it. He'd lost sight of who he used to be. At one point, all he'd wanted was to have a family—to settle down and live a quiet life. He'd had enough excitement during his younger years, and now he just wanted to live in peace. Yet here he was, murdering for someone he both hated and loved at the same time. What had his life become?

"Is everything ready?" Jezz asked, walking up to Max.

Her clothing was covered in fresh blood and she grinned, uncaring of the crimson speckles on her face.

"Yes," Max said in a hard voice.

If he let any of his thoughts into his voice, he'd be dead. She couldn't know that he was having doubts. And why was he even having doubts? He was here, he was alive, and Jezz would keep him alive. He had to believe that.

"Good," Jezz said. "We will set the plan in motion tomorrow. Make sure they find it."

"I will."

Zeke left the rest of the gathered Reclaimers to join Max and Jezz. "Phase two is coming along," he said.

"Splendid," Jezz said.

"I think this'll work," Zeke said, glancing at Max.

It's not like it was Max's plan. He was just the one put in charge of setting up phase one. Jezz had come up with it so he couldn't be blamed if it failed, or could he? Jezz walked off to go talk with the others.

"Best make sure you don't fail," Zeke said, coming closer to him. "The rest did their part, even said it was easy. Those people were completely unprepared."

"It's not *my* plan," Max mumbled.

"Oh, it is. The moment she gave it to you to set up, it became yours."

Max looked at Zeke, noting his hateful eyes. Maybe he should amend his opinion of Zeke. He might even be worse than Jezz. While she was sometimes blind to those who followed her without question, this man seemed to be able to read Max like a book and knew all the doubts he was having. Zeke was dangerous, and he'd have to watch himself.

"It'll work," Max said with false confidence. "I've done everything like you said."

"Might want to double check it all then," Zeke said, walking away with a wolfish grin on his face. "You can never be too careful."

Zeke walked over to where the other twenty

Reclaimers were all standing. Their clothing was speckled with blood, and every single one of them had smiles on their faces, like they'd just done something enjoyable. He was glad Jezz had left him to his own preparations instead of making him join the rest.

Max waited for Zeke and the others to disappear around the corner of the barn before he pulled the piece of paper Zeke had given him earlier out of his pocket. He read through it, checking to make sure he had everything put together right. His eyes searched the page for anything that he might've missed. He wasn't able to visualize exactly what he'd done, so he walked over to the back of the truck. Opening the bed, he examined the small device before him, comparing it to the diagram on the page.

"C4 goes here," Max mumbled to himself. "Red wire attaches there. Blue wire…"

He spent the next thirty minutes checking and rechecking to make sure everything had been done correctly. Finally, he closed the tailgate and folded the piece of paper, stuffing it back into his pocket. Pulling out his knife, he began to look for a small piece of wood in the dusky light. Everything was perfect. He'd been told many times that he wasn't the sharpest tool in the shed, but he'd always been good at following directions. He'd done that now, and he was confident that everything was ready. Finding some dead sagebrush blown up against the side of the shed, he picked out a good piece and began to whittle. Soon, he'd lost himself in memories of better times before the world had fallen apart.

28
RED RIVER

Post-outbreak day 21

Connor slammed the magazine into his ACR, racking the bolt.

"Time to lock and load," he said.

"And rock and roll," James said, climbing into the new and improved Scourge.

Connor looked at the side of the passenger door. Even though Angel looked like he'd made a few bad life choices in his past, Connor had to admit that he was one hell of an artist. He couldn't believe Angel had done this in a single day. He opened the door and climbed in as Tank started the rig.

"Ready boys?" Tank asked.

"Let's do it," James said from the back seat.

Tank pulled Scourge away from their place and drove through town in the early morning light. They drove down North Avenue, heading towards the southern gate out of town.

"Is that Chloe?" Connor asked, noticing someone standing by the side of the road.

"Sure is," Tank said, slowing to a stop and opening his door.

"Morning, guys," Chloe said. "I wanted to take a picture with you all geared up."

Tank looked over at Connor.

Connor shrugged. "Why not?"

"I think a picture sounds awesome," James said, getting out of the back with his ACR.

Positioning themselves to show off Scourge's new paint job, they stood decked out in their Kryptek Typhon uniforms, holding their rifles.

"Now smile," Chloe said as she snapped a few pictures with her phone and then quickly looked through them.

"Connor," Chloe said, "I said smile."

"I don't smile," Connor said.

"Cut the crap and just smile," Chloe said.

"Damn, son, you just got told," Tank said.

They all laughed as Chloe snapped more pictures. "There. Those are good."

"That all?" Connor asked.

"Don't you want one with you all stern and angry looking?" Chloe asked.

"I'm good," Connor said.

Tank walked over and gave her a kiss, saying something as Connor walked around to the passenger seat. Soon, Tank joined them and they started off down the road again. It wasn't that Connor was trying to be a dick. It was just that they weren't on a normal run. They were going to meet with a group of survivors to trade goods. Emmett had told them about the small colony of people living a few miles to the west of Coutts on the Montana side of the border. It was one of those religious communities where everyone shared what they had and lived in a sort of commune. That was a bit weird for him to think about since it was so alien from how he'd been raised, but now, at the end of the world, it honestly made a lot of sense. The interesting thing about the Red River Colony, as it was called, was that they were almost completely self-sufficient. The leaders in Coutts had received a message yesterday that the community had some fresh vegetables they wanted to trade, so the back of Scourge was filled with the miscellaneous items the colony had requested.

Connor watched the mix of Marines and Vindex men guarding the gate. Now that he knew who those men in the black uniforms were, he might be able to discover something about them. They just seemed off, like how none of them could be found when they weren't on duty. Emmett said they'd set up in the large church on the north side of town, but the only time Connor had ever seen them was at the Mess Hall, and even then they came in sporadically. It seemed that they didn't have to follow the same rules everyone else did. He didn't like it when people thought they were above the rules. Maybe that wasn't how they were, but all he'd seen so far had confirmed it.

After leaving through the gate, they drove to the first overpass south of town and turned right onto a dirt road. Connor barely noticed when Tank turned the music on and *Screams of the Undead* by Demon Hunter began to play. His mind drifted back to the night before. It'd felt good to have a night like that with all of them together in a situation that didn't require them to be on guard. It was almost relaxing, and he'd allowed himself to let go and enjoy it.

Emmett had joined them later, although he refrained from drinking. It'd been the perfect night—a night none of them should be having at a time like this. A night that he didn't deserve to have any more, not with the world in shambles and the Reclaimers hunting them. Those good moments just meant that something bad was bound to happen... something really bad. He could almost feel it building in the air around them.

Shaking those thoughts from his mind, Connor focused on keeping a watchful gaze around them. The Reclaimers were out there somewhere, waiting for them to slip up like the last time. Then, they'd spring on them and do their best to destroy them completely, and he wouldn't let that happen. Every time they left those gates, he'd be on his guard, expecting the Reclaimers to pop up around every corner. It would be exhausting, but he wouldn't mess up again. They *couldn't* make a mistake like that a second time. It'd been pure luck that they'd even escaped. He'd be ready this time, and as soon as they had any lead on the Reclaimers, they'd take the fight to their front door. Then he'd kill every last one of them.

Tank pulled Scourge to a stop. Only a few hundred yards ahead there was a collection of white and silver buildings—the Red River Colony. Connor pulled a pair of binoculars from the dash and looked through them as he heard James opening the hatch in the roof. The place looked pristine. Everything was where it belonged and there was no trash scattered around. It looked normal, like the apocalypse hadn't devastated it. The odd thing, however, was that he couldn't see anyone outside—not a single person.

"There's no one down there," James said from the roof.

"Good observation, Captain Obvious," Tank said.

In the middle of the colony sat eight white buildings with random barns and outbuildings scattered around those. Four long apartment buildings with seven doors on each side sat in a square with two other long buildings between them. That would probably be the living quarters, kitchen, and church. No one moved down there, not a single sign of activity. There was supposed to be a population of seventy-five people. They waited another five minutes to see if anyone came out of the buildings.

"Something's wrong," Connor said.

"What's the play then?" Tank asked.

"We need to investigate," Connor said.

"We could just go back and report this," James said.

"And not do what they sent us out here to do?" Connor asked.

"They could just all be inside for breakfast or somethin'," Tank said.

"We have to check it out," Connor said.

"Alright," James said. "But we go in ready."

"I was ready as soon as we left Coutts," Connor said.

They continued on their way, pulling down the driveway into the colony. Not knowing what else to do, they pulled right up to a small building that was away from the main collection. Tank turned Scourge off and they sat there for a few seconds. Connor opened the door and climbed out, scanning the horizon and all the buildings. Nothing—no people or movement. It was devoid of life, or at least it seemed that way. He walked around to the front of the rig, meeting James and Tank.

"I'll take point," Connor said. "Tank, get our six. I have a bad feeling about this."

"Emmett did say they'd be around today, right?" James asked.

"Yep," Tank said.

Connor walked towards the door and knocked on it. No one answered.

"Anyone in there?" Connor called out.

Nothing.

He nodded to his brother, who opened the door for him, and Connor shouldered his ACR, sweeping into the room. The three of them moved inside, checking the whole building. It was clear. This seemed to be an office of sorts.

"Empty," James said.

"We'll try the next one," Connor said.

Outside, they moved to one of the apartment-looking buildings. Connor knocked again, but no one answered so he entered the room with James on his heels. This was someone's home. There was a bench against one wall and a small table with chairs—a living room. Connor split off to a door on the left while Tank went to the one on the right and James took the one in the middle. Inside, Connor found a small bedroom with a single bed and dresser, nothing else. He turned and exited, noticing Tank coming out of a similar-looking room, shaking his head.

"I got blood," James said.

Connor moved to the middle doorway, going

downstairs to the basement. James was crouched at the bottom of the stairs next to three pools of blood on the floor.

"It's dried, but it's not more than a couple of days old," James said, standing up.

"That's a lot of blood," Connor said.

"There's enough there for at least three bodies," Tank said. "I'd be surprised if they survived."

"So where are they?" James asked.

"That's a damn good question," Connor said, looking around the basement.

~~~

James followed behind his brother as they exited the small church tucked between the two northern apartment buildings. They'd cleared the entirety of the apartment building they'd first entered. There'd been more blood in the rooms, and some of the rooms had crimson drag marks going towards the large central building. Connor moved towards there now, with James following close behind. He knew his brother was watching the ground for any traps so James kept his eyes up, looking for any sign of movement. Tank would be keeping an eye out for anything behind them. They arrived at the first door to the building and Connor stopped with his ear to it.

"I don't hear anything," Connor whispered into the microphone of his headset. "Take it nice and slow."

James moved up to the door and waited for his brother's nod before opening it. Connor went into the room and James entered after him. Inside was a large kitchen with commercial-grade appliances and a doorway to the left. In the next room, there was more equipment and some large counters. None of the apartments had had their own kitchens, which made sense now as they apparently used a large communal one. There was a single door leading farther into the building.

"Clear," Connor whispered.

Tank closed the door behind them. "Nuthin' behind us," he said.

"I don't like this," James said.

"Me neither," Connor said, "but we can't leave yet."

James sighed. "Then let's get on with it."

They repeated the process, Connor going through the door first with James following him and Tank watching their six. The next room was more of a long hallway without any windows and dozens of small, square freezer doors set into the left wall. In between half of the small freezers was a doorway leading to a large, walk-in freezer and cooler. Connor went to check those while James kept his gun and eyes pointed ahead and Tank watched their backs. His brother came back out a few seconds later.

"There's a ton of food in there," Connor whispered, "but nothin' else."

Connor took the lead again and they moved into the next part of the room. On the right side, there were a few wooden tables, and the left side was taken up by a large span of windows. Through those windows they could see the mechanical room that housed the generators and such for the whole colony. A couple of utility sinks sat against the far wall next to another door. James was impressed. These people were truly self-sufficient, and just by looking at this building and their apartments, he could tell they lived a simple life. They were probably happier than most people these days since they had less technology and lived with fewer distractions in life. He hoped the dread he was feeling would be unfounded. It would be tragic if anything had happened to this community.

Connor stopped next to the door and nodded at James, who opened it for him. Connor immediately went into the room and James followed. The smell hit him first and almost caused him to empty his stomach—copious amounts of blood and death. Then he saw what had caused it and stopped dead in his tracks just inside the room. They'd found the residents of the Red River Colony.

29
QUESTIONS

Alexis carried two to-go boxes of food up the stairs and over to her desk, where she set one down and turned to the hallway.

"Where are you going?" Dr. Hart asked from behind her.

She quickly spun, almost dropping the other to-go box. His door had been closed and she hadn't heard him come out.

"To give Mark some breakfast," Alexis said.

"That won't be necessary," Dr. Hart said.

"Why not?"

"He's no longer here. The soldiers found his drugs and he wanted to leave so they gave him a car. He's gone."

"He left town?" she asked.

"Of course. You heard him say yesterday that he didn't want to be here. So when I released him this morning, he asked if he could leave and I told him to head to HQ. I heard he left shortly after gathering the rest of his belongings."

Alexis stared at the doctor. Mark had just up and left? She knew he hadn't been content where he was at and that he wanted to be on the move, but she didn't really think he'd leave the rest of his group. He'd known some of those people for years. Why would he leave now and try to survive on his own?

"He just left?" Alexis asked again.

"Yes, Ms. Wolfe," Dr. Hart said with exasperation. "Now, if you're through asking me the same question over and over, I have work to do."

He turned and entered his office, shutting the door behind him. Alexis walked over to her desk in the corner, setting the to-go box on the edge. Why would Mark leave? He didn't have the drugs, a gun, supplies, or anything. Dr. Hart said the soldiers had given him a car. Had they also given him enough supplies to survive? Or had they given him his drugs back? And now, of all times. With the Reclaimers hunting them, it was more dangerous than ever. None of this made any sense. They wouldn't just let him leave and endanger the whole community.

Henry walked out of his office. "You bring that for me?" he asked, pointing to the second to-go box.

"No, but you can have it," Alexis said, handing it to him.

"Thanks," Henry said, taking it. "You bring it for Mark?"

"Yeah," Alexis said. "Dr. Hart said they released him?"

"That's what I heard," Henry said, opening the Styrofoam container and picking up the plastic fork inside.

"You didn't see him released?"

"Nope." Henry took a bite of scrambled eggs, swallowed it, and continued. "Apparently it was all done before I got in this morning."

"When did you get here?"

"A little after seven, I think."

"When does Dr. Hart come in?"

"I think he lives in that office," Henry said with a chuckle. "I've never seen him leave the building."

"You've *never* seen him leave?"

"A few times for breakfast or lunch, but mainly the guards bring our food. I've never seen him leave at night though."

"That's odd."

"The man is dedicated, though I have no idea how he stays so busy. It's not like there's a lot to do around here besides write our daily reports."

"Yeah," Alexis said, only half listening.

"Speaking of things to do, would you mind cleaning up the room Mark was staying in and taking the bedding over to the Laundromat?"

"Sure."

"Thanks for the food."

He smiled at her and walked back into his office, leaving the door open. Henry hadn't even seen Mark this morning. Why did everything about this place make her so suspicious, and why was it so hard to believe Dr. Hart?

She stood up and walked down the hallway to the last door on the right. Opening it, she slipped inside. Mark was indeed gone. The sheets and blankets from the hospital bed were crumpled and hanging down to the floor. Everything else in the room looked the same as it had when she'd left last night.

Grabbing a garbage bag from under the sink, she shoved the bedding inside. After that, she went to the trash can and started to tie up the bag, but something caught her eye. There was a syringe mixed in with the other trash. Carefully, she picked it up and then dug around until she came up with a small glass vial. She examined it, depositing the syringe back in the trash. It was Ketamine—a common sedative.

She instinctively moved to pull out her phone to take a picture but stopped short. She hadn't carried a phone since the cell towers had gone down. Instead, she'd replaced it with her gun belt, which held her Beretta, two extra magazines, a multi-tool, and a flashlight. But that wasn't on her now since she always had to leave it at the gate. In lieu of a picture, she carefully peeled off the label and stuck it in her pocket. She'd have to check on that later. Putting the vial back in the trash, she tied up the bag, set it outside the room, and continued to clean. It only took thirty minutes to disinfect the room.

After she took out the trash, she sat down at her desk with the bag of laundry next to it. She pulled out her tablet and looked through her inventory list. Ketamine wasn't on it, meaning it would be in the locked room. Since Mark hadn't had an IV, the drug would've been injected directly into him. Why would they need to knock him out if he was leaving town? The question only added to her suspicions.

She walked down to the supply closet, intending to gather supplies to restock the room Mark had been in. Once inside, she turned off the light and cracked the door, gazing out. Within a few minutes, she was rewarded as the front doors opened. Two black-clad Vindex men walked down the hallway to the room with the locked door. Pulling the binoculars from a box of gauze she'd hidden them in, she brought them to her eyes and watched as one of the men entered the code—five, nine, eight, three.

The door opened and the men entered the room. This time, there was no one else inside, so maybe there wasn't normally a third guard waiting. The door shut behind them and she stashed the binoculars again. Whoever had used the Ketamine had access to that room. That meant it was one of the Vindex men or Dr. Hart, but why would they need it? If what Dr. Hart had said was true, Mark had left town of his own free will. Or had he?

The rest of the morning passed quickly as she hid her wandering mind by pretended to be busy on the tablet. The questions were eating away at her and she tried not to dwell on them, but she just couldn't quell the unease she felt. There was a silver lining, though. Tonight was her dinner date with her dad. They'd been so busy lately that they'd barely seen each other. It had been difficult to go from seeing him non-stop every day when they were on the road to going a whole day without seeing him at all. She knew he was doing what he had to, but she still missed him, which made the thought of dinner together that night so nice. Her dad had even initiated it.

A little earlier than normal, she left with the garbage bag of laundry slung over her shoulder. The guards let her pass and she collected her gun belt, heading to the local Laundromat. She was thankful Coutts had its own power and water supplies that were able to be kept fully operational.

Dropping the laundry off, she walked two buildings down to where Mark had been staying. In the yard next to the school, she noticed that Neil had the kids outside and that Seth was helping him. There were piles of leaves, sticks, spruce branches, and other similar items around the kids, who'd been paired up and were trying to make a shelter. She felt a small sense of pride when she noticed that Olive and Felix were paired up and already had the best frame built while the rest of the kids were still working on theirs.

Olive noticed her and waved enthusiastically. Alexis waved back, smiling. She didn't want to interrupt Neil's class so she just watched for a bit. It was encouraging to see that they were teaching the kids lessons that would help them survive in this new world, but it was also sad that it was necessary. Because they were so focused on survival, they hadn't fully realized how much they'd lost over the last few weeks. Could these kids ever grow up and have a *normal* childhood again? Or were they destined to grow up too quickly, missing out on what it meant to be a child?

Entering the school, she went straight to Helen's classroom. The older lady was inside, grading papers. Helen had found her place in this new world doing something she loved and had been doing for years. Alexis had hoped the infirmary would be that for her, but after the first day it had felt more like a prison than anything else. This whole town felt that way to her, and she hated to be in a cage, even if it was safe. She wanted to go for a walk out in the woods where no one could see her and just enjoy the peace and quiet. Instead, she was stuck in a town that was maybe a square mile with over four hundred other people.

"Can I come in?" Alexis asked, knocking on the open door.

"Of course, dear," Helen said, looking up from the papers.

"How are the kids doing?" Alexis asked, sitting down in the chair across from her.

"Surprisingly well, all things considered," Helen said. "They're adjusting better than some adults now that they have the semblance of a normal routine again. Most miss their parents and have lost a lot of their friends, but they're pressing through it. It helps that they have others their own age who've been through the same experience."

"How are you doing?"

"Great, actually. It feels good to be teaching again. How about you? I hear you and James are together."

Alexis blushed a little. "Yeah, we are. With everything going on, we've only been on one date, but it feels so natural."

"That's how you want it to be. My husband and I only went on two dates before he asked me to marry him, but our generation was a bit different."

"Wow, just two dates?"

"Yeah, they were long ones mostly spent talking. We hadn't even known each other before the first date; it was all arranged by one of our mutual friends. Within a week, we were engaged."

"How long were you married?"

"Forty-two years before the cancer took him. They weren't always easy years, but we never gave up on each other. That's what you have to remember—no matter how hard it gets you can't give up."

"Thanks, I'll remember that."

"Now, I'm sure you didn't come here to ask for relationship advice."

"No, I wanted to see if you knew anything about Mark."

"I heard about what happened. I had no idea he was taking those drugs. He'd been clean for years."

"Have you seen him today?"

"No, I haven't seen him since he left for lunch yesterday. What'd they do with him?"

"They admitted him to the infirmary. I talked with him yesterday, but now I've been told he left."

"What?"

"Yeah, he left town. At least, that's what they told me."

"Mark wouldn't do that. He had nightmares about being out there."

"That's what I thought, but they said he's gone. Where was he staying?"

"Down the hall to the left. Is that what those men were doing here yesterday?"

"What men?"

"The ones wearing those black uniforms. They said they were looking for the drugs, but they walked out with all of his belongings."

"They took everything yesterday?"

"Yes."

"Can I see his room?" Alexis asked, standing.

"Sure, it's just down the hall," Helen said. "Why are you asking all these questions? They may have just moved Mark to a different house."

"Maybe, but something doesn't feel right here," Alexis said as she left the room, heading down the hallway.

Mark's room was empty. A cot sat against one wall with a small table next to it and a set of shelves against the opposite wall. There was nothing else; they really had taken it all. Why would they take his belongings? Hadn't Dr. Hart said Mark had gathered his things this morning and then left? Maybe the doctor had given him the drugs back, and he left. Or maybe they made him leave, not wanting to have a drug addict in town. Alexis left the room, walking by Helen's classroom.

"Find anything?" Helen asked.

"Nope, but thanks for the advice," Alexis said.

"You're welcome, hon. I'm sure everything is going to work out."

"I hope so," Alexis said.

She exited the building, waving to Olive as she walked by. She and Felix had finished their shelter, and Neil was inspecting it with a small smile on his face.

What had really happened to Mark? Did it have something to do with whatever was going on in the basement? She was tired of guessing. It was time to make a move.

30
MASSACRE

"Holy shit," Tank said, stifling a gag.

Over seventy bodies—men, women, and children—littered the dining area in piles. Almost the entire floor was covered in dark blood that stuck to their boots. This had been the scene of a massive slaughter. No one had been spared, not a single resident. The closest pile contained six bodies, mostly adults, but there was a tiny hand sticking out from the middle of it, stiff with rigor mortis. This was too much, it was all too much. James bent over and wretched up the contents of his stomach onto the crimson floor. When he looked back up, he didn't see just the scene before him but one that was rising in the back of his mind as well.

"Connor," James said, desperately. He needed to let his brother know that he wasn't himself. Leaning back against the wall, he closed his eyes against the scene before him as another one took its place.

Lord help me! James cried out. *I can't do this alone!*

The episode still came, like it always did, but it was less intense this time and had more of a dreamlike quality. He still felt his back pressed against the cold wall and he could hear Connor and Tank talking around him. It passed quicker than usual, too, but left him sweating and feeling drained. He opened his eyes to see Connor standing just in front of him, ACR up and ready. Tank was beside him, watching the room they'd just come from. James took a deep breath and then spit some of the bile from his mouth.

"I'm good," James said, moving from the wall.

"For once, I don't think that could've been helped," Tank said.

"No, this is brutal," Connor said.

"You don't think it was…" James started to say.

"Has to be," Connor said.

"Who else is this heartless?" Tank asked. "You heard what she made Ana do."

"Then they did this because of us," James said, unable to look away from the massacre before him. So many bodies, so much blood. The loss of life was staggering.

"Don't even start down that path again," Connor said with an edge to his voice.

"I'm not," James said. "But why? Just to send us a message?"

"I don't know," Connor replied. "But we need to report this."

"Good idea," Tank said. "I'm ready to get the hell outta here."

"Me too," James said and turned away. "Let's go."

Exiting the door in the dining area, they quickly jogged over to Scourge. They loaded in and Tank took off back down the dirt road. James couldn't get the image out of his head. So many innocent people had died, and for what? Why did the Reclaimers kill all of them? It hadn't been a trap, or they wouldn't have been able to leave so easily. So why?

They didn't fully let their guards down until they passed through the gate into Coutts. They immediately pulled up to HQ where Emmett was outside talking with Cpt. Miller, who was smoking a cigarette. Tank stopped Scourge in the spot closest to them and they climbed out.

"Back already?" Cpt. Miller asked.

Emmett read their faces as they walked over. "What happened?" he asked.

"They're all dead," Connor said.

Cpt. Miller looked confused.

"The entire Red River Colony has been slaughtered and piled in the dining hall," James said.

Cpt. Miller cursed. "All of them?" he asked.

"Every last man, woman, and child," Tank replied.

"We didn't check all the apartment buildings," Connor said, "but the one we did had no one inside, only blood."

"And there were over seventy bodies piled in there," James said.

"Was it them?" Emmett asked.

"Not sure," Connor answered.

"It doesn't make sense that it would be anyone else," James said.

"Assuming makes an ass out of you and me," Cpt. Miller said.

"I agree," Emmett said. "But this sounds like the Reclaimers."

"They had freezers full of food," Connor stated.

"Yes, all of last fall's crops are in there," Cpt.

Miller said, dousing his cigarette. "We need to recover that food before someone else does and then figure out what happened. You three hold tight. I need to get Cpt. Sanders."

"Yes, sir," Connor said.

James slumped down against the side of the building.

"That bad?" Emmett asked, looking at the three of them.

"As bad as the big house back in Meriden," James said.

"That *is* bad," Emmett said. "Did you see anything else?"

"No," Connor answered.

"I just don't get why," James whispered.

"Because she's loony," Tank stated. "She probably just enjoys the killin'."

"That could be," Emmett said. "But she's also sharp. There may be something we're missing."

Cpt. Miller came back, followed by Cpt. Sanders.

"You said *all* of the residents of the colony are dead?" Cpt. Sanders asked Connor.

"All the ones we saw," Connor replied. "There could've been more in the other buildings, but from what we gathered, they killed 'em all."

"So there could be some alive?"

"Yes, sir."

"Then this is part supply run, part rescue mission, part investigation," Cpt. Sanders said to himself.

"We can—" Connor started to say.

"No, you three stay here," Cpt. Sanders said, walking away and pulling out his radio.

"Go get some lunch," Cpt. Miller said. "You look

like you need it. Meet back here in a couple of hours. We may still need your help."

"Yes, sir," Connor said.

Tank helped James stand, and they walked the three hundred yards to the Mess Hall in their gear. How could this keep happening? He'd begun to feel settled in this place. Just last night, he was thinking about how this could be their home, but then something like this happened and caused everything to be turned upside down. The Reclaimers needed to be taken care of once and for all. How else would they ever be able to make a life for themselves? That last question brought up even more questions. How had they found them? How many were there now? And why did Jezz want them so badly? So far, she hadn't tried to kill them. That first encounter had been a trap to catch them, alive. Had there been more to the slaughter out there? Or was Jezz just letting off steam or doing what she called "reclaiming"?

James was still absorbed in his thoughts when they entered the Mess Hall. He numbly took a tray and let the server dish up some food, even though he wasn't hungry. They sat down at a vacant table and he took a long pull of water to wash the rest of the bile down. James forced himself to eat in spite of the queasiness. He could go the rest of his life without seeing something like that again. There'd already been too many of those scenes.

"What would they gain from it?" Connor asked as he took a bite.

"I thought it was gonna be a trap," Tank said.

"Me too," Connor said. "And yet, here we are."

Tank shrugged. "I still think she's just crazy and

likes killin'.""

"It could be for shock value," James said, setting down his half-eaten sandwich.

"If so, it worked on you," Connor said.

"That's low, bro," James said.

"I was okay with your episode back there," Connor said. "But now you have to get up and prepare yourself because I can tell you one thing for sure—shit is about to go down. They wouldn't show their hand like that if they didn't have something planned."

James started to respond, but Tank cut him off, stopping the argument before it began.

"How did Emmett know the colony wanted to trade?" he asked.

"Someone radioed in yesterday," James said.

"It could've been the Reclaimers then," Tank said.

"Yep," Connor said. "It would've been a perfect trap."

"So how are we sitting here?" James asked. "Did we just not spring it?"

"Who knows," Connor said. "If it was a trap, they'd better step up their game."

Cook walked out of the kitchen, heading straight for their table.

"You get my stuff?" asked the large woman, holding a wooden spoon threateningly in one hand.

"No, ma'am," James said. "We went to the Red River Colony, but I don't think they had anything."

"You'd better not forget," Cook said.

"I wouldn't dream of it," James said. "Next time we get a run into town, I'll grab some."

"Good," Cook said. "Now eat the rest of your

sandwich. No one leaves here hungry on my watch."

"Yes, ma'am," James said, picking it up.

She watched him take a bite and then nodded, heading back into the kitchen. "Don't forget," she called as she disappeared through the doors.

"That's one helluva woman," Tank said with a laugh. "You'd better get her soda or she may beat you with that spoon."

"I wouldn't be surprised," James said.

They left the Mess Hall and James decided to go for a walk while the other two returned to Scourge. He still had an hour before they needed to be back. Moving helped him sort through his thoughts, yet no matter how he looked at it, he was having a hard time figuring anything out. On the one hand, he wanted to stay there and hoped that this place was truly safe so he could start a family and put down roots. At the same time, he just wanted to leave and get to Alaska where he *knew* it would be safe. He might be more inclined to leave if they didn't have a group of killers following them. By the time his hour was over and he was heading back to HQ, he hadn't figured anything out.

A couple of soldiers ran from the building, heading for the infirmary while a few Marines exited and stood by the front doors. Emmett stood over by the entrance to the building, talking with Cpt. Miller.

"What happened?" James asked Tank and Connor as he walked up to where they stood next to Scourge.

"No idea," Tank said.

"We're about to find out," Connor said.

The sound of multiple engines coming from the south reached their ears. Were they under attack? He had his answer soon enough as Cpt. Sanders's lead Humvee pulled to a stop right in front of them. The captain jumped out of the passenger seat and walked right up to James, who was standing between Tank and Connor.

"What—"

It was all James got out before a fist slammed into his gut, and he crumpled to the ground as his side exploded in pain. Cpt. Sanders swung again, but Tank stepped between him and James, shoving the little man back. James looked up through blurry eyes, his side on fire. Connor stood next to him with his hand on his handgun while Tank stood in front of him, fists raised.

"I wouldn't," Tank said to the smaller man.

Emmett and Cpt. Miller came running up.

"Stand down!" Cpt. Miller called out.

"Those bastards just got five of my men killed and another four wounded!" Cpt. Sanders yelled, red-faced.

"What?" Connor asked, moving his hand away from his gun.

"I said stand down!" Cpt. Miller said, looking between Tank and Cpt. Sanders.

Tank lowered his fists but didn't move from in front of James. Cpt. Sanders stormed off, walking towards the infirmary where another of the Humvees had gone.

"What's he talkin' about?" Tank asked as Connor helped James to his feet.

"There was a bomb in one of the small freezers," Cpt. Miller said. "It killed five Marines and wounded four others. It seems that it was a trap after all."

"And that's our fault?" Tank asked.

"No," Emmett said. "Sanders just doesn't want to take the blame right now, not that I can fault him much. Losing men is hard."

"Me neither," Cpt. Miller said. "But his reaction was uncalled for. Are you okay, James?"

"Yeah," James said. The pain in his side was decreasing and now his stomach ached. "The captain has one hell of a punch."

"It's surprising for his size," Cpt. Miller said.

A Marine ran up to Cpt. Miller and whispered something in his ear.

"Damn," Cpt. Miller said, looking at Emmett. "Col. Briggs is calling an emergency meeting. He wants you and Cpt. Sanders there."

"You can go ahead," Emmett said to Cpt. Miller. "I'll catch up."

"Roger," Cpt. Miller said. "You boys are dismissed for the day."

"Yes," Connor said, then added, "sir."

Cpt. Miller walked off and Emmett turned to them.

"That could've been us," James said.

"Yes, it could've," Emmett said. "Just like every time you go out."

"How're we supposed to go out on a run again knowing that the Reclaimers could've set up another bomb?" James asked, rubbing his aching side.

"You do what you do every day," Emmett said. "You gear up, walk out that door, and go to war to protect those you love. It's no different than what soldiers have been doing for years to keep our country free and protect their loved ones. Now you do it to protect others from what's beyond these walls—hell on earth. If you don't go out there, someone else will have to while you sit in here unable to come to terms with the fact that every moment you're alive is a gift that shouldn't be wasted. I thought you knew that, being religious men."

"They are," Tank said. "I'm not so much."

"It's just…" James began but didn't know how to put it into words.

"What?" Emmett asked. "Hard? Everything in life that's worth a damn is hard. Terrifying? You bet your ass it is, knowing that every time you say goodbye to your wife, daughter, mother, or brother could be your last; knowing that no matter what you face out there, you'll be bringing some of it back with you, no matter how you deal with it; knowing that even if you survived today, there's no guarantee for tomorrow.

"Don't think for one second that the absence of fear is courage. To quote a great man, 'Courage is being scared to death, but saddling up anyway.' That's what you have to do every single morning, whether you're going out on runs in the apocalypse or raising a family safe at home. Courage is something everybody has to choose every day that they face something that scares the hell out of them. So what're you going to do?"

Emmett locked eyes with each of them, looking at James last. The fire in his eyes and set of his face spoke just as much as his words had. James opened his mouth to respond when Emmett turned. "I know you'll figure this out," he said as he walked towards HQ. "You're warriors."

James stood there, completely shocked. How had Emmett spoken directly to his heart like that? Had what he was feeling been that obvious? He looked over at his brother and Tank.

"Did we just get mic dropped?" Tank asked.

Connor chuckled. "I think so."

James took a deep breath. This was far from over, and he was far from defeated. It had just hit home knowing that he'd walked within a few feet of a bomb that killed five good men. It very easily could've been them, but it hadn't been. He said a quick prayer of thanks and for future protection, as well as for the injured Marines. It'd been a long day already and it was only three in the afternoon.

31
THE GREATER GOOD

Emmett sat in a chair in Col. Brigg's office with Cpt. Sanders and Saul to his right. Col. Briggs wasn't what you'd expect from a man who commanded so much respect and loyalty from his men. He was average, plain even, with no distinguishing scars. He was neither tall nor well-muscled. If he walked down the street in civilian clothes, no one would even realize he was a full bird colonel who'd earned three purple hearts and a bronze star. He looked from Emmett to the other two.

"Sgt. Wolfe," Col. Briggs said, "you're here because you have knowledge about dealing with these Reclaimers, as they call themselves. That and because of your service record and the stellar recommendation of Cpt. Miller here. But make no mistake—your opinion will be taken as just that and nothing else. Is that understood?"

"Yes, sir," Emmett said.

"Good, then we can proceed, off the record," Col. Briggs said, looking to Cpt. Sanders. "What the hell just happened out there? Assaulting a civilian?"

"I'm sorry, sir," Cpt. Sanders said. He'd calmed down quite a bit since his outburst earlier.

"Sorry won't cut it, Captain," Col. Briggs said. "But that's a matter for another time. What happened at the Red River Colony? From the beginning."

"We received a radio call from them yesterday," Cpt. Miller said. "They had extra crops they were willing to trade for various supplies we had plenty of. I made the call to send our Scouting Team."

"Why did you send them?"

"I figured it was a better use of our manpower. They're effective, and it leaves more men here for protection if something were to happen."

"I can see that. So those three get there, then what?"

"They began to investigate the premises when they didn't see anyone around," Emmett said. "After searching one of the apartment buildings, they stumbled onto the bodies of roughly seventy of the residents."

"Seventy-six," Cpt. Sanders corrected. "All of the residents were inside."

"So they came back here, reported what they'd found, and then you got the green light to recover the supplies and any survivors. What happened when you arrived, Captain?"

"We found the colony just as they'd described it. I had men check all of the apartments and outbuildings. They found no survivors and no bodies. Someone, presumably these Reclaimers, had gathered up all of the residents, killing those who didn't cooperate, and put them in the dining hall. There, they opened fired and killed the rest. This was evident from the bullet holes in the walls and placement of the bodies. Quite a few had even been killed with a knife.

"After we'd established that the colony was clear, we began to load all the food into the Humvees. We emptied the walk-in freezer and cooler, then moved onto the smaller ones. It was inside one of those that a bomb was hidden. When Corporal Johnson opened it to empty out the contents, it went off, killing him and four others around him while wounding four more. We immediately gathered up the bodies and the wounded, and returned here."

"I'm sorry for your loss, Captain," Col. Briggs said, true emotion in his voice. "They'll be missed. Did you take the necessary precautions with the bodies of your men?"

"Yes, sir," Cpt. Sanders said. "They won't turn."

"Good," Col. Briggs said. "We have some decisions to make. Sergeant, do you know what these people want?"

It was odd being addressed as sergeant again. It'd been years.

"I don't know for sure," Emmett said. "But my guess is she's after us—James, Connor, and Tank especially."

"Why's that?"

"Most of our group was captured by them a couple weeks back. I and another of our group were able to rescue them, but we lost a few. James, Tank, Connor, and Chloe were following us and ran into the remaining Reclaimers. They killed them all but the leader, Jezz, and at least one other."

"They seek revenge then," Col. Briggs said. "Tell me about their leader."

"She's a psychopath, a truly insane individual.

She's also a clever leader and a cunning killer. If there was a bomb there, it was for a reason."

"It was a trap for those three, but my men were killed instead," Cpt. Sanders spat.

"You said that the incident at the US Customs Building in Sunburst was them as well?" Col. Briggs asked, looking at Emmett.

"Yes, sir," he said. "That one was them for sure."

"They're determined to have your men. How far will they go to get them?"

"I'm not sure," Emmett said. "Maybe as far as they have to."

"And where does that leave us?" Col. Briggs said.

"Caught in the crossfire," Cpt. Sanders said.

"What are you implying?" Emmett said, staring daggers at him.

"That all we need to do is kick those three out and we won't lose any more of our own," Cpt. Sanders said.

"Coward," Emmett growled.

Cpt. Sanders began to stand.

"Sit down, Captain!" Col. Briggs said in a voice that didn't leave any room for argument. He looked to Emmett. "The captain may have a point."

"You just want to kick them out?" Emmett asked, shocked.

"No, but if we asked them to leave, would they go?"

"Maybe, but I don't think so," Emmett said.

"But you could still ask. If they do, then it solves our problem and they get to continue on their way. Didn't they want to get to Alaska?"

"Yes, but things changed when we found this

place. It did for all of us."

"What if they don't want to leave?" Cpt. Miller asked.

"Then we'll cross that bridge when we come to it, but it may be in the best interest of all of us for them to leave."

"Whether they want to or not," Emmett stated, coldly.

"Possibly," Col. Briggs said.

"Whatever happened to 'leave no man behind'?" Emmett asked.

"That's in war, Sergeant, and they aren't my men. They're three strangers who stumbled into our community, bringing their problems with them. You have no idea the importance of keeping this place safe."

"This is disappointing," Emmett said. "I expected better."

"You of all people should understand having to make the hard choice for the greater good, *Sergeant*," Col. Briggs said.

Emmett shook his head. "That was another time and a completely different situation, but I get the hint. Is that all?"

"Yes. I can finish up with these two," Col. Briggs said. "Thank you for your assistance, Sergeant."

"It's just Emmett now," he said, standing and leaving the room.

That hadn't gone at all as he'd expected. Col. Briggs was giving them a choice, but how hard would he push to get them to leave? If Emmett asked them to leave, they wouldn't go. So then he'd explain the situation to them, tell them everything that had just happened. It would be the best choice for the community, but it'd mean almost certain death for them. No, he couldn't allow the colonel to kick them out and he wouldn't try to convince them to leave. They might not be the colonel's men, but they were *his* men, and he wouldn't leave them behind.

~~~

Alexis slumped into the chair, peeling off her bloody gloves and throwing them into the trash can as two Marines wheeled out the man she and Henry had spent the last—how many hours?—trying to save. It'd been fruitless. While Dr. Hart worked on the other three less injured patients, they'd tried to save Private Orden. She'd known from the beginning that he wouldn't survive. The wound in his chest was too severe. They had to try, however, and they'd done their best. Yet as the man's body was wheeled past her, she couldn't help but glance at the emotionless face. For a moment she didn't see the private's face but her brother's. She'd been powerless to save him as well.

This time was different, she told herself. *I tried this time. He just couldn't be saved.*

Even though she knew the words were true, they didn't alleviate the guilt inside of her for not saving Pvt. Orden. There were always questions about if she'd done this or done that, maybe he could've been saved. *Had* she done all she could?

"Was this your first one?" Henry asked, glancing at her.

"Yes," Alexis said.

"It does get easier," Henry said. "There was nothing we could've done differently."

"I know."

"Good. Don't forget it. Now, you need to get washed up and go get some sleep. You look awful."

"Thanks, I'm exhausted. What time is it anyway?"

"Seven forty-three."

"Wow, it's later than I realized."

"Time goes by quickly when someone's life is hanging in the balance. Don't worry about cleaning up. I'll send someone else to do it. You worked hard today."

"Thanks, but it'll help me unwind after all that."

"Suit yourself. I'll be leaving in ten if you want me to walk you out."

"Thanks, I'll be good."

"Okay then, enjoy cleaning."

Henry turned and left the room they used for surgeries. It was surprisingly well stocked. The military must've brought a lot of equipment with them, although it seemed like this stuff had been there for a while. She stood up and went to the sink, washing the blood from her arms. The water turned pink as it ran down the drain, mesmerizing her. If she moved past the guilt and worry that she hadn't done enough, she felt pretty good. She'd tried to help him, and that counted for something. This was what she'd spent her entire adult life pursuing, and she was finally able to make a very real contribution.

After going down to the supply closet to change into clean scrubs and put the others in a garbage bag, she went back upstairs. Henry had already changed, and he threw his scrubs in the bag as well while

Alexis picked Dr. Hart's up off the floor outside his office. After that, she took the garbage bag downstairs and gathered the necessary cleaning supplies from the supply closet. She went upstairs and began to scrub the blood off the floor. After an hour, she had it cleaned up and disinfected. She walked back to her desk and grabbed her jacket off the chair.

"Goodnight, Dr. Hart," Alexis said as she passed his door. He mumbled something in response that she couldn't hear.

Walking downstairs, she realized how exhausted and hungry she was. She just wanted to go home, take a shower, eat a bunch of food, and collapse onto her bed, but she couldn't. Tonight was going to be her best chance. She had an excuse to stay late and she *had* to use it. At the bottom of the stairs, she quickly looked around and then slipped into the partially open supply closet door. She'd been intentionally leaving it partway open since she started working there so people would get used to seeing it that way. Standing by the shelving, she looked through the crack at the lobby and hallway leading to the locked room. If anyone caught her, she'd tell them she was doing some last-minute stocking before she left.

Now the waiting began.

Luckily, it wasn't even an hour before she heard a door open upstairs. A few seconds later, Dr. Hart walked down the stairs, passing just in front of her. She held her breath and didn't even blink. He continued past her and turned into the hallway. At the locked door, he entered the code—five, nine, eight, three—and the door unlocked. He entered the vacant room.

The door closed behind Dr. Hart and she smiled. Her hunch had been correct; the doctor didn't leave the infirmary because he disappeared into the basement.

She gave it five minutes before she snuck out of the room and approached the door. Saying a quick prayer, she entered the code and the door unlocked. She hesitated just a moment before opening it and slipping inside.

32
DISCOVERIES

James sat alone on his cot in their place, the only light in the room coming in from the windows. His side was sore, but luckily the sucker punch hadn't reopened his old wound. The injury had healed past that point, although he still experienced a dull ache if he moved the wrong way. Connor and Tank were up at the saloon, like they were most evenings, but James hadn't been able to bring himself to go with them tonight. Maybe it would help him, or maybe it'd just be an escape. He wasn't there though because he needed to think. He had things to work through. It frustrated him to no end that his emotions were a rollercoaster from hell. One day he was feeling great about the world and the next he was back to feeling like he was completely alone. It was childish, and he needed to do something about it. Or maybe that was the problem—he wanted to do something about it, but he didn't have the control.

Not this again, he thought to himself.

It always seemed to come down to one word— trust. Maybe he should've gotten that tattooed on him somewhere so he could have a constant reminder. When things had gotten tough, even before the apocalypse, he'd always reacted first, getting angry or trying to fix it himself. It was only after he'd made things worse that he remembered it wasn't up to him. He couldn't do it alone then and he couldn't do it alone now. He needed help, but he hated to ask. He needed to surrender and trust, and yet he didn't want to let go of the illusion of control. Thinking back to the hilltop, he remembered he'd been through this before—recently. This same issue had played out just two weeks ago, and he'd forgotten already. Or maybe it wasn't so much that he'd forgotten but that he'd tried to take back control. Whatever the reason, he was tired of this merry-go-round he always found himself on. It was time to change that, so he did the one thing that always helped.

James prayed.

It started off like most of his prayers, asking for protection, guidance, and all that, but as he continued, something changed. He let down the walls around his heart and released his grip. He prayed like he hadn't in years, pouring out his heart before God. There was no surety in his faith, no non-disputable physical sign that his god was watching him or answering his prayer. There was always the chance that he was wrong and that his beliefs were all a sham. Yet, he knew that wasn't true. He *knew* Jesus heard him. He could *feel* a presence next to him, sitting on the same cot he was. His faith had always been the centerpiece of his life, even in those times when he forgot or wandered down the wrong path. But he always came back to the waiting arms of his Father.

As he prayed, his head bowed and tears streaming

down his cheeks, he made a choice. He would walk the straight and narrow path to the best of his ability, leaning on God the entire way. He would continue on past any hardship the world and Satan threw at him. It would be tough and he would have to constantly turn his eyes upward, yet he knew he could do it. With Jesus, he could do anything.

The minutes turned to hours and the room darkened as night settled on the town.

He opened his eyes, looking around the dark room. Wiping the tears from his cheeks, he stood up, stretched, and took a deep breath—a burden had been lifted from his shoulders. He wasn't alone in all this. It'd been tough, but over the last couple of hours he'd dealt with the doubts he held and the guilt he felt from all the deaths he couldn't stop or he'd caused, and he'd come to terms with the fact that these episodes were a part of him. They may be around for the rest of his life, but he wouldn't let them be a dark cloud hanging over him. He'd deal with them the same way he'd deal with everything else going forward—with prayer and faith, leaning not on his own strength but on the strength of one much stronger than he.

Walking slowly so he wouldn't trip over anything in the dark, he went to the switch by the door and turned it on. The light was extremely bright considering he'd been sitting in the dark for hours. A knock came at the door.

"James, you in there?"

It was Emmett, but there was something in his voice that seemed off. Had James done something wrong? He opened the door to see Emmett standing on the porch, the light from inside illuminating his face.

"Yes... sir?" James asked, studying him. He looked upset.

"Is Alexis here?" Emmett asked. James could tell he was trying to keep the anger out of his voice.

"No, sir."

"Are you sure?"

"Uhhh, yes," James said, looking back into the room behind him. "You can come in and check if you'd like."

Emmett marched through the door, looking around. It'd be hard to hide someone in the large, sparsely furnished room. The bathrooms would be the only place someone could hide, and that was where Emmett immediately went.

"Is something wrong?" James asked, shutting the door and walking into the middle of the room.

Emmett came out of the bathrooms. "I can't find my daughter."

"What do you mean?" James asked, getting anxious.

"We had plans for dinner."

"When was that?"

"Six. I expected her to be late with the wounded, but she never showed up. Dr. Nelson came into the Mess Hall a couple of hours ago and said Alexis should be along shortly. She never showed."

"You check your house?"

"It was the first place I looked. Then I checked the saloon and came here."

James cursed, remembering how she'd talked about the locked room in the infirmary. "I think I know where she might be, although I hope I'm wrong."

"Where?" Emmett asked, walking up to him.

"She's been investigating some suspicious goings-on in the infirmary basement. I told her to be careful, but..."

"I know my daughter, and she doesn't drop things easily."

"She's probably still there," James said, grabbing his gun belt and putting it on.

Emmett walked out the door and James followed.

~~~

Alexis looked around the room. Shelves full of supplies, mainly medications and other drugs, sat against the far wall, with the only other thing in the room being the door to the basement. It was a brand new metal door that would be nearly impossible to break into. There was a scanner next to it and no other visible way to open it. Pulling out the keycard she'd stolen from Dr. Hart's office, she held it in front of the scanner. The mechanism turned green and she heard the whirring of the lock as it pulled back into the door.

This was it.

If she got caught now, there was nothing she could tell them as to why she was there. Was this worth the risk? Definitely. There was something going on and she needed to know what. This place could never feel fully safe if they were hiding secrets.

Opening the door, she began to make her way down a circular metal staircase. When she reached

the bottom, she found herself in a long hallway that
stretched out before her. It turned to the left at the
end, with two doors leading to off the left side of the
hall. This wasn't what she'd expected. The whole
place looked immaculate, not like the musty old
basement it should've been. This hadn't been done
overnight, and she realized that the underground
facility had been built before the apocalypse ever
began.

Carefully starting down the hallway, she glanced
through the small window set in the first door. Inside
was a medium-sized room with tables and some
vending machines against the one wall. It looked like
a cafeteria. She moved on to the next door, peeking
through its window. It was a large laboratory with
three people in white coats working at the various
stations. There was a door at the back of the room
with a Vindex guard standing by it, and it appeared
that he was there to keep anyone from getting out of
the room. Moving on, she came to the bend in the
hallway and glanced around it.

There were three doorways going off to the right,
one door going to the left into the laboratory, and one
at the end of the hall. No one was in the hallway. She
snuck up to the first door to the right. This one didn't
have a window and didn't seem to be locked. Easing
the door open, she glanced inside. It looked to be a
small bedroom with bunk beds, two small dressers
and a nightstand. She closed the door and moved
down to the next one. The door at the end of the hall
was open a crack and voices drifted to her from
inside, but she was too far away to make them out. At
the next door, she repeated the process. It was

another bedroom, identical to the first. She moved onto the next doorway but stopped dead in her tracks. She recognized the voices coming from the room at the end. Figuring the last room was another bedroom, she ignored it and moved to the cracked door.

"I grow tired of living in this cage," said a man's voice. It was oddly familiar to her, but she couldn't place who it belonged to.

"The new facility is almost complete," said a gruff man's voice she didn't recognize.

"Good, it'll be a pleasant change from this," the first voice said. She really should know that voice.

"Any new developments?" another man asked. She recognized that one immediately—Dr. Hart.

"None," the first voice said. "I appreciate the new subject. We've been able to study the transformation firsthand."

"Is it as you feared?" asked the gruff-voiced man.

"Worse, I'm afraid," First Voice said. "The virus is evolving even more quickly than we anticipated."

"And you haven't found a way to stop it?" asked Gruff Voice.

"No."

"You developed this and yet you don't know how to cure it?"

"It wasn't supposed to get out. We'd only just discovered that it could be weaponized. There wasn't time to find or produce a vaccine."

"Doctor, time is up. We need you to find a way to stop this," Gruff Voice said.

"I'm trying, but nothing is working," First Voice said.

"You'd better find something, because we need

answers, soon."

"If you'd just let me talk to Emmett and the others, I'm sure they'd have vital information that could shed light on this. His group was out there for over a week. They have to have seen something."

"We can't do that," said Gruff Voice. "They'll have questions we're not ready to answer."

"You may want to think about this one, Clover. Your insistence on secrecy may be what causes our extinction," First Voice said.

"Your concern is duly noted, Albert, but you have one job here and that's to find a vaccine. Leave the rest to me and my men."

Albert? That name, that voice.

It can't be, Alexis thought.

Suddenly, it dawned on her. She *did* know that voice. The first man who'd spoken in the room was none other than Dr. Albert Hashen, her grandpa.

"I have to go," the man named Clover said. "We have a situation at the gate."

"What is it?" Dr. Hart asked.

"Emmett and one other person are here looking for your assistant," Clover said. "She went home, right?"

"I assume," Dr. Hart said. "I heard her go."

"My men at the gate haven't seen her leave," Clover said.

"She's still in the building?" Dr. Hart asked.

"So it seems. She doesn't know about this place, does she?" Clover asked.

"I don't think so," Dr. Hart said.

Alexis was pressed against the wall between the room the three men were in and the last bunkroom. She could tell the conversation was winding down and didn't know if she'd be able to make it back upstairs in time. Acting on instinct, she turned and dashed into the nearest bunkroom. It was empty like the others. Keeping the door cracked so she could peer out, she saw a heavily muscled man with a red beard exit the room.

"You better not hurt her," Albert said. "Your secrets aren't worth her life."

"We'll see," Clover said as he walked past the room Alexis was hiding in. He spoke into the earpiece he wore. "We have an uninvited guest in the building. Find her."

33
ANSWERS

Emmett stood outside the gate to the infirmary, using all his self-control not to barge past the two Vindex mercenaries. He just wanted to see his daughter, but they wouldn't even give him a straight answer. It was just an infirmary. Why was the security so tight? Unless Alexis *was* onto something. James had filled him in on their way down here, and he couldn't help but feel hurt. His daughter hadn't brought this to him. She hadn't even mentioned it when he'd seen her, not that he'd seen her much lately. He was so busy trying to make this place safe for her that he was finding less time to spend with her. That's why he'd planned the father-daughter date that night.

"Just tell me if she's still working," Emmett said to the two guards.

"Someone will be here to answer your questions soon enough," said one of the guards, a young man named Smiles.

"They better be," Emmett said, "or I'll be going through that gate in two minutes, whether you want me to or not."

The two guards looked at each other, gripping their ACRs a little tighter. Soon, the red-bearded

Vindex leader from the town meeting came out of the front door to the infirmary and started their way. The guards called the man Clover, but Emmett knew it was an alias.

"At ease, men," Clover said, walking up. "What can I do for you tonight, Mr. Wolfe?"

"Tell me where the hell my daughter is, Clover," Emmett said.

"That's a question I was hoping you'd have the answer to," Clover said.

~~~

Alexis watched through the crack as Dr. Hart left the room shortly after Clover and entered the laboratory through the door opposite her. She berated herself for forgetting about the dinner date tonight with her dad. In all the chaos of the four wounded Marines, it had slipped her mind. Hopefully, her dad wouldn't do anything stupid trying to find her. And she hadn't needed to hear that James was the other one with her dad. She just knew.

Acting once again on instinct, she left the safety of the dark room and walked into the office the two men had just left. There was a desk in the middle of the room and her grandpa was sitting behind it. A doorway led to a small bathroom on the left side of the room. Judging by the cot sitting against the right wall, she assumed this was where her grandpa was living. On the desk was a picture of her family before Mason's death and the divorce. Her dad and grandpa had always gotten along in the early years. They'd been a happy family back then—Jane, Emmett,

Albert, Mason, and her. It seemed like so long ago.

Her grandpa didn't look up from his desk, not even when she closed the door behind her. He'd always been extremely focused when he worked. Albert looked like he'd aged years in the few months since she'd last seen him. Even though he only lived thirty minutes away, she'd rarely seen him after the divorce because he came around less as the years passed. His skin was even paler than usual, and it seemed as though he'd shrunk a few inches, or maybe that was because he sat with a hunch to his shoulders. He looked defeated, not the excitable old man she remembered.

"I thought you were…" Albert said, trailing off as he glanced up. "Alexis! What are you doing here?" He glanced around nervously.

"I came to get answers," Alexis said, sitting down across the desk from him.

"You shouldn't be here," Albert said, getting up and locking the door behind her.

"How are you involved in something like this, Grandpa?" Alexis asked him as he sat back down. "I thought you wanted to help people."

"I did, and I still do," Albert said, looking down. "None of this was supposed to happen."

"None of what?"

"Any of it."

He looked up at her, staring into her eyes. The once proud way he held himself was gone, replaced by a regretful old man. What'd happened to make him this way? Some of her anger abated as she looked at the man who'd always been kind to her.

"I'm glad to see you're alive, Grandpa Al," Alexis

said.

He smiled at that. "It's good to see you too, sweetie."

"Will you tell me what's going on?" Alexis asked.

"I can't. There's more at play here than even I know."

"Please, Grandpa. We need to know."

Albert gazed into her eyes and then took a deep breath, letting it out slowly.

"Okay," he said. "But can I have a hug first? I didn't know if I'd ever see you again until I heard you'd come into town."

"Of course," Alexis said, standing up and walking around the desk.

He stood up and wrapped his arms around her. Her head rested against his chest, so maybe he hadn't shrunk after all. He held her for a solid minute, slowly stroking her hair. Finally, he broke the embrace and stepped back with tears in his eyes.

"You remind me so much of your mother when she was young," Albert said, sitting down. "Can you tell me how she died?"

"How'd you know?" Alexis said, sitting again.

"I sent men to get her from the house when this all started, but she was gone. I knew Emmett wouldn't have left without you or her, no matter their differences. And when you showed up in Coutts without her or George, I connected the dots."

"She was bitten," Alexis said, surprised at the tears that came to her eyes. "Dad tried to save her, but she died anyway."

Albert just nodded, more tears brimming behind his glasses. "I told myself to reconcile the fact that you were all gone, but when you came into town, I couldn't believe it. How did you get here?"

"That's a story for another time," Alexis said. "What are *you* doing here?"

"A good question," Albert said, wiping the tears from his eyes. "I can't tell you all of it for fear that they might do something drastic, but maybe I can give you enough to make a difference. Just don't tell anyone I told you. If word gets out…"

"Does it really even matter anymore?"

She thought about telling him that she'd already overheard some of their conversation but decided not to. Best if he was kept somewhat in the dark. She thought she could trust her grandpa but not the other men running this place.

"No, I guess not," Albert said with a sigh.

"Who's in charge of all this?"

"The Vindex Corporation. They're the ones who paid for all the research and supplied the protection."

"What research?"

"You have to understand, I did this to help people. I didn't know what was going to happen."

"Just tell me, Grandpa."

She suddenly remembered a conversation with her dad when they'd been locked in the basement at Safe Haven with Ana. When her father worked for LifeWork, he'd seen them experimenting on people and had watched as the patients came back to life. He said it was something about a new drug to cure everything. She almost spoke up again, but stopped. She wanted to hear it from her grandpa first to see if it lined up.

"LifeWork doesn't just produce pharmaceutical

drugs. We also have a division that does testing for new drugs. A few years ago, we were approached by Vindex. They were worried that our enemies were producing a biological weapon that we'd be helpless against. They wanted us to find the vaccine for this new virus. The problem was that they didn't know much about it, just bits and pieces. We started testing, trying to create a virus like the one they were worried about. We stumbled onto something a couple of months ago."

"A virus?"

"Not just a normal virus but one that eventually kills the host. Then, it somehow brings them back, only they aren't the same. They're mindless killers."

"How is it possible?"

"It's not, and that's what scared us. We still don't know what it is, except that it's a virus unlike any the world has ever seen. Even after working frantically for these past few months, we still don't have a vaccine for it, and there's no way to combat it or reverse its effects. We're continuing to search, but time is running out."

"What do you mean time is running out?"

"The virus is evolving," Albert said, his eyes showing true fear. "It's why we haven't been able to figure it out. Every few hosts, it mutates—some small change that's barely noticeable at first. It's impossible to anticipate."

"Then how do you stop it?"

He shook his head and then suddenly looked at her as his eyes widened. "You've been out there. You've seen it. Explain to me all you've seen with the infected—the symptoms they show, the way they act, anything that might help us learn more."

She explained everything she'd seen over the past three weeks—how they only seemed to truly die with a headshot, the way they walked and acted, and anything else she could think of. After she finished, she added, "Some of the survivors I'm traveling with even said some people have turned without being bitten or scratched. And some turn quicker than others."

"Yes, that's very astute of them. The incubation time is different, depending on a lot of factors—the location of infection, heart rate, age, blood type, body temperature, external—" Albert suddenly stopped talking and looked directly at her. "They turned even if they *weren't* bitten? Are you sure of this?"

"No, but they seemed to think so," Alexis said, looking confused at her grandpa's excitement.

"That's it!" Albert said, standing up suddenly. "That's how the cities are being infected from the inside."

"I don't understand."

"It's mutated again," Albert said and looked at her, his excitement fading, replaced by dread. "It's gone airborne. Everyone who comes into contact with the hosts will contract the virus."

"Then why aren't we all turning?"

He cocked his head. "Good point, unless... maybe it's not the same virus, or maybe it's different if you get a direct infection instead of just part of it. Like how airborne particles of peanuts can cause some people to have an allergic reaction, but it's not the full reaction they'd have if they were to ingest it. What if the virus is dormant until the host dies and then it sets off a reaction in the brain that activates it?"

Alexis looked at him, the implications fully sinking in. "So we all have the virus and turn if we die?" she asked.

"That's the assumption, but I need to run some tests."

"Why don't you know more? You created it."

"I didn't. One of my scientists did, and he disappeared just before all this began."

"So how did the virus get out?"

"We're not sure. It started around our facility near home, then suddenly broke out across the nation. The only guess I have is that somehow our pharmaceutical drugs came into contact with the virus."

"You had the virus by your medications?"

"Of course not! It was in a completely different building, but one careless doctor not following protocol could've caused it."

"So you don't even know for sure?"

"That's beside the point now," Albert said, walking towards the door. "You need to go before they find you, and I need to go run some tests. You've given me an idea."

"Wait, how'd you get here?"

"They brought me up in a helicopter from the facility near Hill City once all this started. They wanted to get me as far away from it as possible once containment failed. They even brought Dr. Hart up."

A light bulb clicked in her head. She'd seen Dr. Hart in passing while in Hill City this summer.

"I knew I recognized him! He was the new doctor

in town."

"Yes, you probably didn't see him much since he only moved to town a year ago when you were in school."

"But why is Vindex here?"

"They had this facility ready for us, maybe as a backup plan in case things ended up the way they did. I know they're finishing a much larger facility about an hour from here. Beyond that, they've kept me in the dark."

"Thanks for talking with me, Grandpa," Alexis said, standing and giving him another hug. "It helps to know."

"You're welcome, sweetie," Albert said. "I know you have to tell those close to you, but be careful who you trust. If this gets back to me or you, we'll have some serious problems."

"I'll be careful."

"Now, to get you out of here," Albert said, looking at her and then around the room.

~~~

James stood next to Emmett as they waited on the Vindex mercenary Emmett had called Clover to give them an update. He'd told them they didn't know where Alexis was, but he was going to have his men search the entire building. James could tell that it was killing Emmett to just sit by. Hell, it was killing him, too, but he couldn't do anything about it. Clover wouldn't let them inside, saying something about it being after hours or some other crap. The man was a large, well-muscled weasel, and he didn't trust him.

Then again he didn't trust any of those men. They had their own motives, and he knew it. It was supposed to take only five minutes to check the building, but fifteen minutes later they were still looking.

Clover cocked his head, listening to his earpiece. He glanced at Emmett. "It seems—" Clover began but cut off, turning as the front door to the infirmary opened.

Alexis walked out, yawning and rubbing her eyes. She looked unharmed and healthy, although exhausted. She came down the steps slowly and walked over to them.

"Sorry, Dad," Alexis said, walking past Clover. "I fell asleep in one of the old classrooms. It's been a long day."

"That's okay, honey," Emmett said.

James watched Clover's eyes narrow as Alexis showed the guards her ID card. The guard, Smiles, briefly glanced at his boss, who gave a subtle nod. They let her through and one went into the small guard shack, returning with her gun belt. She took it and walked over to James and Emmett.

"Let's go home," Alexis said, stifling another yawn.

James took her hand and the two of them started to walk down the driveway. Emmett stayed behind and said something to Clover when they were out of earshot. James continued walking and Alexis laid her head on his shoulder as they went, leaning on him.

"You that tired?" James asked.

"It's been a long day," Alexis said under her breath. "I'll tell you more about it once we get home."

"So you did go looking," James whispered. She didn't react, but he knew the answer. "I hope it was worth it because that guy back there—Clover—is the leader of Vindex, and he suspects something."

"Oh, it was."

34
Hornet's Nest

Tank lay in bed with an arm around Chloe, wearing nothing but the sheets that covered them. He smiled as she nuzzled into his neck. How had he gone from trying desperately to get out of Fort Collins at the start of this to being safe with a girl he was quickly falling in love with? He'd known this was going to be a new start for him—hence the new name, no matter how ridiculous some people thought it was—but he'd never imagined that it'd turn out like this, not in his wildest dreams. He wasn't going to complain about it though. He'd take all he could get.

He glanced over at the nightstand where the picture of the Wolf Pack she'd taken earlier today sat in a frame. She'd gotten it printed up at HQ and had a copy for each of them, plus this framed one. Next to it rested one she'd taken of the two of them a few days ago when they'd made things official. She was one hell of a woman.

"Why Tank?" Chloe asked.

"What?" he asked, leaning up on one elbow to gaze at her.

"Why did you pick that name?'"

"Oh, that's easy. Tank was my call sign in the Wolf Pack. We all had 'em. Plus, I felt it summed up my personality and physical appearance perfectly."

"But why even change your name? Why not just go by Allen?"

Tank shifted, looking away from her. Was he sure he wanted to go down this road? He was opening himself up to her and the old fears were returning. What if she cut out his heart? What if she devastated him? What if she left him? The final question really hit home and he felt the fear grip him tighter. He was giving her too much power, showing too much of himself, which could only end one way—a broken heart and years of pain to deal with.

"You don't have to tell me if you don't want," Chloe said, running a hand down his arm.

"No," Tank said, battling down the fear.

He would *not* let himself turn back now, not after all the progress he'd made. The mountain had to be climbed because he was tired of living down in the valley. Things had to change, just like he'd told himself the night he left his old life behind. Not just physical or surface changes, but life-changing stuff.

"Allen is my dad's name," Tank said after taking a deep breath. "He always called me junior, and I both loved and hated it. Then he left, and I wanted nothin' to do with him or that name. I still don't."

"Don't you think some of that anger is misplaced?" Chloe asked in a soft voice.

"How do ya figure that?"

"Maybe you do miss him and wish he was still alive, but you don't want to admit it. Or maybe you wish you'd made more of an effort to see him before all this happened."

"Damn girl, you aren't pullin' any punches, are ya?"

"I'm just trying to help you work through all this. I don't want you to have to run anymore."

"Fair enough. Yes, that's some of it. I wish I'd at least seen him once before all this. All I have are memories of who he was, nothin' about who he is now. Well, now he's dead, but just before this."

"Do you think he changed?"

"It seemed like it on the phone when he called a couple of years ago, but he was always good at fakin' things like that. I didn't trust him then, and I'm not sure if I would now either."

"So you didn't have anyone but your mom growing up?"

"My stepdad was there, but we never connected like he or I wanted. My stepbrother was older by five years and wasn't around much. Of course, once I met James and then Connor, we connected. But other than them, I just had my grandpa."

"You haven't talked about him much."

"It's painful. We were always close. He lived in Michigan, where my mom was from. We went back to see him and our other family there sometimes, and he'd spend summers with us in Colorado. He loved to go fishin' and we spent a lot of time out on the water. Those were some good memories. He taught me a lot about fishin' and life on those trips."

"He sounds like a great man. What happened to him?"

"He died a few years ago, old age. It was hard for my mom and I right after that. We were both really close to him. Shortly after that, my mom found out she had cancer. It was a rough couple of years."

"I can imagine. What was your mom's name?"

"Duh, I forgot to even tell you their names. My mom was Lynda and my stepdad is Grant. My grandpa was Carter. I always loved that name. If I ever had a son, I'd want to name him that."

"That is a good name."

"What about your parents? You haven't told me much of your past either."

Chloe closed her eyes. "I don't like to talk about my past. It's too painful."

"Seems like I'm not the only one."

She opened her eyes, staring up into his. It seemed like she drew strength from the look. "My parents were harsh people. My mom used to abuse me and my dad."

"Wait, what?" Tank asked, raising an eyebrow.

"Yes, I know it sounds backwards, but my mom was a real bitch. She never touched us, but she didn't need to. Her tongue was even more deadly. It broke my dad down to a spineless coward who didn't stand for anything. He was more like a shell of a man than a real one."

"Wow." He was taken aback by the pure venom in her voice.

"You know what my dad used to tell me? 'Trust no one. They'll disappoint you.' Try growing up when that's the most encouraging thing your father ever said to you. I listened to that for years before I realized how messed up it was. Then I did my best to be the complete opposite of them, but it didn't work well. I'm just not a super nice person."

"I think you're nice."

"Shut up," Chloe said, punching him in the shoulder. "I'm not like my parents, but I'm also not going to go out of my way to be kind to people."

"You shouldn't have to. You should be true to who you are. Just look at me—I'm a complete asshole."

Chloe laughed, wiping tears from her cheeks. "You are not. That's not even who you are; it's to cover up who you are."

"Partly, but it *is* part of who I am. You don't see me goin' around shovin' rainbows up people's asses, do ya? They can take me for who I am or shove off."

"That's what I like about you. You are who you are, and you don't try to be anything else. It's endearing."

"Thanks. It took quite a few years of bein' a cynic, but I got it down now."

She laughed and he smiled. All it'd taken for him to find a girl was the end of the world. Better late than never.

~~~

"It's airborne?" Emmett asked, sitting next to James on the couch as Alexis finished telling them about what she'd discovered.

"He's not sure, but that's what he thought," Alexis said, sitting across from them in her living room.

"That would explain how the ones not bitten would come back," James said.

"Then why haven't we all turned?" Emmett asked.

"He thought maybe it was a different strain or not

293

as potent."

"That would explain a lot," Emmett said. "You told him about your mother?"

"Yeah."

"How did he react?"

"He was sad, but he knew it as soon as we came into town without her."

"Can you trust him?" James asked.

"Albert may be in way over his head, but he's not a bad man," Emmett said. "Misguided and sometimes indifferent, but not evil."

"I think they took Mark," Alexis said, speaking the fear she'd had since she overheard the conversation. "They talked about having a new 'test subject.' I think they infected him to study the virus."

"Do you know that for certain?" Emmett asked.

"No, but I have a feeling."

Emmett nodded. "Vindex is capable of that, and so is Albert."

"You sound certain," James said.

"I am," Emmett said. "I've seen them do it before."

"What?" James asked. "How?"

"I used to work for LifeWork as one of their private security personnel. Albert hired me personally to help me out after I left the service. While I was there, I saw them experimenting on people."

"That explains how you were so prepared," James said.

"Exactly," Emmett said. "I saw enough to worry me. I tried to get an investigation into the company started, but they had power high up because it never went anywhere. When I worked there, they said they were developing a drug to cure everything. It makes a lot more sense now that it was a cover-up for the real goal."

"It was never a drug," Alexis said. "It was a virus that somehow came into contact with their drugs."

"They claim it was an accident?" James said. "No way. Has to be more to it."

"Probably is," Emmett said. "Is that all he said?"

"Yeah," Alexis said. "Oh, and Dr. Hart is from Hill City."

"Really?" Emmett said. "I don't recognize him."

"Grandpa said he was new to town, and you know how you could go weeks, sometimes months, without seeing anyone."

"I guess that's true. I need to talk to Saul," Emmett said, standing.

"Dad, he warned us to not tell too many people."

"I trust Saul. If they're experimenting on people, he needs to have safeguards in place," Emmett said, walking over to Alexis and giving her a big hug. "I love you, sweetie. We'll have to do our dinner date tomorrow night."

"I'll plan on it," Alexis said. "I love you too, Daddy."

He smiled at that. "Sometimes I forget you're a woman now and not my little girl."

"I'll always be your little girl."

His smile widened. "That you will."

"I need to go tell my brother and Tank," James said, standing up. "They need to know."

"I agree," Emmett said.

"Come by after a bit and we can go for a walk," James said to Alexis.

"I'd love that," Alexis said, giving him a quick kiss on the cheek.

"Come on, lover boy," Emmett said, holding the door open for him.

"Yes, sir," James said, walking out.

"Daddy," Alexis said, giving him a look.

He shrugged his shoulders and shut the door, walking down the porch to stand by James. "I apologize for insinuating you were with my daughter earlier. Those papa-bear instincts kicked in."

"Nothin' to apologize about," James said, sticking his hand out. "I would've done the same thing if it was my daughter."

"I know," Emmett said, shaking the offered hand, "which is why I'm allowing you to continue to date her. You remind me of myself when I was younger."

James smiled. "Thanks."

"That wasn't wholly a compliment."

James laughed. "I'll take it, either way."

Emmett chuckled, starting off towards HQ. "Be careful, James. We're stirring the hornet's nest, and there's no telling what might come out."

"I will," James said as he started towards his place.

35
BEHIND THE GUN

Connor lay on his cot, embraced in an intoxicated state. It was enough to make him feel good but not enough to make him forget. He didn't drink to forget; he drank to help him think, not to mention that it helped him relax. He needed that, especially after a day like this one. His contemplations were broken after a time as the door opened and the lights flicked on.

"What the hell," Connor growled and closed his eyes against the sudden brightness.

"Sorry, bro," James said, walking in and sitting down on his cot. "Forgot you were a vampire."

"Just enjoying the dark," Connor said, sitting up. He could tell by his brother's voice that he wanted to talk. He hoped it wasn't like the last time.

"I know how all this started," James said.

"The apocalypse?" Connor asked, the sudden spike in interest driving some of the effects of the alcohol from his mind.

"Yep," James said.

James spent the next fifteen minutes telling him how Alexis had snuck into the basement and about meeting her grandpa. He continued, telling Connor about the conversation between them and the leader of the Vindex mercenaries and then what Emmett had witnessed while working there. Connor asked him a couple of questions here and there. It was just as they'd thought—the Vindex Corporation *did* have their hands in all this.

"We need to tell Tank," Connor said after James finished. The whole conversation had been a literal buzz kill, but one that he was glad to have.

"I was going to tell both of you at once, but I assume he's with Chloe," James said.

"Yeah, we can tell him in the morning," Connor said.

A knock sounded at the door.

"James?" Alexis said from the other side.

"I'll be back in a few," James said, standing.

"Take your time," Connor said as he picked up his ACR, checking the chamber and then setting it down under his cot.

James opened the door, leaving Connor to his musings. If Vindex found out they had this information, things could get ugly—real ugly.

~~~

James took Alexis by the hand and they started walking down North Avenue, heading towards the west where he'd set up the bench for their first date. With everything going on, he'd forgotten to take it back, so they might as well use it again.

"How are you doing?" James asked.

"Honestly, I'm doing well," Alexis said. "I was finally able to get some answers. It feels good knowing it's just a conspiracy."

James chuckled. "Yeah, *just* a conspiracy. No big deal."

"It could be worse. A psychotic priest could be sacrificing people to the infected."

"Good point. This is a little better than that. But you ever think about what happens when Vindex figures out that you know?"

"Once they find out, they'll know I've told people and won't kill us all."

"I hope not, but you never know with these kinds of people."

"So how was your day?"

"Pretty bad."

James told her about the run to the colony and then the bomb.

"I knew about the bomb, but I didn't realize it was where you guys had been. How are you holding up?"

"A lot better now. Jesus and I finally had a good heart-to-heart."

"I was wondering when that was going to happen."

"It was a long time comin'," James said.

They sat there in silence for a few minutes, just enjoying the quiet of the small rural town. James looked over at Alexis. The overcast sky made it hard to see as there was no moonlight, but he could make out her features in one of the porch lights a block to the south. She had her hair up in a ponytail, which she usually did when she was working, and her eyes glistened in the light as she turned to look at him. A phrase started to rise in this throat and he almost blurted it out before he could stop himself.

Get ahold of yourself, he chastised himself. *It's only been a few days. You can't say that yet!*

She smiled at him, and it melted his heart. He had leaned in for a kiss when something sounded in the night. At first it was just once, but a second later more joined the first—gunshots.

~~~

Tank was lying in bed, enjoying the warmth of Chloe's body. After their little emotionally intimate moment, they'd enjoyed another kind of intimate moment, which was honestly the best he'd ever had. Maybe that had something to do with them opening up to each other. If it always felt that good, maybe he should open up more often. He smiled at the thought, yawning. Chloe was already asleep and had been for thirty minutes or so. His mind wouldn't let him sleep yet, but he just about had it convinced. That'd always been a problem of his—he was a night owl. His eyelids began to droop and he closed them.

He bolted awake, sitting up. How long had he been out?

Chloe stirred next to him.

"What is it?" she asked, sleepily.

"Shhhh," Tank said, shushing her.

There it was again. It sounded like fireworks going off, and it took a second for it to register. Those were gunshots!

Tank cursed loudly, jumping out of bed.

"What?" Chloe asked again, still groggy but more awake this time.

"Gunshots," Tank said.

"So? They might just be taking down some of the undead," Chloe said.

"They don't shoot them," Tank said, slipping his underwear on and then his pants.

There was more gunfire now, and it was coming from multiple locations.

"Stay inside," Tank said, leaning over and giving Chloe a quick kiss.

"I will," she said. "Be careful out there."

"Will do," Tank said, slipping his shoes on and not wasting time with his shirt. "Love ya, babe."

He was out the door of her bedroom and almost to the front door when it registered what he'd just said.

Ah, hell. I really just said that.

The thought was pushed from his mind when he exited the house, the warm summer night air embracing him. The gunfire was even louder outside, and it was coming from the east. He ran south, and once on North Avenue, he looked to the east. He could see the muzzle flashes outside the fence and soldiers and Marines on the inside, firing back. More men ran from the barracks to the north and south towards the eastern fence where the gunfire was concentrated.

They were under attack.

~~~

Connor climbed into Scourge, decked out in his full kit, with James and Tank's gear in the back seat. He cursed himself for not asking where James was going. His brother could be anywhere out there, and he had no way to find him. The gunfire was coming from the east, so if he went in that direction, hopefully, he'd run into them. It wasn't like his brother or Tank to run from a fight. He started the vehicle and pulled out, speeding down the street.

It was a good thing Tank didn't have his shirt on or Connor might not have seen him and he might have ended up a bloody smear in the middle of the road.

Tank ran around to the passenger side and hopped in.

"Your gear's in the back," Connor said. "Why were you in the middle of the damn street?"

"I was lookin' at the gunfire," Tank said, slipping his plate carrier over his torso. "I'm glad you didn't kill me with my own baby."

"Me too," Connor said, slowing as they approached the other side of town. "You see James?"

"No," Tank said. "Not back at our place?"

"No, he's out with Alexis."

"He have anythin'?"

"Just his handgun."

"That'll have to do. Your ARs are still at the house, if he needs them."

Connor nodded, looking at the scene before them.

It looked like the gunfire was mainly coming from the train tracks southeast of their location. There were train cars that their assailants were using for cover. He pulled Scourge down an alley, shut it off, and hopped out. Grabbing his helmet from his pack, he attached his night-vision goggles to the top. Tank did the same and they slipped their helmets on, heading down the alley. He approached the open street, noticing the soldiers who had taken cover against the solid part of the fencing around town and against the nearest buildings.

Connor took a knee, using the corner of the building he was next to as cover, and scanned the train cars. The people attacking them were skilled, and they didn't show themselves long enough for him to get off a shot. How he wished the goggles had thermal as well.

An explosion rocked the night back to the west. A second later another one sounded more to the north, then one to the south.

"What the hell was that?" Tank asked.

~~~

Emmett crouched behind the cover of an LAPV in the parking lot above HQ. Saul came running out of the building, bringing him an M4. He tossed it to Emmett who caught it. Rising up onto the hood of the vehicle, he aimed to the northeast where the gunfire was coming from and waited. One of their attackers' muzzles flashed in the darkness. Emmett immediately acquired his target and fired a barrage around that location. He wasn't sure if he'd hit the man, but it would have been close if he hadn't. Another muzzle flashed in the night and Saul sent a volley at that one as Emmett waited for the first attacker to shoot again. There were more men further up the train cars, but he couldn't get an angle on them from his position.

Who would be attacking them? Would the Reclaimers be this bold? They had to know they couldn't take on a fully armed town with military support. Then again, they *were* led by a bloodthirsty psychopath.

"Just like old times," Saul said, smiling next to him. "It's been too long since I've been able to hold one of these."

"You've probably lost your touch," Emmett said, firing at a muzzle flash in the night.

"Not a chance," Saul said.

"What the hell is going on?" Clover said, jogging over to them from down the street.

"What the hell do you think?" Saul said. "We're under attack."

Emmett watched the red-bearded man coming towards them. He didn't really like the man, but he could tell that he was former military and respected him for that, even though he was now working for a less than honorable company. Clover suddenly jerked, blood spraying out his back as he collapsed to the ground. The shot had come from the south, and he hadn't even heard it.

"Sniper to the south!" Emmett yelled, running for the fallen man.

"Covering fire!" Saul yelled, shooting towards where the round had come from.

A round slammed into the ground where Emmett had just been. He didn't slow as he grabbed hold of Clover's plate carrier by the shoulder straps and hauled him behind the nearest vehicle. The shooter had gotten him in the shoulder, but the wound wouldn't be fatal.

"Thanks," Clover said as Emmett propped him up against the side of the truck.

"No problem," Emmett said. "Tell your men there's a sniper to the south."

"Roger," Clover said.

"Saul," Emmett called out. "You have a radio to talk to your men?"

Emmett scanned the darkness to the south, looking for a muzzle flash, but he couldn't find anything. Either the man was reacquiring another target or relocating.

"Saul!" Emmett called out louder. "You have a radio?"

Still no answer, so Emmett looked around the edge of the truck. Over by the LAPV they'd been using for cover, Saul lay with blood leaking around his chest. Emmett ran for his friend, grabbing ahold of him and dragging him around the side of the rig. A bullet slammed into his shoulder and he almost lost his grip on Saul, but he held on, grunting through the pain and making it around the LAPV. Kneeling down, he felt for a pulse. There wasn't one. Sitting back on his heels, he grabbed at his shoulder, putting pressure on the wound while looking down at the bullet hole in Saul's chest.

Three explosions rocked the night.

36
ATTACK

James was crouched behind the bench, about to take off towards the gunfire to the east when a grunt sounded behind him. He turned around and looked into the night, trying to identify what had made the noise.

"What is it?" Alexis asked from behind the bench they'd been sitting on.

"I'm not sure," James said, ducking down. "I heard something over by the fence."

"Let's check it out," Alexis said.

"All the gunfire is over there. We need to go help out."

"Maybe the gunfire is to draw people's attention from something else."

She had a good point. "Okay, let's go, but be careful, and stick to cover."

He cursed himself for not having a rifle with him. With the 1911 handgun in his hands, he ran for a line of brush on the side of someone's yard. Once there, he aimed towards the fence where he'd heard the noise as Alexis came up behind him. They moved from the brush to a shed next to where a dirt road was cut off by the fence. Setting his shoulder against the shed, he poked his head out. Was that a body lying just inside the fence?

He crouched and came around the side of the shed in a run as Alexis made it to him. A head popped up over the other side of the solid base of the fence and James raised his handgun, firing as he ran. The man shouldered his rifle and let loose a fully automatic barrage at him. James dove for the dirt, landing hard. He crawled into the ditch on the side of the road, which didn't offer him a lot of cover but was better than nothing. The man stopped firing so James aimed in his general direction and let off a few rounds. He needed to be careful since he only had two extra magazines with him. At that moment, he wished he had a 9mm Glock with double-stacked magazines that held seventeen rounds each.

The man behind the fence fired back at him, and James covered his head as bullets slammed into the dirt all around him. None hit him, which was a first. Usually, he was a bullet magnet. Maybe he shouldn't return fire since that seemed to make the bad guy shoot at him, but if the guy didn't want to kill him, what was he doing? He got his answer a second later when an explosion blew up the fence twenty yards in front of him.

Instantly, his ears started ringing and a bright light dominated his vision. James lay there, completely disoriented as someone came over and grabbed him. He weakly fought back, not understanding what was going on, but he stopped struggling when he realized it was Alexis dragging him back to the cover of the shed. Smoke and dust filled the air as debris rained down around them. Finally, he gained his feet and she helped him to the shed where he slammed against the wall, slumping down.

"Are you okay?" Alexis yelled, but James barely heard her.

He shook his head, his senses slowly returning. He'd been a dozen yards away from that explosion, but it still rocked his world. Standing up, he checked his holster. His handgun wasn't there. It'd been in his hands when the explosion went off. He glanced out and saw it lying in the middle of the road only a few feet away.

"Cover me," James said to Alexis.

Not waiting, he ran out and scooped up his handgun, then ran back to cover. The man hadn't even shot at him. That was weird.

"What's that?" Alexis asked, cocking her head.

It took James a moment to realize she'd heard something.

"I can't hear," James said. "What is it?'

"Sounds like a big engine," Alexis said, looking worried. "It's coming this way."

James glanced out from the side of the shed and saw something glinting in the darkness a few hundred yards out. He could hear it now as the ringing in his ears began to abate somewhat.

"We need to get back to that house we passed. We're too exposed out here," James said. "You go first and I'll cover you."

"Okay," Alexis said, taking off at a run.

James leaned out from behind the shed and emptied his magazine in the man's direction. No one shot back. After Alexis had made it to the house, he ran after her, reloading once he was there. Going around to the front of the house, James glanced at where the explosion had gone off. There was a large gap in the fence, and out of the darkness, a shape materialized. A semi-trailer was backing up through it. Once the entire rig was inside the fence, two men jumped out. They ran to the back of the trailer, one covering the other while he began to open the large door.

"I go high, you go low," James said.

Alexis nodded and he took a deep breath.

James swung around the corner at the same time Alexis did, but she was on her knees. He fired at the man opening the door to the trailer, thirty-some yards away. Alexis must have been aiming at him as well, because bullets thumped into the door around him and a couple tore through his body. He fell to the ground and the second man opened fire at them with a combat rifle. Bullets slammed into the side of the house, throwing up splinters of wood. James ducked back behind cover and checked his magazine. He only had three more rounds, plus the one in the gun. Slamming it back in, he looked down at Alexis.

"You okay?" he asked.

"Yeah," Alexis said. "Ready?"

He nodded and they leaned around the corner, opening fire again. The man who'd been shooting at them had the door ajar and used it for cover as it swung open. Zombies began to pour out of the back of the trailer. James's magazine ran dry and he swung back behind the house. He ejected the spent magazine and slapped in a new one. By the time he was aiming again, the man was gone and the zombies, drawn to their gunfire, were stumbling towards them. There were dozens of them and still more piled out, falling the few feet to the ground.

"We need to get to my place," James said, slipping back around the corner.

"Wouldn't that take us right past them?" Alexis asked while reloading.

"Yeah, but we can cut through the field and keep a good distance," James said. "We just need to go now."

"Lead on," Alexis said, determination in her eyes.

Damn, I love this woman, James thought.

"Keep up," he said, smiling as he burst around the corner of the house, heading towards his place.

The zombies had swarmed the road around the semi, and all of them—around fifty—were either coming at them or heading straight into town, drawn by the gunfire to the east. The ones that *weren't* coming at them were more of a problem since they were blocking the path to James's place and his rifle that waited inside. Those zombies soon adjusted their paths when they caught sight of the two of them running from the house. Even though the things were usually slow, they were in a frenzy at this point and had picked up a little speed. Given their numbers, James and Alexis wouldn't make it to his place before they were swarmed.

"Change of plans," James said to Alexis, who was beside him. "Cut across the field into town. We'll take the long way around."

Alexis nodded as they adjusted their course, running across the grassy field. A Marine came from the south along the fence. He opened fire, picking off a few of the zombies and causing more to veer for him. Another Marine soon joined the first, and James was grateful for the help. But from the darkness beyond the fence, a muzzle flashed in rapid succession and the Marines fell.

"Get down," James said, grabbing Alexis and falling to the ground as bullets flew over their heads.

James landed first with Alexis on top of him, driving the air from his lungs. He gasped as she rolled off, staying low to the ground. She began to crawl through the knee-high grass towards the backyards on the other side of the field. He rolled over and followed her, his ribs aching. The zombies were still coming after them, and they were closing fast. They wouldn't be able to out-crawl them.

"You stay down and keep going," James said. "I'll give us some space."

"Got it," Alexis said, continuing to crawl.

James rose to his knees and sighted on the nearest zombie, only three feet away. He squeezed the trigger and its head exploded in a spray of bone fragments and blood. Aiming at the next one only a foot behind the last, he fired again. It dropped, then another, followed by another. Soon his slide locked open. He was out of ammunition and there were still two dozen zombies only a few feet away.

He rose to a crouch and started to run towards where Alexis was jumping over a wooden fence into a backyard. Bullets flew through the air around him and he picked up his speed. Something pulled at his pants but he didn't look down; he just kept running. When he reached the fence, he didn't even slow as he dove over it. He landed hard, trying to roll to absorb the impact, but it just left him sprawled on the ground, looking into the sky.

"That was graceful," Alexis said, crouching next to him. "You hurt?"

"No," James said, getting to his knees while picking up and holstering his empty handgun. There was a bullet hole in his pants leg. It must've just missed him.

"Good, then let's go," Alexis said. "They're almost here."

James glanced through the slots in the white picket fence and saw two dozen zombies only a handful of yards away and closing steadily. He didn't notice any more muzzle flashes beyond the perimeter fence.

"Let's go," James said as they stayed low, running beside the house and out the front gate to the street beyond. "Head north. My place is on the next street."

"More of them?" Alexis asked in exasperation, looking to the south where more zombies were coming up the street. A group of townspeople, armed with an assortment of makeshift weapons, were trying to take them down.

If we're not being shot at, maybe I don't need my rifle, James thought. *These people need our help, now.*

"Hold on," James said, running into the backyard.

Going to the shed he'd seen earlier, he opened the door and quickly grabbed an axe and a machete. Returning to Alexis, he handed her the machete and hefted his axe. Together, they ran at the growing horde of zombies the townspeople were trying to fight off.

"Aim for the head," James yelled as he reached the edge of the horde.

He accentuated his point by slamming the axe into an unsuspecting zombie's head. The thing dropped and he pulled his weapon out, blood and brain matter coating the axe head. Alexis dropped one next to him. Lifting the axe, he brought it down again on another.

This is surprisingly a lot like splitting wood, he thought, *although these pieces of wood move and want to devour my flesh, so maybe not so much.*

Now that they knew to aim for the head, the townspeople were more effectively taking them down. He was amazed they hadn't known that simple fact, which was the problem with living in a safe town since the beginning.

Headlights shone on them from the north, and James pulled his axe out of a shattered skull. He couldn't look back, however, because another zombie took its place immediately. They were making headway, but it wouldn't be enough. There were too many.

"Move, bitch, get out the way!"

The voice was instantly recognizable—Tank. James quickly backed away from the zombies and moved off to the side, making sure not to turn his back to them. The rest of the townspeople were already on the sidewalk and Alexis was next to James.

Tank revved the engine as the front end of Scourge slammed into the zombies. Multiple sickening crunches could be heard as the LAPV mowed a path through the horde, taking down almost twenty in one pass. Once in the clear, Tank whipped the vehicle in a sharp U-turn, using the e-brake to make it slide across the pavement with his blood-covered tires.

James worked his way along the sidewalk towards the other townspeople with Alexis at his side. Tank took Scourge on another pass, finishing off the rest of the zombies in the middle of the street and leaving the ground littered with bloody body parts. Finishing off the stragglers on the sidewalk, James walked up to the townspeople, noticing Greg was with them.

"Everyone okay here?" James asked.

"Mostly," Greg said. "She was bitten." He was pointing at a young girl armed with a kitchen knife.

James knew what needed to be done, but looking at the other dozen men and women gathered around, he faltered. This wasn't his call to make—not here, not now.

"Anyone who's wounded needs to go to the infirmary and get patched up," James said. "Greg, can you escort the girl and anyone else who's hurt?"

"Sure," Greg said, sharing a look with him.

James gave a subtle nod. Greg would know what needed to be done if something happened before they made it to the infirmary.

Scourge sped back from the north, sliding to a stop on the gore-covered pavement.

"Catch a ride!" Tank said, opening his door to holler out.

James ran over to the back door and opened it for Alexis as he went around the other side and climbed in. He noticed his gear sitting in the backseat, and he quickly put it on.

"Thanks for the assist," James said.

"You guys rock," Alexis said.

"Ain't nuthin'," Tank said.

"There're more zombies in that field to the west of us," James said, pointing.

"Then let's go get 'em," Connor said from the passenger seat.

37
REBEL SOULS

Post-outbreak day 22

James's eyelids kept drooping and he had to slap himself to stay awake. The sun was beginning to brighten the horizon. They'd been at it all night. He ducked through the open hatch in the roof of Scourge, entering the cab.

"I don't think there're any more," James said, yawning.

"Don't start that," Tank said, yawning in turn.

"I think you're right," Connor said. "We need to head back and see if they have anything else for us to do."

"Got it," Tank said, turning the rig and heading back to HQ.

"What a night," James mumbled.

After clearing the main three hordes of zombies, they'd gone to HQ to see what they could do to help. Vindex had spent most of the time protecting their helicopters and the infirmary. They learned later that the mercenaries had barely helped in the fight. The military had dealt with the main force of attackers to the east and then had sent patrols outside the fence into Sweet Grass to get rid of the snipers. They'd found two and been able to capture one of them. The other went down fighting. That left the Wolf Pack to drive around town, looking for any more zombies while some of the Vindex men went door to door. They'd found two people who'd been bitten and took them to the infirmary. There were also three houses where zombies had broken in and killed the residents. The military had escorted Greg and some of the other welders to do a temporary fix on the three holes in the perimeter fence.

The whole thing had been a well-executed assault. They'd started off by attacking from the east, drawing most of the soldiers and Marines there. After that, they'd started sniping to keep them locked behind cover. Then came the three explosions and three holes in the fence where the semi-trailers had let the zombies loose. At some point during the confusion of trying to deal with the zombies, the attackers had just faded into the night. James spent most of that time leery that they'd return, but they never did. The attack had been vicious, but what had been the goal? They'd taken quite a few lives, but they hadn't taken the town.

It has to be the Reclaimers, James thought. *No one else would attack a well-defended town like this.*

After stopping to pick up Chloe, Tank pulled Scourge to a stop in the parking lot by HQ and James practically stumbled out. He was bruised and bloody, his side hurt, his ears were still ringing, and he was about to pass out. It'd been a *long* night. Alexis left her dad's side—a new bandage on his left shoulder, thanks to one of the snipers—and walked over to

James. She wrapped her arms tightly around him. They'd dropped her off with Emmett earlier in the night.

"Ouch," James said and she loosened her grip.

"Sorry." Looking up into his eyes, Alexis said, "I'm just glad you're safe."

Emmett walked up. "Col. Briggs called an emergency meeting with the leaders of the town."

"Why aren't you in there then?" Connor asked, coming around the side of Scourge.

"I wasn't invited," Emmett said crossly.

"Well, hell," Tank said. "That ain't good."

"No, it's not," Emmett said.

"What do you think they'll do?" Chloe asked.

"I'm not sure," Emmett said, "but it doesn't look good."

"Did they interrogate the man they captured?" James asked.

"Yeah," Emmett said. "From what I can gather, it was definitely the Reclaimers, and Jezz made it explicit that they were here for us—mainly you three."

"Well, hell again," Tank said.

"So what?" Chloe said. "Will they turn us over to them as a peace offering?"

"I doubt it," Connor said.

"Easiest thing would be to kick us out," James said.

"That'd get rid of all their problems," Tank said.

"Roger," Emmett said.

Cpt. Sanders and a few other Marines came out of the front door. The captain walked towards them while his men jumped into a couple of Humvees and drove into town.

"What's going on in there, sir?" Connor asked when he walked up.

Cpt. Sanders looked Emmett straight in the eyes. Then he looked away and answered. "You'll know soon enough."

"Those Marines went to gather the rest of our group, didn't they?" James asked.

Cpt. Sanders didn't answer. He just looked towards the sunrise.

"Answer us, you bastard!" Tank said.

"Calm down, son," Emmett said. "He's not worth your breath."

"After all we've done for you, you're just going to kick us to the curb?" James asked.

"All you've done for us?" Cpt. Sanders said, turning around to face him. "You killed six of my Marines with the bomb and then we lost another thirty men last night, including Cpt. Miller. Vindex lost four men and we count at least two dozen civilians killed or infected. For what? We killed ten of theirs and captured one. No, we don't need any more of your *help*."

Anger rose in James, but it was quickly replaced by resignation. In a way, the captain was right. The fact that they were there *had* caused those deaths. He wouldn't take the blame for it, not anymore, but the simple fact was that if they hadn't been there, those people would still be alive. Everyone remained silent after the captain's little speech, and he went back to looking at the sunrise. He hadn't realized Cpt. Miller was dead. James glanced at Emmett standing stoically next to Alexis, who had her hand in James's and her arm through her father's.

A few minutes later, the Humvees pulled up, carrying all the survivors from their group except for Helen, Margaret, and the kids. Greg was there along with Beverly, Neil, Lucas, Troy, Abby, and Seth. None of them looked very pleased. They walked over to where the rest of them were gathered.

"What's goin' on?" Greg asked.

"We're about to find out," Emmett said as the town leaders began to exit the building.

They looked sullen, which wasn't a good sign. Col. Briggs walked at the front of the group and stopped as the rest of the survivors from Burns walked up to James and his group. The colonel looked at each person in the group, while most of the other leaders tried not to look directly at anyone.

"Good morning, ladies and gentlemen," Col. Briggs said, beginning his little speech. "When you came to us two weeks ago, you were desperate and weary from your travels. We gave you a place to rest your heads, eat, and start a normal life, but unknown to us you brought with you a dark shadow—the Reclaimers. It was them who attacked last night and killed over sixty of our citizens, while we only took down a handful of theirs. The attack was well planned and well-orchestrated. They somehow disabled our perimeter sensors and managed to get three semi-trailer loads of infected into town. They did all this just to get to you, which they failed at, but not before taking a heavy toll on our people."

He paused and James could practically feel the hammer about to strike the anvil.

"It's with a heavy heart that I and my fellow

leaders have made this decision. For the safety of our own people, we must eject you from our community. We do this not just for ourselves but for the greater good of this safe harbor and of the country. This base must stand as a beacon of hope to others, but that isn't possible when we're harried by an enemy that wants only you. We'll give you as much aid as we can and send you on your way, well-armed. You'll need to leave by noon, today."

James smiled. He walked right up to Col. Briggs and held out his hand. The colonel looked confused for a brief moment, but then he took his hand and James shook it firmly.

"On behalf of our group, I'd like to thank you for the hospitality you've shown us. You did indeed bring us in and help us rest up and get ready for the journey ahead. It was a pleasure to stay in your town and meet your people, but we'll be glad to get on the road again."

Col. Briggs nodded, and James turned and walked past his group, heading across town to the building that had been their place. It'd never been a home to him. He hadn't even thought of it that way. Deep down he knew this wasn't where they were meant to be. It was just a short stop on their journey to Alaska, and now it was time to get back on the road. Even though the trip would be dangerous—more so since they were being hunted—he'd be glad to see the open road ahead of them. They still had a long way to go.

38
AS THE DUST SETTLES

Emmett was beyond shocked by James's words. The kid had acted like a true leader, and whether he'd meant to or not, he'd set the tone for how the others would respond.

"Thank you, sir," Connor said to Col. Briggs before he turned and walked off, following his brother.

Tank cursed under his breath and looked at the colonel. "Peace," he said.

He walked over to Chloe and put his arm around her. She looked up at him with tears in her eyes and they climbed into Scourge, turning it around. Tank drove up beside Connor and slowed down so Connor could jump onto the running boards. Then he took off down the street towards James. The survivors from Burns looked around with a multitude of expressions on their faces—shock, anger, resignation.

"You can't kick us all out!" Seth said, speaking up first. "The Reclaimers are after them, not us!"

"I concur," Col. Briggs said. "We're allowing all the children and women to stay. That means the majority of the group will leave, including the ones they want."

"That's very generous of you, Colonel," Emmett said, a little surprised. The man did have tact and maybe some semblance of a heart.

"But I have two daughters. I can't just leave them," Seth said, begging.

"I'll trade spots with him," Beverly said, stepping up.

"No," Neil said, looking at her.

"I won't stay here knowing you're all out there," Beverly said firmly.

"If that's your choice," Col. Briggs said, "I think that could work."

"Thank you," Seth said with tears in his eyes.

"Thanks," Beverly said and turned to Neil. "We need to go pack."

Talking animatedly, the two of them walked off, closely followed by Lucas, Troy, and Greg. Seth hesitated, then turned and walked away quickly, probably hoping the colonel wouldn't change his mind.

"Will you let us take some supplies? Or can we at least have what we came in with?" Alexis asked.

"We'll return enough firearms from the ones you brought in to outfit your group with a rifle and sidearm each. We'll also return all the tools you had, and supplies, as well as send more food and medical supplies with you. Sadly, we can't give back everything that belonged to the Vindex Corp. but we'll make sure you're well supplied and ready to make the trip north."

"Thanks," Alexis said, turning and walking back towards their home—at least, what had been their home for a short time.

The rest of the town leaders dissipated.

Clover walked over to Emmett. Both men had bandaged shoulders, but Clover's arm was also in a sling. His wound was a lot worse than Emmett's. "Thanks for last night," he said. "I wish it could be different."

Emmett shook his outstretched hand. "Me too," he said.

Clover walked off, leaving Emmett standing there with Col. Briggs.

"Well, Colonel," Emmett said, walking up to him, "it wasn't unexpected, but it was disappointing. You and I both know you have the means to find the Reclaimers and finish them off rather easily."

"Indeed," Col. Briggs said, "but at what cost? It's not worth the lives of my men. Most of your people seem like they want to be back on the road anyway."

"That's a bunch of bull, and you know it."

"Maybe, but our mission is not to hunt down groups of hostiles."

"And what is your mission? To test the virus on unsuspecting drug addicts in hopes of finding a cure?" Emmett had the satisfaction of watching the colonel's face reveal his shock for a brief moment before his stern mask was back in place. "How many lives is it going to cost for you to *save* humanity?"

"As many as it takes," Col. Briggs said, back in control.

Emmett stared into his eyes. "So be it. I'd ask if you could spare one of your birds to watch over us for the first day, but I know your answer."

"Indeed, you do."

"Colonel, I can't say it's been a pleasure getting to

know you since that would be a lie. Make sure Saul gets a proper memorial."

"He will," Col. Briggs said, offering his hand.

Emmett looked at it for a few seconds but then shook it and turned to walked off, adjusting the bandage on his shoulder. Never had he thought he'd give up this place so easily. Just a week ago, he'd been willing to fight tooth and claw to keep it for his daughter—somewhere she could be safe and have a life—but the events of the last twenty-four hours had changed all that. He knew now that his daughter had a life whether they were safely behind these fences or out on the road. Her life involved him, James, and the rest of her friends. It wasn't so much about where they were or whether they were safe. It was who they were with and how they spent the time they were given. That was what it meant to truly live.

~~~

It took James a total of five minutes to pack because he'd been prepared for this day since they'd gotten there. Looking at his duffle, he noticed the folded picture Olive had drawn him sitting near the top. He unfolded it and looked at it. They'd come so far since then and yet they still had a long way to go. He slipped the drawing into his back pocket and closed up his duffle, loading his gear into Scourge.

During that first week of the apocalypse, he'd worn his tactical vest and then his plate carrier almost non-stop. By the time they arrived in Coutts, he'd mostly grown used to it, but during their time there, he'd only worn it on runs. That had made him soft, and when he stepped out into the mid-morning sun at ninety-some degrees, he almost felt like dying.

A couple of Marines brought them some rations of MREs, a few ammunition cans, a big medical kit, a couple of tents, and some cots. They had some supplies in Scourge already, but only enough for a few days. With these, they'd be set for a week, maybe two if they rationed and didn't run into too much trouble—which they would. It was inevitable at this point, but until then he'd enjoy every moment and face head-on whatever trials came their way.

Connor and Tank finished packing up around the same time James did and they stood there, looking back at the old store they'd been staying in.

"I'm gonna pick up Chloe and then swing by the saloon to see if Durt's willin' to part with some whiskey," Tank said, climbing into Scourge.

"I'll join you," Connor said.

James shut the door to their place and then jumped into the back seat. "Can you drop me off at the orphanage?" he asked.

"Sure thing," Tank said as he pulled out.

A minute later, James hopped out and walked towards the front door as Tank drove off. He stopped outside, preparing himself for what was ahead. It would be hard—really hard—but he knew it was the right decision.

~~~

Alexis packed up what few belongings she had with a light step. Call her crazy, but she was glad to be leaving this place. She was under no delusions that it would be easy going forward. It would certainly be

326

harder than anything they'd faced so far, yet she knew they'd face it together. Her dad, James, Chloe and the rest were a large, dysfunctional family now. As long as they had each other, they could get through anything, so it was with optimism that she packed up all of her things and loaded them into a duffle.

Taking the duffle out to her dad's truck, she threw it in the bed. Laying on the tailgate was a plate carrier vest already loaded with magazines and an M4 rifle with a Trijicon scope and attachments. She picked up the rifle and checked it quickly, refreshing herself with the setup. Taking the plate carrier—which was heavy—and the rifle, she set them on the front seat. She was wearing the same gun belt she'd worn since she'd been there. Pulling out the Glock, she looked at it. This was the same one Ana had given her the night she'd rescued them from the Reclaimers.

Alexis had been avoiding thinking about Ana over the past couple of weeks. It was easier that way. She regretted the way she'd acted toward her friend. In the moment, she'd felt hurt and betrayed, but after spending many nights thinking about it and talking with her dad and James, she realized that Ana had done what she'd had to. Alexis didn't ever think she'd be able to do it, not like that anyway, but she couldn't fault Ana for it. Maybe Ana would find them somehow. She could only hope.

"You ready?" Emmett asked as he brought his own duffle out of the house and threw it into the bed of the truck.

"Yep," Alexis said.

Her dad shut the tailgate and walked over to her.

Gazing down into her eyes, he smiled. "I'm proud of you, honey. You did what you had to in the infirmary, and now we have answers. I just want you to know that you've grown into such an amazing woman, and I love you."

By the end, his voice broke a little and a single tear leaked down his cheek.

"I love you too, Dad."

She embraced him and he held her like he always did. The contact with her father bolstered her strength and gave her courage for what lay ahead. As long as they had each other, the whole world could be falling apart around them and she wouldn't care. They were a family, and nothing would change that.

~~~

Connor sat in the truck while Tank went in to help Chloe pack. She was taking it the hardest. In her mind, this had actually become her home, whereas for Connor this was just another stop. He wasn't thrilled about at how they were leaving, but he was excited to finally make some progress again. They'd been stagnant for too long.

This next leg of their journey would be the hardest. The Reclaimers would be dogging them every step of the way. They'd have to be on their guard—and stay on their guard—the entire time since they didn't know when or how they'd strike. But they would strike. Whether it was when they first set out that day or the following days, Jezz would return to finish the job. Maybe flushing them out had been what the attack was about the night before. It was a risky move that might not have worked, but after the bomb and then the attack, they hadn't left the colonel with many choices. Either the leaders of Coutts would have to hunt down the Reclaimers and kill them all or cut the ones they were hunting loose. Connor would've chosen to hunt them down, but the colonel had taken the other option. Did that make him a coward? Maybe, or perhaps he knew something they didn't. Either way, the choice had been made and they'd have to roll with it.

~~~

Tank grabbed a shirt and handed it to Chloe. She had to go through every single piece of clothing she owned, which was a lot considering she'd had nothing when they'd gotten there two weeks ago.

"Where the hell did you get all this?" Tank asked, tossing her a pair of blue jeans.

"I bought some, and people gave me some," Chloe said. "It's not like I could wear the same outfit every day like I did out there."

"Well, you could. You just didn't want to."

"Yeah."

She held up two tops, looking from one to the other. They looked identical to him, but she seemed to find some small defect in the one because she tossed it aside. Immediately, she regretted her choice and picked it up again, comparing them a second time. Tank sat next to her, taking both shirts and setting them down. Grabbing each of her small hands in his, he looked into her eyes.

"Stallin' won't change the outcome," Tank said.

"We're leavin'."

"I know," Chloe said, tearing up. "I was just starting to think of this as home. I felt like maybe I could pretend things were normal."

She broke down and the tears flowed freely. Tank took her in his arms and she grasped him desperately, crying onto his shoulder. He held her, stroking her hair as she let it all out.

"It's okay," he said, when her sobs began to subside. "I won't let anythin' happen to you. Once we get to Alaska and out to the lodge, things'll begin to take on a new 'normal,' I promise."

Chloe pulled away slightly, looking up at him with glistening eyes. "You *promise*?"

"Yes, I promise," Tank said, wiping some of the tears from her cheek. "You and I are together now and I'm not goin' anywhere."

~~~

James walked through the doors of the school and was immediately greeted by Olive standing next to one of the tables with a packed bag beside her. Neil walked by, loading a suitcase into the van they'd stolen from the mine.

"She's determined to join us," Neil said as he walked by. "Good luck."

Taking a deep breath, he approached Olive. She noticed him and set her jaw. It almost made him laugh out loud.

"Look," Olive said, as he came to a stop before her, "I know it's not safe out there, but Neil has been teaching us how to survive. And it's not any safer in here. What if more bad people attack? Or what if someone gets bit and comes into the orphanage? Or—"

"Olive," James said, trying his best to hide his smile.

"No, you listen to me, James," Olive said, and a tear started to slip down her cheek. "Everyone I have is gone. All I have left is you. Please don't leave me."

More tears followed the first, and it broke his heart. He bent down and picked her up, wrapping his arms around her.

"I wouldn't ever leave you," James said, holding the little girl in his arms. "I was trying to tell you that I'd like you to come with us, if you want to."

"Really?" she asked through the tears.

"Of course. You're allowed to make your own choices. Just know it'll be a lot harder out there, and we might not make it."

"That's okay. Jesus has our backs." She wiped the tears from her eyes and James set her down. "Let me go say goodbye to Squeezer and my friends."

"Sounds good," James said, smiling as she ran off.

Helen looked out the door of her classroom after Olive and then turned her gaze to him as she walked over. Now for the hard part.

"You can't expect me to allow you to take a child back out there," Helen said in a stern voice. "Even if she wants to go, she's just a little girl."

"I know, and that's why I have this," James said. He pulled a folded piece of paper from his pocket and handed it to her. She unfolded it and began to read. That thing had been in his pocket for a week, and he'd just been waiting for the right time to use it.

Now was that time.

"You can't be serious," Helen said. "This isn't a legally binding document."

"No it's not, but it's as official as it can be. It's the end of the damn world, Helen, and I don't need an official document. That right there works just fine for me. It states my intentions and has my signature, along with Cpt. Miller's."

"James, you don't know the first thing about raising a child," she said, but her voice had softened somewhat. "And that's not even considering the state of the world out there."

"No, I don't, but I do know that I love that little girl and I'll do everything in my power to protect her and care for her. That's all I need to know. Now, if you're going to try and stop me then go ahead, but when she returns, I'm leaving here with her, one way or another."

"I'm not going to stop you. I just want to make sure you know what you're doing. This may condemn her to a death that could've been prevented."

"I'll give her the choice one more time, but it's ultimately her decision to make."

Helen nodded. "I won't stop her if she wants to leave."

James let out a sigh. He hadn't been sure that was going to work, but he'd been determined. Olive returned a few minutes later, carrying her backpack. Then she looked back at Mrs. Olger's classroom.

"I forgot something in my desk," Olive said, running inside. After a minute or so, she returned. "Will you take care of Squeezer, Mrs. Olger?"

"Yes, honey I will," Helen said. "Mr. Andderson had something to ask you."

Olive looked at James and suddenly he was nervous. What if she changed her mind?

"Olive, I need you to be sure you want to come with us," James said. "It'll be hard, and it may result in all our deaths."

"I already told you," Olive said, "I'm not afraid. I want to go."

"Good, then I have another question for you. I'd like to adopt you. It's not official or anything, but for all practical purposes, it will be. Olive, do you want to be my daughter?"

39
ALWAYS ON THE RUN

James opened the door to Scourge, letting Olive and Felix climb into the third row of seats while he threw their bags in the back. He then climbed into the back seat. Felix had come out shortly after Olive with his bag packed. He was determined to go as well, and Helen could do nothing to dissuade him. So now they were both coming along.

"We good?" Tank asked.

"Yep," James said.

"You're bringing them?" Connor asked quietly.

"They wanted to come," James said. "I told you my plan."

"I know, but still."

"Tank, Connor, Chloe" James said, raising his voice. "I'd like to introduce you to my daughter, Olivia!"

Olive rolled her eyes. "Hi, guys," she said. "It's just me."

"Nice to meet you, Olive," Chloe said.

"Hi," Olive said.

"We only met briefly," Tank said. "I'm Tank."

"Hi, Tank," Olive said.

"And of course you know Sir Felix," James said.

"Just Felix, Mr. Andderson," Felix said.

"Hi," Chloe said.

"Hey, Felix," Tank said, pulling away from the orphanage.

They headed to the parking lot beside HQ where they were going to meet the rest of their group. James was legitimately excited to be back on the road soon. Pulling up beside Emmett's truck, James climbed out.

"You ready?" Emmett asked.

"Yes, sir," James said, coming up to his window. "We have all our gear and people."

"Same here, enough for at least a week. Just waiting on the others."

"How did they do after their escape from the Reclaimers?" James asked.

"A lot better. They really stepped up, especially the ones who're joining us. Greg, Lucas, and Neil have taken to it well."

"Good."

"You still gonna take charge?" Emmett asked.

"I was hoping you'd do that."

Emmett nodded. "You've grown a lot. You sure?"

"Yes, sir," James said. "I think you can do a lot better."

"You did a damn good job before, but yes, I'll take charge from here."

"Thanks."

Alexis walked out of the HQ building and up to him.

"You ready for this?" he asked.

"Oh, yeah," Alexis said, smiling. "I have my family with me."

"That you do."

"Anyone need to use the bathroom?" Alexis asked.

"Me," Olive said, climbing out.

"Have you met my daughter?" James said as Olive walked up.

"James," Olive said, giggling.

"This is Olive, my daughter," James said.

"What do you mean? You adopted her?" Alexis asked.

"Yep, it's as official as anything is these days," James said.

"I would say I'm shocked, but I could see it coming," Alexis said, giving him a kiss on the cheek before leading Olive back inside.

Felix climbed out a moment later. "Might as well go too, I guess," he said.

"Very true," James said, following him inside.

When they came back out, the rest of their group had arrived. Greg was driving the truck they'd taken from the mine on the last leg of their trip. Lucas and Troy were riding with him, and there were a few supplies stacked in the back seat. Neil and Beverly drove the van they'd also taken from the mine, and the rest of the supplies were packed in the back. Connor was going around putting a small CB radio into each of their rigs, sticking the magnetic antenna on their roofs.

"Everyone set?" Emmett asked.

"Yep," Greg said.

"Good to go," Neil said.

"Good. The Wolf Pack will be taking the lead in the LAPV. Greg, you go next, and then Neil. I'll bring up the rear. We stay tight and we keep a sharp eye out. The Reclaimers are out there somewhere and we need to be ready for them. The CB radios are set to channel seven. Keep 'em there and always on when we're driving. Take these as backups. There's enough for everyone to have one," Emmett said, handing them each a small radio and headset. "Keep in touch. If you see *anything,* report it. We can't be too careful."

"Will do," Neil said.

"Got it," Greg said, grabbing three sets of radios.

James walked over and climbed into Scourge, noticing the head mechanic, Tom, talking with Tank on the other side of the rig.

"Remember what I told you, son," Tom said.

"I will," Tank said, shaking the man's hand.

"Safe travels," Tom said, moving away from the rig as Tank climbed in.

"We ready?" Emmett asked once everyone had loaded up.

"Yes, sir," James called from the hatch on the roof of Scourge.

"Time to roll out," Emmett said.

James slapped the roof and Tank started off, taking the lead. He watched behind him as Greg followed in his truck, then Neil in the van, and finally, Emmett. He waved at Alexis in the truck, and he could see her smile and wave back. That might not have been very smooth, but who cared if he was a little dorky? The girl he loved didn't mind it.

The girl he *loved.*

The thought should have come as a surprise, but he remembered thinking it the night before during the attack and it felt right. He did love her. It didn't matter that they'd only been on one "official" date. They'd known each other for a couple of weeks, and that was all the time he needed.

The caravan pulled out onto Alberta Highway 4, heading north. The sun was high in the sky, promising another hot, sunny day. Even though they'd been there for a couple of weeks, it almost felt like they'd just rolled into town yesterday. When he thought about all that had happened, he knew it'd been longer than a day, but it still felt like it. They were finally on the road again, heading to their true home. They just had to traverse more than two thousand miles of zombie-infested, apocalyptic landscape to get there. No big deal.

James climbed inside the rig and shut the hatch.

"Isn't this the part when you put on some oddly fitting song?" Chloe asked from beside Tank.

"She does have a point," James said.

"Damn, I'm losin' my edge," Tank said, slamming on the brakes.

"What do you see?" Emmett's voice said over the CB radio in the middle console.

Connor picked it up as Tank swiped through his iPod. "Might've forgotten somethin'. One sec."

"We're not even five miles out and you already forgot something?" Emmett asked.

"Got it," Tank said, starting to drive again.

"Never mind," Connor said through the radio.

"If I find out you stopped to play one of your stupid songs, I'll skin you alive."

"Never," Connor said, smiling.

Olive giggled in the third row of seats.

"Over and out," Emmett said.

"Here we go," Tank said, turning the volume up as *Bad Company* by Five Finger Death Punch began to play.

James smiled. What a perfect song. With the open road ahead, his friends and family around him, and a new hope in his heart, he looked forward with a certainty that everything would work out—one way or another.

EPILOGUE

Ana watched the farm from atop a hill across the small reservoir. Right then, she wasn't even sure anyone was there. The whole place was silent and nothing moved. This had to be the right place. It just had to be. She'd been trying to catch up with them for the past couple of weeks, but it'd proven a lot harder than she thought. They were heading north, she knew, but where exactly? Which route would they take? She'd basically been wandering around all that time, going on hunches and educated guesses. Until last night, at least.

She'd heard the explosions off in the distance, and after climbing a hill she'd been able to see the flash of muzzles and hear the sound of faint gunfire to the north. That would be them. They were always involved in trouble, and if something was going wrong, they wouldn't be too far away. The town at the border had been easy enough to find after that. She'd just followed the sounds of a firefight. She'd had to be careful when she'd gotten closer. In the dark, she couldn't tell who was who, so she stayed back, waiting. Finally she'd seen vehicles driving off into the night towards the south. She'd followed them to this farm, and unless they'd evaded her in the night, they were still there.

As the sun rose, a black truck drove down the dirt road from the west, pulling onto the farm. It parked in the barn and a man hopped out. He shut the barn door and ran over to the house across the driveway. Was it them? Had she finally found them? The man was gone for a couple of minutes and then came out with three more men. They each went respectively into the garage, barn, and stable. Soon, four vehicles pulled out—the black truck from before, a red truck, a green Jeep, and a black SUV. The man driving the SUV pulled it right up to the house and then jumped out, going back inside.

A woman walked out onto the porch. Ana's heart rate picked up, and she moved the scope to her eye. The woman's midnight black hair shone in the sunlight. It was her. There was no doubting it. This was Jezz.

Ana steadied her breathing as she aimed at the woman, but before she could even think of squeezing the trigger, Jezz climbed into the driver's seat of the SUV. Ana cursed in Russian. She continued to watch as more men and a couple of women came out of the house, loading gear and supplies into the vehicles. They were heading out, leaving this place for good. What exactly was Jezz doing? Was she trying to rebuild her gang? Or was it as she feared—that Jezz was trying to find Ana's old group and kill them.

Ana had been looking for them for days, and yet she still didn't know what she truly wanted. She told herself that she wanted to end the life of that monster down there, that she wanted to keep her from creating more pain and death in the world, but a small part of her wondered if her motives were completely different. She ignored that part, just like she ignored the voice that whispered in her head. After that first day on her own, she'd never been able to shut the box she'd kept locked for so many years. Now the voice was always there with her, a constant companion. She could ignore it all she wanted, but she knew it was there, and it scared her more than Jezz or anyone else ever could—even more than her mother had.

There were nine Reclaimers down there, plus Jezz and the one she recognized as Max. It wasn't as if she'd memorized all their faces, but these Reclaimers didn't look like the ones from before. Had something happened to them? Or were these just members she didn't recognize, like the ones who'd been stationed at the ambush spot? Either way, there weren't many of them anymore, and she assumed they'd lost a few in the fight the night before. Once they were all loaded up, the vehicles left the farm with the black truck leading.

She'd finally found them. Now she just had to keep up with them, but if her hunch was correct, she knew right where they were heading. Climbing down the back side of the hill, Ana got into her black Ford Raptor. The irony wasn't lost on her as she set her Dragunov SVD rifle in the seat next to her—a Russian with a Russian sniper rifle. She would've picked something different if she could, but right then all she had was the Dragunov and the AK-47 from the Reclaimers, plus a Glock 19 she'd taken from the corpse of a man back in Yellowstone National Park. Going there had been a big mistake. Looking at the map, it had seemed like a good shortcut, but she hadn't accounted for all the tourists that were in the park when the apocalypse started. She'd barely made it out of there alive.

Pulling out from behind the hill, she drove across the field and onto the dirt road. She could see the dust a mile or so ahead from the Reclaimer's vehicles. Going slowly, she began to formulate a plan in her head as she followed. What would she do when she caught up with them next? Jezz needed to die, and Ana couldn't rest until that happened. But then what? She didn't know, and that scared her. She should just kill them all and then catch up with her old group, but that didn't feel right anymore. She'd been through too much to go crawling back to them.

You can lead the Reclaimers like they're meant to be, the voice said in her head.

Ana ignored it as she continued to drive. The voice had planted that idea in her head days ago, but unbeknownst to her, it had taken root and begun to grow.

ACKNOWLEDGEMENTS

I couldn't have finished this book without the help of numerous people. Huge thanks to:

Jesus, you keep guiding me down this path and providing for me.

My wife, you inspire me like none other!

My family, thanks for the constant support.

Guildies in the FRG, you keep helping make these stories better!

My awesome editor, you are the one who takes a *very* rough draft and makes it readable!

My cover artist, I've never had someone so perfectly bring to life an image that was in my head!

And last, but certainly not least, to my awesome readers. You all continue to amaze me with your support and kind words. As long as you continue to read, I'll continue to write!

THANK YOU!!!

ABOUT THE AUTHOR

Joshua is a Jesus Freak and follower of the Way. As an adventurous nerd, he loves the outdoors and when he's not found high in the mountains of Alaska, he can be observed living on the rolling plains of eastern Montana with his wife, guns and two katanas. He has a passion for all things imaginary and finds inspiration in the wilderness, away from all the distractions of life. Some of his other passions include hunting, shooting, board and video games, hard rock, movies, reading and the Walking Dead.

Learn more about Joshua at:
www.joshuacchadd.com

Also by Joshua C. Chadd

The Brother's Creed Series
Outbreak
Battleborn
Wolf Pack
Bad Company
Last Hope (Coming Soon)

Made in the USA
Columbia, SC
10 July 2018